The Arsonist

The Arsonist

Poet, weaver, seer, blasphemer

Kiran Nagarkar

juggernaut

JUGGERNAUT BOOKS
KS House, 118 Shahpur Jat, New Delhi 110049, India

First published by Juggernaut Books 2019

10 9 8 7 6 5 4 3 2 1

P-ISBN: 9789353450366
E-ISBN: 9789353450373

Typeset in Adobe Caslon Pro by R. Ajith Kumar, Noida

Printed and bound at Thomson Press India Ltd

Nobody knows for certain when exactly the Bhakti saint Kabir was born. But the fact is Kabir is timeless. Which is why he is always timely. He is the contemporary of every age. And his time is forever 'now'.

He was illiterate. And yet his dohas, as his poems were called, are beyond literate. They are the very essence of wisdom, often the opposite of received wisdom. The most curious thing about him is a separate oeuvre of his which introduces a radical surrealism into his meditations on God. His mordant wit, his sense of irony, sees through it all: life and death, faith and God, the banal and the profound, the spiritual and the mortal. His observations, his insights and his commentary on every aspect of our term on earth make us question our most revered beliefs and the humbug that often passes for religion or philosophy.

This book found itself being written because every now and then the ghastly things that were happening in Kabir's own country, India, and across the world compelled me to ask how he would have responded to events that were occurring centuries after his death: the lynchings, the hate campaigns, the loss of humanity, sanity and compassion; the stupendous double-and-triple talk; the bottomless greed and mendacity; the wars, riots and ceaseless violence. The endless mass murders in the name of God and religion. And the wilful ignoring of the very real possibility of the extinction of mankind itself.

Would Kabir have managed to shake us awake and rise?

1

'If you had to choose between a woman you loved and God, who would you choose?'

And the Weaver said, 'The woman. Is there any doubt about that?'

And the mullah asked him, 'If you had to choose between a song and God, what would you pick?'

And the Weaver said, 'The song, of course.'

And the priest from the temple asked him, 'Weaver, if perforce you had to choose one or the other, a beautiful sunset or God, what would your choice be?'

And he said, 'Isn't it obvious? The sunset.'

And they asked him how he could blaspheme so.

And the Weaver said, 'Why sirs, God has eternity on his side, he can always wait. Will the woman, the song or the sunset wait for me?'

And they asked in desperation, 'If you had to choose between sin and God, Weaver, what would you choose?'

And he laughed and said, 'Sin, always sin. Sin is fun, sin is forbidden, sin is, what shall I say, so sinful. They should forbid God as they forbid sin, then maybe he would become far more attractive and we would all be drawn to him.

'What a bunch of buffoons you have for your devotees, oh Lord,' he laughed out loud. 'The fools would sever you from your creation.'

Kabir yeh ghar prem ka,
Khaala ka ghar naahi.
Sheesh utaare bhuin dharey,
Tab paithe ghar maahi.

Kabir, this is the dwelling of love,
Not the home of your aunt.
Bend your head (ego) low, all the way to the floor,
Only then can you enter it.

2

One afternoon when the Weaver was taking his siesta, two of his pupils, Ismael and Ananda, rushed into the house and woke him up.

'I hope you've found God or something as important, Ananda. For if you haven't, I'm going to beat the living daylights out of you.'

'Is it true–' Ananda was still out of breath, 'that you were an ascetic and lived alone in the mountains?'

'Is that why you woke me up, you fool?'

'Answer the question, Master,' Ismael said tersely.

The other apprentices left their looms and gathered around the Weaver.

'Oh, I don't remember. It was such a long time ago. And how does it concern you, anyway?'

'No ascetic with any self-respect would ever return to a normal life or go back to his wife,' Ismael sneered.

'I guess I have no self-respect. Now may I go back to my nap?'

'Why, why would you come back when you were supposed to be the greatest maharishi in the country?'

'Can't we talk about it some other time?'

'Now,' the pupils said impatiently.

The Master sat up and shook his head in disbelief and resignation. 'Who is the Master here? You or me?'

They laughed and Ananda said, 'We don't know about you but we outnumber you thirty to one. So I guess we must be the boss-men here.'

The Master said:

When I was your age, I set out in search of God. Not small- or medium-sized gods but the big one, the Almighty Himself. I was a pretty persistent sort and over the years I acquired a reputation as a holy man. They called me a sage and a seer. Some said I was a siddha and had miraculous powers.

I lived in the Himalayas in those days, some fourteen thousand feet above sea level. It was my seventh year of standing on one leg. My eyes were closed and my mind was focused on Brahman. People from far and near, from neighbouring principalities and distant kingdoms, trekked to the mountains to fall at my feet and receive my blessings. Sometimes they would wait for days, even weeks, to see me, for there was no telling how long my devotions and meditations would last.

Why do people go to see holy men? Because they believe the enlightened ones can make God bend down all the way from heaven to lend an ear. For them a sage is a go-between, a middleman, and, who knows, God may be on the take. But I promised nothing. If I had, as was rumoured, magical powers, I was keeping them to myself. And yet they kept coming, an endless march of pilgrims, the rich and the poor, men, women and children, the lame and the halt and the handicapped, those who needed their lives fixed and those who needed nothing. They came to sit in the shadow of saintliness and be touched by someone who, for all they knew, was privy to God's thoughts.

One day the blacksmith's wife from a nearby village came to see me with her son. He was of an indeterminate age, he could have been twenty-five or maybe he was close to forty. His mouth was open and there was a vacuous smile on his face.

'Don't just stand there, you fool. Touch the Master's feet,' the mother snapped at him.

He bent down and lay prostrate in front of me, his hands joined prayerfully for a full five minutes.

'Bless him, Master,' the mother said. 'I've seven daughters and one son. His name is Suraj. He's a good boy and his heart is in the right place but he's a little simple. He's slow to learn and gets a beating from his father almost every week.'

'Tell the blacksmith to beat iron and not the boy,' I told her. The simple of heart, I suspect, are closer to God than all the subtle scholars of the world. 'Rise, my son.' I put my hand on his head. 'May God be with you.'

'Likewise,' Suraj said and laughed as if he had said something vastly funny.

He would come by from time to time and watch me from a distance. I would forget him and then hours later realize that he was still staring at me.

It was the beginning of February and a cold, nasty wind was blowing, the one they call the Intruder. It whistled inside your bones and froze your blood. The blacksmith's son came up to me and wrapped a shawl around my shoulders.

'I thank you for your kindness,' I told him, 'but I must return your gift, for I have vowed that whatever the season, however inclement the weather, I will endure it.'

The blacksmith's son looked puzzled. 'Why would you do this, Master?'

'A small token,' I said, smiling self-deprecatingly, 'of my devotion to God.'

'I have brought you some bread that my mother made and raw chillies. They'll bring warmth to your shivering body.'

'That is kind of you, Suraj. I'm touched by your concern but I'll not touch food for the next three weeks.'

'And why would you do this, Master? Are you unwell?'

'Nothing of the sort,' I said. 'Just another small token of my affection for the Almighty.'

'Does it give God pleasure then when people starve or freeze to death?' he asked innocently. 'Is that why people scourge themselves?'

'Oh no, no. The good Lord doesn't ask anything of us. It's just a way of showing my love for him.'

'Is that why you stand on one leg?'

'Yes, that is the very reason.'

'You have a rather funny way of showing your love, Master. For if God wanted us to be one-legged, he wouldn't have given us two.'

I smiled at his naivety but decided to humour him. 'Maybe you've got a point there.'

'What else have you given up, Master?'

'Not much really. I shaved my head, left my young wife

and my child of two months. And my elderly parents. They didn't want me to go since I was their only child and the sole breadwinner. "Who will run the workshop and who'll look after us?" they asked.'

'God will,' I told them. 'He takes care of his own.'

'What workshop? Are you too an iron-master?'

'No. I was Chief Weaver by appointment to His Majesty. All the princesses and queens wore fabrics woven on my looms.'

'All this you gave up? No wonder they call you maharishi.'

'Just a trifle. Nothing more. I bade farewell to my job as the village mukhiya. The villagers said, "Who will save us when the floods come and who will listen to our troubles?"

'And I told them that power is an unquenchable thirst, and high office a pair of shackles. I will have nothing to do with them. Everything I had desired, I parted with.'

'Surely then you must part with the Almighty too.'

I laughed and asked him, 'Pray, why should I part with the Almighty?'

'Because you desire God more than anything else in the world.'

I was nonplussed. Was this man just stupid or was he the devil incarnate? 'You think that I would forsake the most precious thing in my life?' I spoke with suppressed rage.

The blacksmith's son fell at my feet and clung to my ankles. 'Mercy, Master, have mercy on me. I will not get up till you've forgiven an ignorant man with a loose tongue.'

'Rise blacksmith,' I said, 'I bear you no ill will.'

'Your love of God is indeed great, Master. Greater than

any other man's,' the blacksmith's son said and bowed. 'I'll take your leave now.'

'May God be with you,' I said.

He never showed up again. It was I who visited him some months later. He was in the smithy and cleared some cast-iron scrap off a bench to make room for me to sit and asked his mother to get me a glass of buttermilk.

'What can I do for you, Master?' he asked me.

'Will you be my teacher, my guru?'

'Me?' He seemed astounded by the suggestion.

'Yes. You have more wisdom than all my years of searching for the Almighty have given me. You taught me that one can get a little too attached to selflessness. You taught me that at the end of the day a man must renounce renunciation itself.'

The blacksmith smiled. 'I taught you, Master? You are pulling my leg.'

'I'm not,' I told him emphatically. 'I've never been more serious. Be my guru.'

He laughed then, a loud guffaw that shook the smithy. 'You've got to be joking,' he said. 'Do you think I've nothing better to do?'

Ja ghat prem na sancharey,
So ghat jaan masaan,
Jaise khaal lohar ki,
Saans let bin praan.

That pot which is not filled with love,
Beware, it is as barren as the burial grounds,
Just like the blacksmith's bellows,
It breathes bereft of life.

3

Shantaprasad Chaturvedi was not happy. In truth he had been highly upset for the last eight months. As his surname told you, he not only belonged to the highest class of Brahmins, he knew all the four Vedas. Not just that, he knew them better than anybody else in the country and could recite them front to back and back to front even when he was running a temperature of 105 and was delirious. There was not a day when he didn't get up at five in the morning to take a dip in the Jamuna after he had finished his other morning ablutions. When he got back to the Weaver's workshop in Shantipura, the capital of the state of Panchananda, he spent the next hour and a half bathing the family gods, doing pooja, and praying to them.

Like most of the other disciples, Shantaprasad had enrolled in Kabir's studio because he was considered the finest weaver in the country. But that was not all, the Weaver was also known to be the ultimate repository of wisdom. Shantaprasad, however, was no longer so sure about his choice of a master-weaver. As a matter of fact he was certain that the Weaver was perverse and an unrepentant heretic. He was bent on destroying all the traditional values that had made the country great. But enough was enough. Just because the Weaver was eccentric and spoke in conundrums didn't mean that he could get away with destroying the very fabric of Hinduism.

Shantaprasad Chaturvedi got up even earlier that day, finished his prayers and woke the Master up.

'Ah Shantaprasad, to what do I owe the great privilege of being woken up by no less a personage than one whose family and he himself have mastered all the four Vedas?'

'There's something which has been bothering me since the time that I joined your workshop.'

'This is most unfortunate. Why have you waited so long? Tell me what it is and I will do everything in my power to help you. You know very well that I cannot bear to see any of my pupils unhappy.'

'You have untouchables working here.'

'Yes, and some of them are exceptionally gifted.'

'That's what I was coming to. The untouchables are not here to do their traditional duties like cleaning up our, how should I put it delicately, our waste matter, or cart the dead bodies of our cattle away and skin them. They work at the looms alongside us. Mind you, I make sure not even their shadow pollutes me.'

'That is truly admirable,' the Weaver said though Shantaprasad was not quite sure whether the Master was pulling his leg.

'Thank you, but I fail to understand why you break the laws sanctified by our holiest books, the Manusmruti, the Puranas and the Bhagavad Gita, and allow the filthy shudras inside the workshop.'

'I mean no disrespect to your great learning,' I told him, 'but you do know that they are admitted to heaven too.'

'What absolute rubbish. What would they be doing in the residence of the gods?'

'I understand your anxiety and anger. But would you be happier if the divine beings arranged for a separate enclosure for them?'

'Of course not. What business do they have up there in the holiest of holies?'

'Well, the gods as you can imagine, like to welcome all the good folks to their heavenly abode. But they are rather particular about ensuring that this most wholesome of places in the universe remains the sanctuary of perfect bliss. So obviously it stands to reason that when someone had to get rid of trash like you who think God came up with the idea of a caste system, He begged the very people whom you so glibly called untouchables to throw the likes of you out of heaven.'

Kabir kuaan ek hai,
Panihaari anek,
Bartan sab ke nyare nyare,
Paani sab mein ek.

Kabir there is but one well,
But many draw water from it,
The pots come in all shapes and sizes,
But all contain the same water.

4

That morning they were trying to do a warp and woof count for a complicated woven fabric for Shyamsundar Purohit's son's thread ceremony bash when Jalaluddin, the new apprentice, interrupted the tricky calculations with an odd question. 'Some people say you are a Hindu, others insist you are a Muslim. Who are you?'

'Thanks for the break, Jalal.' The Weaver heaved a sigh of relief. 'I find the maths in weaving exhausting. Who am I, you ask. Good question. Unfortunately let's just say I'm confused. I'm half and half, something like a chhakka or a eunuch of religion.'

'It's a simple enough question with a one-word answer.'

'It might be a bit more complicated than that. I think the more relevant question might be what is God's religion? Is He Muslim? Christian? Hindu? Jewish? Jain? The Buddha himself, I'm told, ignored the Almighty altogether. Is it any wonder then that the good Lord must be going through a severe identity crisis? The poor guy doesn't have a clue about who he is. He's utterly confused. Imagine, He spends sleepless nights wondering whether He's a Roman Catholic, a Protestant, a Hindu Brahmin or a shudra, a Jew, a Parsi, or a Muslim; debating whether he's a Shia or a Sunni; a Buddhist or a Moonie. Or if he exists at all, does he have a form, human or divine? Or is he formless?

'His plight is truly tragic. Think about it, the Hindus were trying to undo the all-encompassing hold of the Buddhists in the name of their own gods. What better way to wipe them out, the Hindu kings figured, than to start wantonly destroying Buddhist iconic sites. Imagine, Shashank, a seventh-century monarch, chopped down the Bodhi tree under which the Buddha received enlightenment. Pushyamitra Shunga not only wiped out the Mauryan Buddhist dynasty but he also knocked down the Ashokan pillared hall and Kukutaram monastery in Pataliputra. He didn't just stop there, he smashed and wrecked the Sanchi stupa itself.

'Needless to say, there were innumerable attacks on Buddhist temples and stupas over the decades. No less an authority than the great Patanjali of the Yoga Sutras compared the relationship between the Buddhists and Jains on the one hand and the Hindus on the other as that between a snake and a mongoose. I need hardly add that the Buddhists retaliated, despite their sworn allegiance to the creed of ahimsa or non-violence. But as was often the case, Hinduism had the last word. One of its branches swallowed the Buddha whole by making him one of the ten avatars of the god Vishnu.

'There was, however, a new faith on the horizon. Islam. Its followers were even more fanatical and many a time the marauding Muslims razed Hindu temples and massacred thousands of the locals.

'How times have changed. Things have indeed come

full circle. The Sri Lankan and the Burmese Buddhists, not to mention the Hindutva fanatics, seem to think that murdering Muslims is an article of faith laid down by the Enlightened One himself. As to the Jains, they won't harm even the tiniest living creature and yet I can hardly think of any other community whose intolerance is often worse than overt violence. The good Christians have been persecuting Jews for crucifying Jesus, the Son of God, for centuries. And then when Christianity bifurcated, the Catholics and the Protestants tried to wipe out each other.

'As you can see, the good Lord has good reason to be bloody confused. I think for the time being we should just let Him take care of himself and sort things out. Till then I prefer being a human being, one of those without a label. Not the dead sort bumped off in His name though. But just someone who's allowed to breathe freely and live and let live.

'As you have just seen, all religions seem to have a murderous streak in them. But have you noticed one other thing? There's a common factor here: God ends up as the mass murderer in every faith.'

Man ke mate na chaliye,
Man ke mate anek.
Jo man par aswaar ho,
So sadhu koi ek.

Don't let the mind lead you,
It's pulled in every direction by desires.
The one who rides his mind,
Now that is a rare saint.

5

'Everybody wants a guru to show them the way,' the Weaver said. 'It's not such a bad idea, I suppose. You may not be able to see without a guru. But then, more often than not, you cannot see beyond the guru either. The guru is vision and the guru is blinkers. It is easy to forget that one is not searching for the guru but for God. Once you've found a guru and understood his teachings, it's time to think of leaving him and making your own way.

'If I could teach you anything,' he told his pupils and apprentices, 'I would teach you irreverence. Irreverence towards your guru, irreverence towards all and sundry, but most of all irreverence towards yourself and your solemnities.

'I may have found the true path, if such a thing exists, but the truth, like all of us, has a short lifespan. Somebody must then find another path, and another truth. And the one will not cancel the other.'

Boond samaani samand mein,
Jaanat hai har koi,
Samand samaana boond mein,
Jaanat birla joi.

The drop becomes one with the ocean,
Everyone knows this,
It's the rare soul who grasps,
That the ocean fits into the drop.

6

It was curious how often heaven and paradise were hotly discussed and debated at the Weaver's workshop in Shantipura, the thriving capital city of the kingdom of Panchananda. The apprentices were mostly in their late teens, and regardless of the fact that they belonged to different faiths, their bonding was intense. And on the rare occasion when there was a flood or some dreadful calamity, they stood as one and often risked their own lives to save a classmate or colleague. But when the talk veered to paradise or hell, the camaraderie suffered a drastic setback and often serious fights broke out.

'Saeed says those who follow Islam have access to seven orders of jannats,' an overwrought Abhishek told the Master, 'each one more beguiling and tempting than the previous ones. Which means we Hindus will be packed into just one swarg even though we are nine times their population. How come they have so much more space than we do? We are the larger community by far. So our heaven should be nine times the Muslim one. One other thing, as the larger community we should have the best locations.'

'You've got it all wrong,' Saeed retorted before the Master

could respond. 'We have just as many jehannums as heavens, each one more terrible than the previous one. All of you infidels and idolators, Christians, Jews, Buddhists and Jains, will go to the seventh hell. It's all there in black and white in the Quran. The angel Jibrael himself revealed all this to the Prophet.' The other apprentice weavers had left their looms and gathered around the two disciples, listening intently to the heated discussion.

'What rot.' Abhishek's fist made contact with Saeed's chin and felled him. 'Our holy books spoke about heaven thousands of years before your Quran did.'

'How dare you contradict the Prophet?' Saeed bounced up and lit into Abhishek. Within minutes it was a free-for-all. The Weaver watched the proceedings with keen interest. When matters began to get out of hand, he cleared his throat loudly several times. Since none of the combatants paid him any heed, he went over to the dyeing tank and filled a large bucket with deep purple water and flung it at his assistants. 'Forgive me for interrupting such a crucial controversy about our afterlife but, Saeed, I'm not quite sure you've got your facts right. The Shias won't admit any Sunnis in their jannat and neither will the Sunnis let the Shias in. The same goes for Catholics and Protestants. Perhaps I should also add a footnote to that. This morning's breaking news said that deadly territorial wars had been going on for the past seventy million years amongst the various heavens and their bosses. Mind you there's no dearth of space there since you can't measure infinity.

'There's one other wrinkle to the problem. With earthlings like you and me, even if we can never reach a settlement, the conflicts are likely to peter out or cease altogether because fortunately we are all of us time-bound and, like it or not, will be terminated. But since all the residents in the various heavens are immortals, this is a permanent world war.'

Patthar puje hari miley,
Toh main puju pahad,
Taase toh chaaki bhali,
Pees khaaye sansar.

If one found God by worshipping a stone,
Then I would worship a mountain,
By that measure a grinding stone is far better,
The whole world consumes what it grinds.

7

The Master was in great form today. It was Lord Shiva's birthday and along with his students he had already had three glasses of thandai, the milk drink with bhang which the god himself loved to quaff. It gave you a lovely high and made you feel well disposed even towards your enemies. They were sitting on patchwork quilts spread on two dozen charpoys. The coir strings on the cots had been restrung tightly just a few days back, and when someone got up to go take a leak or stretch his legs, you could have played noughts and crosses on his criss-crossed bottom.

The Master was in a 'those were the days' mood and reminiscing about his childhood and how he had given his parents a hard time when he learnt that he was a foundling.

'I was a pretty smart kid even then. Perhaps mean or nasty might be a more accurate description. If I didn't have my way, I made a scene. I mean the whole village could hear me as I screamed that my foster parents had kidnapped me from my mother's lap and I was about to report them to the police. They were simple folk. Just the mention of the police would frighten them and they would cave in to my wishes.'

'Why did your real mother abandon you?' Devendra enquired. He seemed to want to take the matter up with the Weaver's biological mother, wherever she was.

'No mother is given to getting rid of her child unless she is in dire straits. Or unless her child is the devil himself. I suspect I qualified for the latter and made her life impossible. My foster parents, however, went to great lengths to portray my mother as a visionary Sibyl. They claimed she put me in a wicker basket because she foresaw me as an incarnation of Moses, who as you may recall was sent down the river in the same manner.'

'Some Moses you turned out to be.' Bismillah snorted. 'We hear you were a real ladies' man. The stone tablets you brought back from the mountain must have had an extra commandment saying "Thou shalt not keep thy hands off any woman."'

'No, no no,' the Master roared, smiling modestly at the same time. 'It was the other way round. The ladies couldn't keep their hands off me. And of course since I was a chivalrous gentleman, I had no option but to oblige.'

'Oh poor you, how you toiled and suffered doing so much social work,' Bismillah retaliated.

'You won't believe this but I was perpetually on call. There were times when two, even three, ladies wanted my services simultaneously. I remember it was the rakhi festival when the zamindar's wife, the military commander's daughter-in-law and the priest's daughter came to visit me, saying they wanted to tie a rakhi on my wrist and declare themselves my sisters. So I stretched out my hand, and the first thing they did was untie my salwar. I remember protesting that this would amount to incest. They were shocked that I should interpret pure sisterly love in this fashion and got on top of me.'

'And what about your wife?' Inayat was in charge of the drinks and he made sure that the Weaver's glass was not allowed to stand empty.

'What about her?' The Master countered Inayat's question with one of his own, suspecting that he was needling him.

'How did she respond to your philandering?'

'What choice did she have?' The Weaver was getting more than a little shirty. 'I'm the man of the manor, the breadwinner. She had no choice but to do my bidding.'

'Is that why she threw you out of the house?' Inayat asked archly.

The Master threw the glass of thandai at his oldest pupil but Inayat ducked his head and the missile missed its mark and splintered on the ground. 'How dare you insult your Guru? I have half a mind to sack you from your post and let you starve.'

Inayat knew the Master's temper was nothing but hot air but he pretended to be contrite and fell at the Weaver's feet and rolled on the ground begging for forgiveness.

'Spare us the melodrama, Inayat,' the Master ticked off his pupil. 'You are a bad actor and a worse ham. Get me another glass of thandai.

'Now that you've exposed me,' the Master said as he sipped the thandai, 'I guess I have no option but to tell the truth.

'My wife Kashmira was an illiterate woman and it was easy for me to think of her as infinitely inferior to me and look down upon her. Rather late in life I discovered that literacy or scholarship rarely signify wisdom.'

'Can we skip the profound philosophical ruminations and just get to the point, Master?' Inayat was not about to let the Master off the hook.

'Sometimes I wonder who is the Master here and who the pupil. It was the same with my wife. It took me time to learn that she was the one who wore the pants in the family. But lest you tick me off again, let me tell you how I was kicked out of the house. I was coming back home one morning after a night of revelry. I was still a little high and in a good humour and singing a ditty: "Why, oh why is there daylight / All I want is the night / A woman on my left and another on the right." I was at the gate in our compound wall when I saw my wife coming out from our house with a man in tow and bidding him goodbye.

'I was suddenly wide awake. "Who's that?" I asked sharply.

'"That, my dear, is one of my lovers."

'"One? Are there others?"

'I looked at the man closely. I couldn't believe my eyes. It was the kind of coincidence that only a writer of the most trashy stories would dare to pen. He was the husband of the woman I had been with all night long. What was this? A fair exchange programme?

'"Am I to understand that you have been entertaining another man while I've been away?"

'"Yes. You see I have an excellent teacher," my wife retorted.

'"Who's that?"

'"You," she said.

'"Hey you, piss off." I screamed at her companion who was still hanging around. "If I ever catch you with my wife again, I'll skin you alive."

'I should have been a little more circumspect in my threat. The man was twice my size and he was all muscle and no fat.'

'"Well," the man said, "you are going to have to do a lot of skinning. Your wife is a connoisseur of men." He was already advancing towards me. "Come to think of it, I should be the one peeling your skin off for ruining my reputation and turning my wife into a whore."

'My wife ran her hand over his back as if to calm him down. "Go home, Salim. The Weaver's no match for you." She laughed. "One whack of your backhand and he will be out for the count."

'"Khuda hafiz, Kashmira. It's been a night I will never forget. Any time you want me to come over, I'll be more than happy to abandon whatever I'm doing and be in your arms." He kissed my wife on her cheek and waved a cheery goodbye to me.

'"How dare you show your face in public without your burqa? And that too in the presence of another man?"

'"I don't see you wearing a burqa in the presence of another woman. And I am sure you are not wearing one while you are fornicating either."

'"I'm a man. I don't need to. The mullah at our mosque will vouch for that. He'll tell you that the burqa is a paak woman's identity. It is a pure woman's armour and shield against the sinful gaze of men. A woman without a burqa is a whore and deserves to be stoned to death."

'"Oh really? Obviously it suits you that the barely literate mullah in our tiny town insists that the black burqa is our identity and how as paak women we must proudly exhibit it. But don't forget, many of the scholars of the Quran insist that that's absolute nonsense.

'"The menfolk try to persuade us that seeing the world through a narrow aperture between the forehead and a little below the bridge of the nose is a wonderful gateway to the world. My blind sisters are only too happy to believe that God wills it so without ever grasping how unjust it is to the Almighty, and to all of us. Do you think God is so ashamed of his own creation that he needs to hide our faces? Do you know what the burqa is? It's a coffin. Frankly I wouldn't want even the dead to be buried in it either.

'But I have not yet touched upon the most infuriating and utterly unfair burden we place upon the shoulders of two and three year old girls when we make them wear the hijab, telling these innocents that we are doing this for the greater glory of God.

'"But let me clarify a few, what shall I call them, home truths, facts, whatever. There's no mistaking my identity. It is the face that God and my parents gave me. No, nobody else in the world has my eyes, my nose, my delicate ears and my gorgeous lips that you love to lick and kiss. No man's going to imprison me or my body in black. These pert boobs are mine and so are my nipples which you can't have enough of. They are all God-given just as the vertical slit at the fork of my legs is and no man is going to tell me any different. A marriage is a covenant. Both husband and wife swear fidelity to their partner. When one party breaks the compact, the other too is free to engage with anyone he or she wishes.

'I don't believe in a tit-for-tat one-upmanship but I gave you a long rope to hang yourself by, Kabir. It didn't occur to you that your neck would ever get caught in the noose, did it? What men want of course is that they should have all the freedom in the world while their wives should be locked up at home and be grateful for being imprisoned. No more.

'"This body is my property and I alone can and will decide what to do with it. Isn't it marvellous that that same vertical line can be tightened and will keep out whoever it wants to keep out and yet grows large enough to let a newborn child out into the world? I rejoice in me.

'"God is God because he does not discriminate. If He stands for all that is fair and just, he knows that it's the menfolk who are perpetually ogling women and dying to get inside their skirts. And that's why they keep the ladies in perpetual purdah. However, let me not overstate the case for the ladies. When they get going, they too can have a swinging time.

'"I have heard the mullah say that in the old days women were never allowed to step out of the house and that it was sheer goodness on the part of the men to permit them to go out anywhere they wanted so long as they wore the burqa. Oh, the magnanimity of the menfolk. Thank you so much.

'"Have any of the men, especially the mullahs, ever experienced the joys of being in that hothouse called a burqa, preferably a black one, for just a week? Forget the sweating or the terrible body odour, TBO for short, that issues from being encased in black in temperatures that fluctuate between 37 and 45 degrees centigrade. A week, however, would be enough for the men to also discover that there are far greater joys in the black robe like ghastly rashes, skin eruptions, and even better, the most disgusting skin diseases.

'"If the menfolk had the least sense of decency, they would give women as much freedom as they themselves have. But that's out of the question, isn't it? God should have had the sense to make all men blind. Then they wouldn't go chasing every piece of arse. And a woman could choose the man she wanted to be with instead of the menfolk sitting on their high moral horses and deciding the fate of their wives and daughters while raping women, in the flesh or at least with their inner eye. And then have the gall to say talaq, talaq, talaq and disown all responsibility towards their wives and the children they had begotten.'

'"Excellent timing, my dear Kashmira. I've had my fill of your blasphemy and I will say the three glorious words which will set me free once and for all at this very moment. Talaq, talaq, talaq."

'"Oh, thank you so much, Kabir." Kashmira smiled, one of her caught-you-with-your-pants-down smiles, and hugged me. I knew instantly then that I had put both my feet into my mouth and would live to regret it till the end of my days.

'"Ah freedom." She threw her hands up in the air and did a little jig in front of me. "I feel lighter by a dozen years, almost like a teenager.'

'"May I have the keys to my home, please?" I cut in sharply. "I want you and all your belongings out in the next hour. Because if they're not, I'll light a bonfire and throw all your stuff into it and celebrate your departure in the company of my friends and neighbours."

'"Ah Kabir, poor, poor Kabir." Kashmira sighed and looked at me full of sympathy and pity. "I'm afraid there's a slight misapprehension here. You gambled your house away when your parents were alive and living with you or rather we were living with them. And then we moved into the home which my father had left for me. So I am afraid you will have to look for another place for yourself. Shouldn't pose any problem, you have so many women friends. They are bound to beg you to stay and make a lovely threesome, I suspect. And don't worry about your paraphernalia, all your unwashed clothes and socks, your shoes, your phentas and your pressed kurtas, angarkhas and salwars and sherwanis, not to mention your looms. I'll make sure they are outside the gate within the next thirty minutes."

'I blanched. I had to retrieve ground immediately or all would be lost, but Kashmira was already hollering for the household help.

'"Bajrang, oh Bajrang, ah, there you are. Get Rabia and Rakhi and Yusuf and collect all the Master's clothes and leave them outside the gate.'

'They stared at her as if she had lost her mind.'

'"Is the Master travelling today?"

'"Yes. All the way from the house to outside the gate."

'"No, no, no, no." I guffawed. It was a good imitation of a laugh but there was no conviction in it. "You know very well how the Mistress loves to pull my leg. And yours too. She's such a funny lady, but don't worry, she's just joking."

'No joke, this. I want him and his entire wardrobe and shoes and those clickety-clack, clickety-clack looms of his out on the street in the next fifteen minutes or all of you will be out on the road with him."

'The servants ran helter-skelter into the house and you could see them through the windows ransacking my clothes.

'Tell them to stop, Kashmira. You know very well I would never throw you out. I was just playing the joker."

'"Maybe you were, but I am not. Out of my sight and out of my life, that's where I want you."

'"What will people say?"

'"They will call you cuckold, that's all. For years now I have heard the women snigger when they saw me at the grocer's or in the marketplace. Did you see that poor thing, they would say, her husband's philandering the whole night while she's at home pining for him."

'"How will I show my face to anybody in our city?"

'"Don't. Wear a burqa. No one will know who it is. I can lend you one of mine. I am through with them."'

'All the neighbours were out watching this once-in-a-lifetime grand show. They sneered and there were hoots of laughter and catcalls and clapping.

'Kashmira, my wife, looked at them and said, "You find this funny, don't you? I know even funnier stories about most of you. Would you care to hear them?"

'It was amazing how rapidly Kashmira and I were left alone with just the servants packing my stuff in trunks and bringing them out.'

'What happened then?' Charatram asked.

'What do you think happened? I had made an ass of myself and was the laughing stock of the whole town. QED. Finis.'

'How did you get back home?'

'I grovelled and I begged my wife to take me back. I swore I would behave myself and never look at a woman again.'

Charatram got up saying, 'That's a whole load of poppycock.'

'How would you know?' The Master looked daggers at his pupil.

Charatram looked at his companions as he walked out. 'Don't move, any one of you. You need to hear the whole story.'

'But he just told us the whole story,' they said.

'Only half the story.'

A few minutes later a smiling Kashmira Mai came out of the house with Charatram and asked the apprentices and assistants, 'Is my husband still in denial?'

The Weaver cringed and tried to slip out of the back door but his wife pinned him to the spot.

'No,' they all said together, 'on the contrary he said he had made an ass of himself.'

'Oh, that he certainly did. But Charatram is right. He left out the most important part. Don't ever underestimate this man. Would you care to hear the rest of it?'

And they all shouted with one voice. 'Yes. Yes. Yes. We want to hear every last detail.'

Kashmira Mai was quiet for a few moments and then spoke softly. 'He disappeared without taking a single kameez, salwar, kurta or pyjama. No razai or blanket. Not even a comb or a razor. Weeks passed but there was no word of his whereabouts. I was caught in a fine quandary. I had done what no woman in the state of Panchananda had done, thrown my husband out, and now I was going out of my mind searching high and low for him. One moment I was sure he had taken up with some other woman and the chances of his coming back were nil. And the next I was convinced he had committed suicide. I went to the police and lodged a complaint about his disappearance. A week later they told me they had combed every nook and corner of the city. They had made forays into the neighbouring towns and villages and across the river into other kingdoms.

'I knew then that he must have committed suicide. I kept asking myself what exactly I had expected him to do.

Or rather wanted him to do. The answer did me no credit. I wanted him to suffer hellfire and worse for shamelessly carrying on with other women even after I had thrown him out. And the next instant I wanted him to crawl on his knees and beg for forgiveness. But I would continue to ignore him and make him pay for his endless betrayals. And then maybe, just maybe, I would consider, nothing more, no promises, maybe I would take him back. But what if, what if . . . he was no more?

'I had given up my burqa. I could have slept with almost any man I wanted and I did. But I have to confess I wanted my man back. The awful truth was I missed him. And how. The fact of the matter was most men bored me to tears once the deed was done. They were pompous, perpetually self-absorbed and it was always me, me, me, me, me. They had no notion of give and take in any aspect of life but most of all in sex. It was their pleasure and theirs alone that mattered. The woman's role was to please them and never the other way round. But what I missed above all else was Kabir's sense of humour. God knows he could elicit a laugh out of a rock and he most certainly could laugh at his own idiocies and follies.

'Humour is not just fun and laughter, it is a call to sanity. It exposes all our inanities, platitudes and solemnities, our insufferable egotism, our endless self-regard and hubris. The curious thing is that it is as much a mirror to the follies of others as it is a dressing down of oneself. The moment it's infected with sentimentality, it turns squelchy. Even stark poverty and starvation can then be romanticized and made to look desirable. It also comes in handy when you want to pass the buck to someone else or disown responsibility. On the contrary, when it's clear-eyed, it can see through all kinds of sham and chicanery. It may be harsh but it's also healing.

'Hindu women stop wearing the red tikka on their foreheads when they become widows. Muslim women have no badge to mark them as widows. But how does one pinpoint a woman who has no idea whether she is still married or is a widow?'

'How did you find the Master who had vanished it would seem from the planet itself?' Inayat asked Kashmira Mai. 'And where was he hiding?'

'I think that's a question you should ask him rather than me.'

All the apprentices and assistant weavers sensed that they had reached no man's land, and while they looked askance at the Master, they left it to him to decide whether he wished to talk about the black hole in his past. It was a curious aspect of their relationship with the Master. They could talk to him about any subject in the universe, they could cross-question him mercilessly and expose his flaws and tics; they could rib him and they could pull his leg and laugh in his face as they exposed his high falutin airs. But they instinctively also grasped that there were certain lines you never crossed.

The Weaver was looking at his wife Kashmira with an odd expression, an amalgam of disbelief and unease, a sense of wonder as if he would never be able to fathom the mystery that she was. He was shaking his head as he said, 'What do I do with this woman? She makes a fool of me, exposes my follies and throws me out of the house and here I stand thanking her for the great favour she did me.

'I have always felt uncomfortable when people confess.

They may confess to intense jealousy, a lack of compassion, terrible arrogance, appalling betrayals and even dreadful crimes. Yes, it takes guts and unsinkable honesty to do so but often there's also a hidden core of pride there, an overweening consciousness of courage. What Kashmira does with honesty is something very different. I know of no other human being who is so totally transparent. She bares her soul, all her fears and hopes, and her struggle to make not just herself but her adversary a better human being.

'When she kicked me out I had the sum total of three emotions: hate, rage and the wrath of a man willing to wipe out the entire female species. She had had the gall to see through me and my macho lies and expose me in public. I had no choice but to vanish. Oh, make no mistake. I would return. Vengeance would be mine. I would make her suffer and plead for mercy.

'Her words were scorched on my brain tissue. I regurgitated them every few minutes to keep the temperature of my vengeance at inflammable heat. Oh, I would wait even a lifetime to get back at her and humiliate her. I was the man of the family. I would prove what that meant. She would have to crawl the rest of her life. Unfortunately there was one small problem: a low but constant hum that I had to keep scotching all the time. As the weeks and months passed the noise kept rising and distracting me from my avowed aim. Kashmira's voice kept intruding in my ears, telling me of the airless coffin called the burqa, the sweating and the awful body odour and the skin diseases, the utter and all-encompassing lack of freedom or say in any matter that is the mark of a paak woman, the triple whammy called talaq, talaq, talaq that men in our country had to merely utter and their marriage would be instantly null and void.

'For the sake of argument, I told myself, let me for a minute – mind you a minute and no more – grant that maybe, just maybe, Kashmira had a valid case but so did I, a very solid one at that. She had not only kicked me out of the house but humiliated me in front of the whole town. What can I say, I was a house divided against itself and my mind was a battlefield. I was at the end of my tether. It seemed the war would go on forever.

'I was exhausted. The fact is I got so fed up after a few months, I just couldn't take it any more. I caved in. I began to listen to the very woman who was anathema to me. For the first time I actually paid heed to her words. Over and over again. Oh, the horror of it: she was making sense. I could just lie down and die. She was holding a mirror to me and my deeds and that included the whole tribe of men, especially the men of God, the mullahs, qazis and maulanas. She unmasked how they had deliberately misread, reinvented and distorted the word of God and the simple, unalterable concept of equality between women and men.

'What choice did I have? I would never admit it but she was right and I was wrong. Months passed and my guilt became unbearable. No, I was never going back to her. My pride would never allow that. But the day dawned when I decided I owed it to her and to every woman since the time of Adam and Eve to make amends, by promoting and propounding the Gospel according to Kashmira, though I was wise enough to change the nomenclature since I did not want my wife to find out that she had won and I had lost. As a newborn convert I was far more of a fanatic than her. I renamed the new doctrine "Boot him out". Him as in the husband or any man who would not treat a woman as his equal.

'I toured the whole of Panchananda and intended to visit every lane and by-lane of the subcontinent. I knew that I was a good mimic and a damn good raconteur. It didn't happen overnight but there was no denying my flair for theatre. Over a period of time I added comic turns, drama and scathing commentary to the original presentation. I began to draw huge crowds of both men and women who guffawed and clapped as I told them the story of how my dear wife had thrown me out. Slowly over the months I built up a devoted group of disciples and followers. I must, however, confess that not everybody in the audience was sympathetic. Sometimes a gang of men would descend and things could get nasty.

'I had lost count of how many months or years I had been travelling across the whole country and come almost full circle when I found myself on the border between Samadhanpur and Panchananda. It was a cold evening but there were already at least a thousand people and with every passing minute hundreds more joined. What was unusual was that there were more than fifty women in black burqas close to the stage. This was encouraging. I thought to myself that maybe they would go home that night and throw their husbands out.

'I was in splendid form and my audience was a highly receptive one. It dawned on me after a while that there was a studied refusal in the burqa group to react to the bawdy dialogue and join the fun. Suddenly two women tried to clamber on to the stage. It was a difficult manoeuvre but a large group of their companions pushed them up by the buttocks and they were finally standing across from me. As they threw off the flaps of their burqas, I recognized the two mullahs from my own masjid. Before I knew what was happening there was a shower of stones and bricks. One of the rocks smashed into my forehead and opened a rich vein. I was blinded by the sudden flow of blood when a wooden pole whooshed in the air and made contact with the side of my head with such force that I felt my neck snap and I was lying on the floor. The last thing that my brain registered was a woman in black trying to save me by shielding me as a group of burqa-clad ladies stamped and danced over her body.

'I think you know the name of the lady who flung herself on me and took the ghastly beating. Kashmira had heard of this crazy man who had started the "Boot Him Out" campaign and had been on the lookout for him for months. I leave it to your imagination to connect the remaining dots.'

Kankar pathar jod key,
Masjid liye banaaye,
Taa chad mulla bang de.
Kyaa behra hua khudaaye?

Putting stones and rocks together,
You build a mosque,
Then climbing to the top the mullah sings the azaan.
Does he think God is deaf?

8

'But why is there so much suffering?' one of the Weaver's disciples, the one they called Gunidas, asked. He was so earnest and solemn in his quest for God, the Weaver wanted to kick him down the stairs to get a laugh out of him.

'Why does a child of two die of diphtheria? Why do the poor starve while the rich only get richer? Why is there no justice? Why is there pain, Master?' There was no stopping Gunidas.

'What a silly question,' the Weaver said. 'Because God is evil.'

Gunidas and his fellow pupils were aghast. The Master was always being heretical, partly to shock them, partly because he liked to speak in puzzles and enigmas, but today he had gone too far; he had crossed all bounds, even those of irreverence. He had to be taught a lesson. They would all leave him.

'Good riddance,' the Weaver shouted as they walked out on him. 'I'll have some peace now.'

But blasphemy is always tempting. It is, after all, the first expression of freedom. One by one, they came back.

'We are here on one condition and one only. You'll stop

saying terrible, heretical things to merely provoke and torment us. Is that a promise?'

The Weaver gave his word that he would never say anything shocking again. He looked contrite.

'I swear by Satan I shall not be heretical again.'

It was pointless talking to him, they said, and walked out again.

'Is Satan not the creation of God?' he shouted after them. 'Are there departments up there, one for evil and one for good? You, Michael, you are in charge of all plant life. Gabriel, I'm shifting you to the department of prophecy and prophets. As for you Uriel, from now on you are in charge of the full spectrum of plagues and the research institute for new and more horrific diseases. We haven't had anything grand and deadly since smallpox. And you, Lucifer, the portfolio for evil, I'm entrusting it to you. I don't want any dirt to stick to me. You are the bad guy and I'm the good one. It's very primitive and simplistic, but take my word for it, good against evil is the best theatre in the world. People will flock to see us. The bishops, qazis and rabbis will philosophize interminably about the tree of knowledge and the doctrine of free will, and how God in his wisdom created polarities and each human being must choose between Him and evil. They'll love it, Lucifer.

'Have you noticed something else?' the Weaver asked. 'Something bizarre? Satan, I mean Lucifer, has all the time in the world, and I mean quality time, for all of us. He is always available. Not just that, he takes the initiative, he's patient, he's persevering and, most of all, he never gives up on us. He's always there, even when we don't need him. In fact, especially when we don't need him.

'How do you think original sin came about? God was sitting on his high horse, acting all mighty and remote and unapproachable while the devil was holding Adam and Eve by the hand in the Garden of Eden and making them feel wanted.

'You'll admit that it's a little odd that while the devil is always on call, the good Lord seems a little preoccupied.

'Why does God get all the credit for good,' the Weaver asked, 'and why is all evil attributed to Satan? If God is the Creator, he can handle both. You must decide who's in charge here, my friends. Only then will you understand that all polarities and divisions are sacrilege. God, if I may use one of these newfangled academic terms, is the unified theory of the universe. Good and evil, warmonger and pacifist, Hindu, Muslim, Jew, Christian, Buddhist, materialist and preacher, atheist and believer are all encompassed in Him. He's large enough and wise enough to accommodate all contradictions.'

Karni kare toh kyun dare,
Aur kari kyun pachhtaaye,
Tune boya ped babul ka,
Toh aam kahaan se khaaye.

Having committed the deed,
Why would you be afraid, and then repent,
First you sow the thorny babul,
Then how come you expect to eat mangoes.

9

The Master was a late riser and was often cantankerous and tetchy till he had finished his bath and had a hefty breakfast, though sometimes he could be perverse and be ill-tempered for a week or two and make everybody's life miserable. But if his pupil Indra Dhanush from Gulmarg, who obviously had an old-fashioned music guru, woke up at four-thirty in the morning, took a dip in the river and sat under the banyan tree with his tanpura, closed his eyes and hit an unhurried mile-deep first note, and magisterially swept up all the treasures that lay at the bottom of the raga Bhairavi, the Weaver would be instantly awake and totally switched on. There was no telling what he would do next. Sometimes he folded his long legs in a padmasan, closed his eyes and went missing for hours. It was impossible to tell whether he had slipped into a trance or was meditating. Often it felt as if he was dead.

Indra Dhanush's voice was nothing less than a gift of God. As his name suggested he was the rainbow that spanned the distance between God and earthlings. When he sang a bhajan or the raga Malkauns, the Weaver was certain that Allah himself put everything aside, even urgent matters that had to be dealt with right away, stretched out and wandered into a sublime reverie.

No one could predict the effect that Indra Dhanush's intense singing would have on the Master. At times even as the sky was developing a million hairline fractures while the sun shot forth from under the line of the horizon, he reached out for his pad and a stick of charcoal. He was like a man possessed, his right hand moving so swiftly capturing the whole cavalcade of life, you could barely track it. Within minutes, the flock of swallows sweeping over the sun was down on the paper, and now he had caught the wind flirting with each and every leaf of the banyan tree and trying to seduce it.

There was no fathoming how a magisterial Darbari Kanada sung past midnight on Dhanteras turned into a million tiny lamps riding on the river on his drawing pad and how each of the minuscule flames was flickering on the paper. One thing was certain. Everything that the Master caught on paper he would turn into a series of the most complex but precise constellations of digits and figures for the looms and then miraculously transform them into images of the crowded ghats of the Narmada or peacocks in heat at sunset or the Bodhi tree under which the Buddha gained nirvana, and these would one day be converted into motifs that would become the warp and woof of His Majesty, the Maharana of Panchananda's wardrobe.

The Weaver's relationship with his liege Ramdeo Singhji was something of a conundrum to most of the courtiers in the capital. How did a nonentity like a weaver-tailor from the backwaters not just make it to the capital but seemed to have a highly personal and private relationship with HM?

The Weaver never spoke about it nor did the Maharana. Once in a while someone or the other would corner Kabir and would ask, supposedly in jest, how come an outsider and that too a johnny-come-lately like him had got so close to a ruler who was known all over the subcontinent to be an extremely private person who did not suffer fools and toadies.

'What's to wonder?' the Weaver would ask with an earnest and intense look on his face. 'I'm just your textbook sycophant.' Almost invariably the questioner would suspect that the Weaver was putting him on and pump him for more information, which of course got him nowhere. The smart guys, however, suspected this was nothing but a strategy adopted by the Weaver to deflect attention from his relationship with Maharana Ramdeo Singhji. The fact was the Weaver loved to make an ass of whoever poked his long nose into his private affairs.

It was the festival of Holi and the previous night the Weaver and his pupils had lit a huge bonfire to symbolize the burning of the demoness Holika and the miraculous escape of her nephew Prahlad, the devotee of Lord Vishnu. The next morning the Weaver's pupils were already on the banks of the Jamuna, pouring powdered colours into separate vats filled with water and stirring them till they had all the seven hues of the rainbow and many more.

Further down the riverbank the young women of the village too were cleaning brass syringes, filling them up and getting ready for a hectic battle with the menfolk. The Weaver, who was usually master of all the Holi shenanigans, had been down with some bug in the stomach and was in a terrible humour because the local hakim had given strict orders that he was not to leave his bed.

The colour wars were at their peak. The young men were high on thandai, and so the women could keep them at bay with their miniature water cannons aimed steadily at their eyes. Though no one would admit it, the courting rituals of Holi were also at an advanced stage with both the men and the women managing to signal their preferences while maintaining an air of 'What, me? Cross my heart and hope to die, never even heard of a gender called male or female.'

A feisty young woman who had partaken of the milkshake laced with cannabis, spices, ghee and mangoes burst into song. She had a raw but full-throated, enchantingly melodious voice. The song spoke of the first meeting between Radha and Krishna, where else but right there on the banks of the Jamuna. When the demoness Putana had breastfed the child Krishna with poisonous milk, he had turned blue and ever since he'd had a chip on his shoulder about this and was certain that the fair and beauteous Radha would never even look at him. 'Jamuna tat, Shyam khele Holi, Jamuna tat / Dor dor pichkari chalawat . . .' Within minutes, nay seconds, the Weaver sleepwalked out into the open.

That classical musical form called the hori which celebrates Holi had wound an invisible rope around his neck and was dragging him willy-nilly to the singer. Even as he drew closer to her, you could see that his body had turned into song and he was now Krishna himself wooing Radha with a sensuous, erotic dance that wrapped itself around the singer like a twisting, swirling vine. The tension between the two was electric, each egging the other on and accelerating the pace. And now the pupils too had joined the delirium of the dance.

In the distance the shahi imam, the seniormost mullah in the kingdom, was walking briskly holding a large folder, along with three elders from the community. It was Anurag, the new acolyte, who first spotted them and wondered whether they were headed to the lighthouse, the masjid across the river or for a private heart-to-heart on the banks of the river. And then before he knew it, they had stormed into the pulsating throb of the whirling mass and had interrupted the Master.

'Stop this profane spectacle at once. Are you even aware, Weaver, that it's Friday today, a day of prayer and introspection, and here you are dancing to some satanic song dedicated to a heathen god. Just imagine, some of our own people think of you as a saint-in-the-making. Don't you know that our faith forbids singing and dancing?'

'The Lord gifteth and the mullah taketh away.' The Master was dripping with sweat and spoke breathlessly. 'Do you have even the vaguest idea, Shahi Imam, what a divine gift the human voice is? Do you know that you have to be the recipient of special grace to be able to do a cosmic dance for none other than the Almighty himself? Why are we forbidden to rejoice in the very gifts the good Lord has presented us with, gifts which become wonderful gestures of thanksgiving and bring us closer to him? How dare you have the arrogance to censor God?'

'Put a leash on your tongue, Weaver, lest the Almighty strike you dead for blasphemy. As if this cavorting with the ladies was not shameful enough, one of your apprentices furnished us with your original drawings.' The Shahi Imam undid the knot of the folder he was carrying and flung the drawings and paintings on the sand. 'Imagine our shock and horror at seeing these paintings of heathen gods and goddesses. And worse still, the depiction of human beings in every conceivable situation including the privacy of the seraglio and other scenes of intimacy when our people have been expressly forbidden to duplicate the myriad creatures who inhabit our planet, most of all the very apotheosis of creation, mankind itself.

'You know perfectly well that there is but one Creator and that is God. And that is why it is forbidden to create the simulacrum of life for that is the privilege of God and God alone. Be warned, Weaver, you have committed the unforgivable crime of pretending to be the Creator Himself.'

'May I ask you a question, high priest? Do you have children?'

'You know very well the answer to your question but let me enlighten you again. Allah has blessed me with four wives and twenty-three children.'

'In that case you have committed the unforgivable crime of pretending to be the Creator Himself.'

'I know your tricks well by now, Weaver. You are as usual attempting to deflect our attention from the main issue.'

'Are you denying that you undertook the role of the Creator twenty-three times?'

'Indeed I did nothing of the sort. The children are the Almighty's gift to a devout disciple.'

'I don't doubt it but the Lord didn't bed your wives. You did and brought forth twenty-three little tykes, each with her or his precious soul and thus imitated the act of creation.'

'May you rot in jehannum, Weaver, but even that will be too kind a punishment for the likes of you.'

'Thank you for your generous offer to find accommodation

for me in hell, mullah. But perhaps you can enlighten me about a rather delicate matter. Who gave some of us the incredible benediction of a singing voice? The boon of dancing feet? And the gift of transcribing the sky, the Himalayan peaks, or the sheer extravagance of the flowers in the Kashmir valley or the intimacy between a man and a woman? The miracle that conjoins speech with language and thus allows us to communicate with each other and tell marvellous stories? Certainly not you but our Maker. And now you have the gall, Shahi Imam, to place yourself above God himself and pass fiats and diktats in His name. You claim obeisance to the Almighty but in fact are shamelessly usurping his role.

'What is one to make of the fact that you and your brothers in the priesthood insist that all women and men cover their heads? If God had disliked mankind's hair so much, he would have made not just women but all of us men also bald. After all, as you never stop repeating, He is the Creator and He knows best.'

'Yes, Allah knows best. But the problem is you, Kabir. While I am the apostle of Allah and keeper of the Quran, you are nothing but a stooge of Satan and will rot in hell for all of infinity.'

'Now who's playing God, mullah? Every Friday you go berserk raising Cain and making your congregation quake with fear as you wax eloquent about the terrible conflagrations of jehannum to which all sinners will be condemned. But let me enlighten you, maulana, the divine one is the very epitome of joy and mercy. He loves beautiful things. Look at the sunrise. On every day of the year, each one is brand new and unlike any other. Look at the

Himalayas, the Ganga or any river, the birds and the trees. Or women for that matter. Each one of them is nothing less than ravishing. Your tribe's excuse is that covering the head is a sign of respect. And hence you have compelled women to extend the black over their body. Did God come and whisper in your ear that he's ashamed of his own creation?

'Do you know what your problem is? You want to be God. Because then you can pretend to be all-powerful and all power rests between those two words: "yes", but mostly "no". Your notion of religion allows geometric designs to be depicted in paint, tile and stone. If one is to grant your reasoning, then geometric forms like parallelograms, rhomboids, circles, triangles, octagons are mankind's inventions. But Imam, however intricately we might interweave them in our mosques and tombs, they are not the handiwork of man. Have you never paused to look at the seed-head of a sunflower, or the whorl of a seashell? This sacred geometry is there all through nature. For everything we are comes from the Almighty. It is He who installed that most precious of the Lord's gifts, our brains, in our heads.'

Jab main thaa tab Hari nahi,
Ab Hari hain main nahi,
Prem gali ati saankari,
Taa me do na samaayi.

When I was, the Almighty was not,
Now that He is, I am not,
The path of love is very narrow,
Two cannot fit in it.

10

The Master's morning bath at the height of winter had by now gained something of a legendary status. Even as he woke up, he had Ram on his tongue. As you know, he referred to God more often as Ram but his Ram was very different from the Hindu god Rama. His Ram had no affiliations with one particular faith. When he called upon Ram, it was the Almighty minus religion. Occasionally he would be composing the tune for one of his own songs early in the morning and start singing while pulling the bucket filled with freezing cold water up from the well before turning it over his head and then stand tottering with the shivers and cursing himself for his masochistic streak.

'Cross my heart and hope to die,' he promised Kashmira, 'never again will I take a cold shower in winter and that too in the open.' He meant every word except that come next morning . . . Believe it or not, on two occasions he was shaking so badly, he had fallen into the well and Kashmira Mai had had to summon the pupils and they had to pull up the Weaver, who had nearly turned to ice and had to be brought back to life. Not that it made any difference to the man's cussedness for the next morning's bucket too went crashing down, was pulled up rapidly and before you knew it, it was sitting upside down on the Weaver's head while he recited the hundred names of Allah with a shaky death rattle. He was fully awake now and ready to take on God.

'Doubtless there is no greater mystery in the universe than God. The sad truth is He will remain so forever.

'Death in the singular, I need hardly mention, comes to all of us whether we want it or not. When Yama, the god of death in Hindu mythology, comes calling, you know that your term on earth is over. It's goodbye and finis. Most of the time Death comes unannounced. It's like coitus interruptus. You have no say in the matter. Your life is terminated never to be taken up again. QED. It's a fait accompli.'

Sometimes the Master would slip into some other world of his own. He would be sitting on a mound watching the sun set on a winter evening behind banks of swollen clouds and start a monologue addressed to no one knew whom. Some of his pupils were convinced that he was in private converse with the Almighty. Others thought that he was, to say the least, a little touched in the head. Maybe he was lost in a reverie, an introspective moment, a questioning of himself and all that he believed in. Some of the elders claimed that they were witnessing a mind trying to come to terms with the infinite.

What difference did it make? The fact was he was no longer conscious of where he was or if he had an audience. Half the time they didn't understand what he was talking about. But whatever it was, it was so intense that they didn't want to miss out on a single word he uttered while he was right there with them and yet in some other sphere or universe.

You would have thought the Master's pupils would have a ball making fun of his philosophical ramblings and his intense questioning but somehow they seemed to instinctively sense that this was not an occasion for tomfoolery or jesting. It might take a little time for them to notice that the Weaver was on one of his solitary jags but within seconds the workshop would fall silent. The pupils and the apprentices would drop whatever they were doing and quietly listen to his philosophical wanderings and quandaries.

The Weaver had a full-throated voice, a tad on the harsher side, but it could suddenly turn mellifluous and wrap itself like a shahtoosh shawl around you. It was marvellous to hear him at that very early hour. In truth it seemed so uplifting, his pupils felt at one with nature and the universe. But try and unravel the meaning of the words and they would be arguing about it for the next week or fortnight.

'When the fatality numbers rise to hundreds, thousands and hundreds of thousands, what you get is a pestilence like the plague, cholera or the pox as in smallpox. Murder, however, is a different kettle of fish. The top honcho on earth, none other than man himself, is the agent of perdition here. This nefarious tradition was started almost at the beginning of time if one follows the Biblical calendar. As the story goes, Cain offered the Lord the fruit of the soil that he cultivated while Abel presented the firstborn of his flock of sheep to God. And here's the puzzle: Why did God welcome Abel's gift while ignoring Cain's? Indeed the question the Omniscient One asked the firstborn was inexplicably naive. "Why are you incensed and why is your face fallen? For whether you offer well or whether you do not, at the tent flap sin crouches and for you is its longing, but you will rule over it."

'Cain, it's not hard to believe, was at a loss to fathom the Almighty's query. On the face of it at least, Cain's gift was the more innocent one. There is no violence or blood-letting in grain or fruit, whereas a lamb is usually meant for slaughter. As it turned out, God seemed to have little understanding of human nature for Cain was not able to "rule over it", it as in sin, as the Lord had forecast. I guess it did not occur to him that God of all people would play favourites. He was so deeply hurt, Cain was the very first human to be possessed by jealousy and it drove him to spill Abel's blood.'

It was hard keeping pace with the Master's track changes. But even more to the point, no one so far had cast such a different light on Cain's actions and made you wonder if God had been unfair and partial to Abel. But the Weaver was not yet done with Cain and Abel.

'Apart from the fact that God ignored Cain's gift, surely the One and Only Omniscient One would have known what was in store for Abel and could easily have averted the calamity with a little bit of forethought. The reason given for this bizarre non-interference is that institution called "free will".'

The sun had set by now, and since winter twilights were very short, it was already pitch dark and the temperature was plummeting rapidly. The apprentices and the novice students didn't realize that those two last words the Master had uttered would set him off on another track altogether.

'The consequences of those two single syllabic words have

been monumentally disastrous when they apply to that man-made category of mass murder named genocide. Sometimes I think of God as Emperor Nero sitting entranced at the site of his kingdom going up in fire and flames. How else can one explain the good Lord sitting on his throne and passively watching a naval captain take over a whole continent and start the trend of destroying almost all the First Nations in the Americas? How come the Almighty chose to be a mere spectator while the European nations discovered slavery, transported millions from the African continent and made it the most profitable business proposition ever? And of course there is the luminous example of the dictator from Germany who took such a shine to the Jews, he could not rest till he had gassed six million of them along with the Roma tribes and the weak of mind. And let's not forget the top honchos from Russia and China who murdered over forty million each. Surely it must take tremendous patience and a satanic love of bloodletting to witness so many genocides.

'With what serenity the good Lord watches the inheritors of the Prophet's teachings and legacy, the Shias and the Sunnis, trying to wipe out each other. Or the bizarre spectacle of the Catholics and Protestants waking up one morning and deciding that though they shared the same Father, Son and the Holy Ghost, the "other" needed to be eradicated.'

Kashmira Mai had raised her voice and was yelling at her husband to come and pick up a shawl or he would catch some awful lung infection. The Weaver needless to say was impervious to any and all calls while he was hauling God over the coals regarding his thesis about free will. Mai must have got fed up of calling her husband and stepped out into the garden. There he was, sitting leaning against the trunk of a raintree. One look at her husband and she realized he was too far gone to listen to anybody. She handed the shawl to one of the Master's youngest supervisors, Divyajyot, and whispered, 'Just wrap this pashmina around his shoulders, will you?' and left.

'In defence of the Almighty, men have always put forward the argument that God gave mankind the gift of free will and hence it was up to every generation of humans, both men and women, to choose between good and evil, between right and wrong and thus gain the high moral ground. How come this omniscient God doesn't ask himself, wouldn't it have been infinitely better if he had thought matters through and dropped the doctrine of free will altogether, or at least when it came to the practice of violence, and thus avoided such horrendous bloodshed? Frankly, He could still do that. After all, just as we dropped our tails as we evolved, he could switch off the killer instinct.

'Instead at some point in time when things got completely out of hand and millions were butchered, God winced and turned his head away even as he closed his eyes. He has not opened them since then. It was clear that he couldn't take it any more. See no evil, hear no evil and speak no evil might have worked for the three monkeys but what else was it but a desperate attempt on the part of God not to face the truth? Instead his resolve to deflect all criticism and thus avoid responsibility by deliberately turning blind is not going to solve anything.

'It's no secret that the world is imperfect. What we don't know, or perhaps we would rather not know, is whether God is imperfect. And there is one other niggling question: Did God make man or was it the other way around?'

That was the problem with the Master. You never, but never, could tell when he would drop a bomb; the kind of bomb that would rock the very foundations of everything you had believed to be sacrosanct and had never thought anyone would have the gall to question. The odd thing was that you couldn't even accuse him of playing to an audience or being deliberately provocative for he wasn't even aware that he had company.

Often the Master could carry on in this fashion, picking holes in the very notion of Godhood. And then at the end of it, he could blithely negate every single thing he had said or implied. Believe it or not, he would fall to the ground and say a prayer. Sometimes out of the blue, having put the whole institution of God into serious doubt, the Weaver would go down on his knees and pray to the Lord, 'Hey Ram, I know I just questioned your very existence. But life, as you are well aware, is full of contradictions. And it's best to play it safe. I know I am a gadfly and I have behaved badly, very badly with Kashmira, but God, I beg you, please make sure that I die before her. This is all I ask of you. I cannot survive without her. Or rather I can but it will be hell. Don't let me down. I will take it very ill if you did.'

Mala toh kaar mein phire,
Jeebh phire mukh mahin,
Manwa toh chahun dish phire,
Yeh toh simran nahi.

The beads move between the fingers,
The tongue rolls in the mouth,
If the mind wanders everywhere,
That surely isn't meditation.

11

It was a winter evening and the Master and his pupils were sitting wrapped in shawls around a bonfire. The disciple Sagar, who had been renamed Athangsagar because there was no plumbing the depths of this infinite sea, was perpetually preoccupied with all-consuming metaphysical questions about life and death, not to mention those relating to the afterlife. His speciality was something called the scientific temper and he claimed his great strength and weapon was research. He did research on every conceivable subject: he looked at the colour of your stools and told you whether you had jaundice, typhoid or worms. And when you said, 'But I am fine, nothing whatsoever's the matter with me,' he looked dolefully at you and told you, 'Ignorance is bliss till you discover it's too late and you are about to breathe your last.' It was amazing, he could analyse a woman's pee and foretell not only whether she was pregnant but what the foetus's gender was. He would stare at the distant skies and the rolling clouds and predict whether there would be a drought or a rich harvest in the coming year.

He came in late that day and asked a colleague sitting

next to the Weaver to move to some other place and began to speak in his portentous voice as he settled down in the just-vacated seat.

'I have to talk to you about a matter of the gravest importance. As you know, Master, human life is but a blip on infinity, which is the only spectrum that God deals in. As if that was not dire enough, death rarely gives notice before it douses the flame.'

Kabir sighed as he listened to this disciple whom he often referred to as the Prince of Banal Profundities and decided to play dumb.

'Why, Athang, we have a roaring bonfire here and no rain or frost is about to kill the lively flames.'

'Ah sire, how opaque can you get. I was referring to the flame of life. There's no knowing whether I will be here tomorrow or–'

'I had no idea you were planning to travel tomorrow. Where are you headed?' The Weaver was in a perverse mood and bent on trying Athang's patience. 'Ah yes, your brother did mention that your parents were looking for a bride for you. I hope you will not forget to invite us . . .'

'Master, how can you think of nuptials when we humans are faced with the most critical choice of our lives? This life will last at the most sixty or seventy years if one lives the full term. But the choices one makes now will decide the quality of one's afterlife which runs into infinity. Which is why, as you know, I have been doing the most extensive comparative studies of different religions. My aim is to find out what each faith has on offer and which is the best on a scale of a hundred on the basis of several parameters.'

'What a truly ambitious project. Absolutely astounding.

Imagine measuring divinity and heaven itself through a scientific lens. How far has your research come?'

Athang looked suspiciously at the Master. You could never trust him and that childlike but totally fake innocent look. But the Weaver was suddenly sitting up and was all ears. 'Perhaps you can fill me in on the indicators against which you are testing the different faiths.'

'What we are looking at actually is how each religion sees heaven or paradise. And of course its obverse, hell or jehannum. The whole field is so full of misinformation, myths, fairy tales and misreadings. Everything's vaguely defined and is full of holes and hence mostly misunderstood. So ours is going to be the very first comprehensive project to get down to the nitty-gritty analyses that will help portray the precise picture.'

'Let's get down to the "nitty-gritty" of your research, Athang. Give me some major factors to chew on.'

'Here are some of the salient ones. Ease of admission to heaven. How much preparation is required before you are found eligible and how rigorously is the applicant tested. The concepts of sin, confession, the tests for the genuineness of repentance, and forgiveness. The intervention of priests. The role of prophets and messiahs. And most important of all, the facilities.'

'The facilities?' The Master sounded bemused. 'What's that?'

'The precise list of what each faith has to offer in terms of heaven and hell. Accommodation is a major concern. How many bedrooms and the view; what kind of locality; is it in a tonier part of heaven? We definitely don't want to be in the company of people from the wrong class. The most frequently asked question is, how close will my residence be to God's? The general feeling is that the saints hog all the limelight and get the best of everything while the others are seen as mere also-rans.

'The oriental religions like Buddhism, Hinduism and Jainism have a cyclical system. One is born endlessly in different forms like trees, reptiles, roaches, all kinds of animal and fish species. Hopefully, at the end of this endless cycle of rebirths, one finally arrives at nirvana or enlightenment and the soul is set free. Its great merit is that it spells escape. But for better or worse, this business of nirvana appears to be a static concept.'

'I beg your pardon, moksha as a dead end?' the Master interrupted Athang.

'Yes, precisely. Once you've reached this goalpost, where do you go? It's the end. Does enlightenment translate into some kind of happiness? Maybe. You remain enlightened for the rest of eternity. That's it.

'The Hindus seem to have the possibility of a swarg or heaven but prior to getting admission there you have to do due diligence, go through the whole gamut of incarnations and only when you are past all desire or temptation, can you end up in swarg. What is unclear is whether this is a soul-state or does the physical body still exist. Of the three peoples of the Book, Christians and Muslims are the ones who have a better idea of the afterlife. All the great painters of Europe have depicted heaven and hell as if they had spent decades in both the places. And of course Dante and Milton not to mention the Bible itself have held forth on the subject.

'Curiously enough the majority of Jews who at one

time were so gung-ho about heaven and hell, can't seem to resurrect their earlier certainties. Time and again you hear of a place called Sheol which is some kind of pit, a land of forgetfulness. Cut off from both human contact and God, it is, however, a place devoid of judgement, punishment or reward. The current crop of Jewish scholars play it safe and prefer to dwell on the life here and now which in the best of circumstances will last a hundred years at the most, but skirt around the subject of the afterlife and thus turn their backs on nothing less than eternity.

'It's Islam which has gone to great lengths to catalogue the exact benefits available. Both jannat and jehnoom have a pyramidal structure. Seven rungs each, one better than the previous one in the matter of paradise or jannat but exactly the opposite in the case of hell. As you progress down the gradient, the level of torture, brutality and fires becomes infinitely more intolerable and the suffering unbearable.

'But there's one other feature which is unique to Islam. They have this institution called houris. It's a service industry and the most important feature of their paradise. They even spell out just how many houris each male resident is entitled to. Of late there's been a serious controversy regarding the exact numbers. It appears that as the residents in heaven increase, the number of houris has been going down. At last count it was forty-three.'

'And what about the ladies?' Kabir enquired. 'I trust they too get free gigolo service and a wide selection of cherubs to choose from.'

'No laughing matter, Master.' Athang looked disapprovingly at the Weaver. 'Women are inferior beings and they should know their place in the scheme of things.'

'Wouldn't it be interesting to find out if there was any connection at all between God and religion?'

Athang looked at the Weaver suspiciously. 'What mischief are you up to? Are you trying to tell me that God and religion are at odds with each other? That they are incompatible?'

'It's something of a conundrum, isn't it,' the Weaver asked, 'as to why God would create mankind and then divide his putative greatest creation through so many internecine faiths, to the point where each one claims sole rights to Him and the truth and is busy murdering and massacring the other?'

'You're straying away from the crux of the matter, Master. The only relevant question is who gets admittance to heaven. The Hindus, or rather the Shaivites or the Vaishnavites? The Sunnis or the Shias in Islam? And the Jews, the Sephardics or the Ashkenazis? And amongst the Christians, the Catholics or the Protestants? The corollary to the central question is: Does each denomination get a separate space?'

'Your research, Athang, has thrown up amazing facts and insights. You've made a comparative analysis of heaven and hell in different faiths. It's exactly like a shopping mall, a commodity or real estate marketplace, and put God up for sale. When it comes to the afterlife, you no longer need to stick to the God of your parents. You study the paradise market and choose the one that suits you best. If what you say is true, all the other heavens are going to empty out and almost everybody will opt for the Islamic variety. Think about it, an eternity of sex. What more can we men ask for? Do you see what man has gone and done? Reduced heaven to a brothel. You don't even have to pay for the services. You get a free ride.'

'Hold your horses, Master. I haven't posed the most important question yet to the Christians. How long will mankind have to wait for that final event, the moment when Jesus will resurrect the dead? For let's not forget that the resurrection alone makes void death itself (1 Corinthians 15:54). Millennia have gone by and yet there's no sign of it. How can one forget that the afterlife is nothing but a mere figment of the imagination without the resurrection.'

'What do you propose then?'

'It's about time we gave God an ultimatum and asked him to set a date. Or else . . .'

'Wow Athang, this is really getting to be an edge-of-the-seat kind of spectacular show. Mankind can now read the riot act to God, how about that?'

Pothi padh padh kar jag mua,
Pandit bhayo na koye,
Dhai aakhar prem ke,
Jo padhe so pandit hoye.

Reading the holy texts time and again,
Didn't ever produce a great scholar,
The one who lives by the four letters of the word love,
He alone will become a pandit.

12

Kashmira woke me up late one night and told me that a stranger whose face was covered in a thick silk scarf except for the eyes had knocked on the door and had asked for me. I looked at the clock groggily and asked, 'At this time of the night? It's past one. Ask him his name and tell him to come tomorrow morning.'

'I asked for his name and he just shook his head and whispered, "Trust me." I was about to tell him that now that he had spoken those two words, my one and only instinct was to distrust him altogether. But something about his voice and manner seemed familiar. I don't know what kind of spell he cast over me but here I am, waking you up.'

I was about to ask her if she had gone out of her mind. 'What if he's a thief and has already entered the house and is about to hold us hostage?'

'I knew I was doing the wrong thing and for all I know he may already be in the house but . . .'

What was the point of my getting mad with Kashmira now? The first thing I needed to do was to tell the man to beat it and lock the door. Just to be on the safe side I shoved a pair of nine-inch scissors into my pocket and grumpily walked out. There he was standing exactly as Kashmira had said: hiding his face behind that expensive scarf. The sheer gall of the man. I was about to ask him if this was any time to visit and anyway I had no time for the likes of him.

'Why don't you close the door, so that we can go for a little walk?'

My answer was on the tip of my tongue: 'You take a walk. Got that? I am not going anywhere. With or without you.'

What was it about him that gave me pause? The voice, the breeding, the politeness? Or was it the air of despair?

'Kashmira,' I hollered, 'you go back to sleep. I'm stepping out for just a few minutes.'

I closed the door and followed him. He must have been fairly well acquainted with the area for he led me to the Amrutsagar lake just about half a furlong from our home and patted the top of a marble bench for me to sit on next to him. We watched as several antelopes trooped out of the forest and slurped the water. Soon a herd of African elephants and a blackbuck couple turned up. What was going on? Had this weirdo woken me up in the middle of the night to watch every species of animal trooping down to the waterhole?

Oh no, oh no, no. All the bells in hell were tolling wildly now. How could I not have recognized him?

'Majesty, I have no idea how to apologize to you for not recognizing you?'

'But that was precisely the intention, Kabir. Why else would I have undertaken to visit you past midnight and not even greeted Kashmira Mai? Well, sit down now that you know who your nocturnal visitor is.'

I was in shock but there was no way I was going to sit down next to His Majesty.

'Forgive me, Kabir, but I needed to have a very confidential chat with . . .'

'Majesty, all you had to do was send for me.'

'So that everybody else would have known that I wanted to discuss something which I did not care to share with anyone else? For God's sake, stop being so damned formal and sit down. Otherwise we can't talk.'

I sat down.

'I am most likely going to hate myself for confiding something so personal to you. But here I am and I am going to talk to you since you are one of the three people who knows that my marriage started off on the wrong foot. It took me time to understand how sensitive and intuitive the woman who became my queen was. The fault was mine, and mine alone. The first couple of years I was wary and not very open with her. That's an understatement. Any other woman would have walked out on me. But she has proven to be someone infinitely patient and caring and I'm truly blessed. And now I want to celebrate her but don't know how.'

'Sire, I'm confused. Why all the secrecy? Why not tell HM Anagha Devi how much you value her?'

'Time does strange things, Weaver. Our actions, or rather inactions, silences and coldness, all have consequences. She has withdrawn into a place I cannot or don't know how to reach. I try every now and then but I'm so clumsy she shrinks further into herself. The fact is I don't know how to break the ice.'

It was ironic, I had behaved like a lout with my wife

Kashmira and yet she had forgiven me. I don't think HM had ever been crude or cruel to Her Majesty, Queen Anagha Devi, and yet they seemed to have reached a dead end. He had come to me for help and all I could manage was silence.

'Don't play coy with me, Kabir. I must know the truth. Is the situation beyond hope? Have I lost her for good?'

'Sire, I'm no Sibyl, and cannot predict the future but one thing I am certain about. If as you say she's a good woman and has a heart of gold but is badly hurt, you'll have to bend over backwards to heal her. Do it clumsily and she'll freeze even further. What it needs is a subtle touch and finesse. It will take time, but all the more reason not to give up on her.'

Ramdeo Singhji smiled and shook his head. 'I must confess, Weaver, that I'm none the wiser, for you've shown me the way but haven't told me how to get there.'

We walked back, both of us lost in thought. I was going to accompany him to the Alakhnanda Palace but he stopped me.

'I came alone and I'll return alone.' He wished me good night and left. The door had been left unlocked and I went in. It must have taken me a few minutes to wash my feet and I was about to get into bed when I rushed out and caught up with HM.

'Majesty, I have nothing profound to say nor have I found a solution to your quandary. In truth, whatever I have to say is a little banal and devious. Perhaps the best way to reach out to HM Anagha Devi is through Prince Satyanam Singh.'

'What are you suggesting?' Ramdeo Singhji looked suspiciously at me.

'Sire, since your wedding was such a fraught affair, if I recall correctly, you and the Maharani have never visited Samadhanpur. I'm sure they would love to see their daughter and first grandson.'

'Are you suggesting I visit my in-laws?' he asked in a barely audible voice.

'No sire.' I knew I was stepping on a landmine. 'I think it would be a good idea if all three of you took a week or two off and enjoyed the hospitality of . . .'

'I've never prevented Anagha from seeing her parents.' HM's voice had turned into an antagonistic hiss. 'Over the last five years she's been there twice, and that too very briefly.'

'Do you think that was because she sensed that you don't care for your in-laws?'

'Quite likely. I think I told you she's very perceptive.'

'I've little doubt that Maharani Anagha Deviji suspects there was a serious falling out between her parents and you. At the same time I don't think her mother, Ameera Devi, would ever want to reveal the true reasons why the relationship between your in-laws and yourself turned cold and sterile overnight.'

'What's all this about? Why are you bringing my in-laws into the picture?' Ramdeoji was obviously getting impatient and short-tempered with me.

'Sire, this is not about your in-laws and the past. They are merely a means to an end. You expressed the desire not merely to initiate a thaw between you and Maharaniji but to establish a deep new relationship, perhaps bond is a better word, that will withstand any and every stress and crisis. There's no guarantee that this game plan will work but it's the only chance there is of persuading Anagha Deviji that you are willing to go more than halfway to let bygones be bygones. Or to put it baldly, that you value her to the point where you will not permit anything to come between her and you.'

I was sure Ramdeo Singhji was livid with me but I had said my bit and would have to take the consequences.

'I know that I came to you of my own free will to ask your advice.' RamdeoSinghji looked at me with distaste. 'I keep wondering if it was nothing short of a blunder on my part since I can no longer tell whose side you are on. Wish I knew what the morning will have in store for both you and me. Goodnight Weaver.'

I could understand his resentment and antipathy against Samadhanpur. They had played him dirty, and he preferred to keep his distance. Unfortunately I had stuck my neck out and touched a raw nerve and very likely there would be hell to pay.

I spent more than thirty-six hours in limbo, not knowing whether I was going to be persona non grata and wondering where the hell I would go if the Maharana threw me out. Why was I playing coy? The fact was fate and HM might have much worse in store for me than exile. The deadline I had set for myself passed and I knew that the end was nigh. Don't ask me how I continued to breathe when all I wanted was to put an end to the suspense.

Dear Kabir,

I'm unable to fathom why I listened to all the poppycock that you dished out even though I knew that you are a quack and a popcorn psychologist. Truth to tell I feel as if I am trapped in a mud-bog and the only way to get out and breathe freely is to get over with your abracadabra.

So here's my POA. If I am to go with Her Majesty and Prince Satyanam to Samadhanpur, then I'll be constrained to order a whole new wardrobe for her, and even the little one must have designer-ware nappies even though he prefers not to wear them since he's perpetually busy playing with his little thingummyjig.

Don't forget, the new wardrobe must outshine the best that you may have woven or designed so far. Needless to say it must be infinitely superior to and utterly different from whatever the denizens of Samadhanpur think of as high fashion. Don't forget we are talking about Panchananda's pride here.

Luckily the city of Dharmabhoomi will be hosting its annual all-India clothes fair in the next week and you can choose whatever fabrics and designs you wish. The question is, after spending all that money and visiting my in-laws despite my resolve never to do so, what if I am still unable to find my way into the Maharani's heart?

For my sake and especially yours, I hope your voodoo works. Because if it doesn't . . .

PS: I suggest you get down to work immediately.

This was the first time he had sent me a letter without signing it.

I read the letter and realized that asking HM to go to Samadhanpur had been a dicey suggestion. He was utterly stressed out and hoping that passing the buck and blame to me would help him regain his sense of balance. It also suddenly struck me that he may rightly fear that the thorny relationship between Panchananda and Samadhanpur may deteriorate dangerously. But I have always had a good feeling about our Maharani. I doubted very much that she would allow any harm to come to her husband or our nation. What bothered me most was that Ramdeo Singhji seemed to have forgotten the most crucial thing in a marriage: after years of being married, come what may, he had to win over his wife. Or rather let her see and know that she meant the world to him.

I went to Dharmabhoomi along with five of my pupils. Let's just say it was no honeymoon.

We left very early in the morning to avoid the heat and the mirage-like vapours that could conjure up entire cities along with snow-peaked mountains. It was almost noon by the time we got there. I was on my way to the annual cloth fair in the Muslim mohalla. I couldn't believe my eyes. I hadn't been here for at least five years and all I could see was that it had grown to seven or ten times the original size. There were wagonloads of cloth from as far as Simla, Calcutta, Travancore, Amritsar, Dhaka, Kochi, Indore, Kanyakumari. I could go on and on.

What I had not factored in was that it was also market day. Vendors of vegetables, fruits, bangles, lentils, grains, heaps of turmeric, garlic, chillies were sitting on the pavements grabbing the attention of passers-by by shouting at the top of their voices or singing a ditty about their wares. Suddenly the scene underwent a frightening change. Gangs of men with swords and knives turned up in the marketplace and began to hack, slice and decapitate any and every man, woman and child who happened to be out and within reach in that crowded area.

Before I could grasp what was happening three of my

apprentices had been butchered. A raging youth yanked me off my horse and held a knife to my throat. He slashed the knife down my kurta and within a second he had opened the skin over my sternum and the beige silk was already bloody. A crowd had gathered by now. As you know, I rarely wear a prayer cap but the sun had been beating on my head and I had clapped it on my pate. They were swearing all kinds of obscenities about my being, pardon my language, a bloody fucking Muslim.

'Take your salwar and underwear off,' they screamed at me.

I tried to laugh and make a joke of it. 'I've got the same goods as you. Nothing different.'

From the corner of my eye I could see that some of the mob were setting fire to the fabric fair with flaming torches. What was I going to tell HM, or more to the point, how was I going to deliver the set of clothes he wanted to gift his wife when he took her to visit her parents in Samadhanpur? I must have smiled at my willingness to delude myself about surviving not till the next day but the next minute, for my tormentor asked me in a towering dudgeon, 'You find me funny, you arsehole? You are going to find me hilarious as I cut you up into small pieces.

'I'll wager you're a landa. Your pecker has been foreshortened from the time you were born.' The knife had ripped open both my salwar and underwear and I was now naked as the day I was born. I was about to be stabbed to death and yet my vanity was in fine fettle and the uppermost thought in my mind was not about seeing my Maker but about my pathetic humiliation; that the world had seen my limp and shrunken bleeding penis. Isn't it strange how the mind works? We sleep with our wives or spend the night with a lady of easy virtue baring all we've got and then suddenly we discover modesty and want to cover up Adam's guilt.

As luck would have it, that's when my badge which said Chief Weaver to His Majesty Ramdeo Singhji fell out of my pocket. The effect was instantaneous. My torturer and his companions abandoned me and rapidly migrated to the other parts of the bazaar. When I finally managed to get up, only two of my students, both Hindus, were still standing. They had had to prove that they had not been circumcised.

I was in no condition to travel and, more to the point, one of my two surviving pupils was severely wounded and needed immediate care. Besides, how could we forget that we had to collect the bodies of my three pupils who had been murdered and give them a decent burial. Our clothes were so badly torn, there was no question of covering our manhood. Not just that, our horses had been stolen and I had lost my shoes. We took refuge in a dank inn run by an ancient couple in a neighbouring village and managed to pick up some ill-fitting, ready-made clothes from a local shop. Luckily the landlord knew Ranjandas, a shoemaker, who came over and took the measurement of my feet.

It was the middle of the night when someone slipped into my bedroom from the window and woke me up.

'Why . . . what . . . what's happened? Where am I?' It took me time to get my bearings and remember that this was the man who had measured my feet the previous day. 'Why did you have to come in from the window and that too in the middle of the night, Ranjandas?'

'Had I come by the main door, the police sentry on duty

would surely have put me behind bars for God knows how long for loitering on the roads in the middle of the night during these terrible times. Besides, I had to deliver your pair of shoes; perhaps the last one you will ever wear.'

'At this time of the night?' I asked groggily. 'And why my last pair?'

'Because even if it's leather cured from the skin of a dead cheetah, deer or a camel, they now accuse us of killing a cow, eating her flesh and using her hide to make leather goods.'

'So how are you supposed to make a living?' I enquired as I tried the dark brown mojaris and paid five silver coins to him.

The leather worker looked at me with more than a whiff of disbelief. 'Is that a serious query or is this your idea of being funny?'

I must have looked baffled by his question as well as his tone.

'Have you forgotten that we are outcastes, achhoots or untouchables? But since you are so keen to know, let me fill you in on what we are going to do. We are going to starve and die as we have done for centuries.'

I lit a candle and could see him now. He had a gaunt, wrinkled face. There were just two yellow teeth standing aslant in his mouth, and when he spoke, the occasional speck of spittle landed on my hand or arm and he quickly tried to wipe it with his hand. His chest was sunken and every rib seemed on the verge of being dislodged. He was wearing a torn dhoti and nothing more. I had never come across anyone as ancient as him and tried to guess his age – ninety-three, more likely 102.

'I didn't mean to upset you. As you can see I'm not

thinking straight. But if you'll forgive me, I've one more question for you. Do you have any idea what triggered these riots?'

Ranjandas had a wry smile on his face. 'When did the higher castes need a pretext or permission to persecute the lower orders?'

'But we are talking about Muslims just now and not the so-called outcastes.'

'How come you don't know that there's something lower in Dharmabhoomi than us outcastes? For better or worse, we still fall in the Hindu fold. The followers of Islam are a very different kettle of fish. As His Excellency the governor never tires of saying, hate is too mild a word for them. They need to be uprooted from our very soil. It's a sentiment shared by almost all the people of Dharmabhoomi.'

'What about you? Where do you stand?'

'When did anybody ever care about what we think? Besides, we're supposed to be so stupid, it's taken for granted that we don't have any opinions.'

'You haven't answered my question.'

'The majority of Muslims are butchers by trade or, rather, used to be. While we've always had to wait for a buffalo, cow or bullock to die before we got to eat its dead meat and convert its hide to leather and then to footwear or belts, beef was the staple diet of the Muslims. So if nothing else Muslims and we shared common business interests. Now that beef is taboo, Dharmabhoomi is at great pains to make Muslims too taboo.'

'What are you trying to suggest? That they want to do away with all Muslims?'

'That's a tall order but they have been doing their best.'

He paused and looked at me quizzically. 'They call you the Great Sage, the Wise One, don't they? Some even think you are the Enlightened One. Now I've a question for you. Why don't you din some sense into these so-called high-caste folks and tell them that if they don't stop this nonsense, they will have to go barefoot to heaven?'

I was silent for a long time.

'Forget it.' Ranjandas must have got tired of waiting for my answer. 'I've got my answer. You don't want to have anything to do with us folk.'

'I give you my word, Ranjandas, I will try, try my best. But that's about it. Will it work? If I knew the answer, you would have to fall at my feet and call me God.'

He was almost over the window when I asked him, 'What's your age, Ranjandas?'

'Who knows? Never learnt to count beyond ten. But the village mukhia tells me he and I are of the same age.'

'And how old is he?'

'Forty-three.'

I guess I should have known better. Three midnights later Ranjandas was back the same way he had come the earlier time, through the window. There was no mistaking the bitterness in his voice. 'You don't need to keep your word when it comes to dealing with us folks? I mean the outcastes, right?'

This time around I was up before the leather-man could tick me off further.

'Yep, you are dead right. Never touch an untouchable issue if you want to be on the right side of the law in Dharmabhoomi.'

'Well, thanks for nothing.'

Ranjandas got up to leave. It was obvious that life had taught him time and again that the one unforgivable crime was to expect a helping hand from a so-called caste Hindu or Muslim. I could see from the expression on his face that he was kicking himself, metaphorically at least, for asking that stupid question.

'You are welcome. Since you've broached the matter, you will be pleased to know that it's the first night I've been in this inn since we last met. Till this evening I was the government's guest. For the crime of sedition.'

'In prison for sedition? On what grounds? I had no idea you had committed any crimes against the state.'

'It appears I did. My offence, they claimed, was to approach the courts to speak on behalf of a man who they accused of killing a cow and eating beef and making footwear out of her hide.'

Ranjandas sat down on his haunches on the floor and kept shaking his head. 'Did they really put you behind bars? Because you spoke up for me? Forgive me for putting you through that ordeal.' He looked blindly at the shabby room and got up with an effort. 'I can't. I can't make sense of the world any more.'

I saw the despair on his face and I hated myself for being so helpless. What would I have done if I had been a leather worker?

'May I ask you a question which has been on my mind for decades?' I patted him on his back to console him and confided in him. 'Frankly, it's been bothering me for a few millennia.'

'Are you making fun of me? You're the educated one while I can't even read or write. Do you really expect me to have answers to questions which the likes of you have not been able to resolve for centuries?'

'Just a minor correction. Whatever gave you the idea that literacy guarantees wisdom? But be that as it may, how often have you and your people suffered terrible injustices at the hands of the caste Hindus? You sweep the streets, pick up their shit, clean their toilets, are forced to stay outside a village or town where you have little or no access to water, so that your shadow does not pollute them. And if it does, then they need to bathe with the waters of the holy Ganga. And now you've discovered that you can't even earn a livelihood picking up dead animals to cure leather.

'In their eyes you are indeed the dregs of society. It's no different with the adivasis, the original inhabitants of the subcontinent, or with the Muslims. They treat all three communities like subhumans. Muslims too daren't touch any animal for fear that they will be accused of butchering cows. As to the adivasis, or tribals as we call them, this land and this subcontinent are rightfully theirs and the rest of us are the real intruders but they have no rights, none whatsoever.

'What intrigues me is how come it never occurs to you that if you joined hands with the adivasis and the Muslims, you would account for at least a third of the population? Do you have any idea what that would do to your status? You would become the most powerful trinity in Dharmabhoomi and turn the caste world upside down. Not just that, you would occupy the highest seats of power and dictate policy.

'I admit it's not going to happen overnight. No way. Every single member of the privileged castes will try to destroy the trinity.' I paused to see the effect of my impassioned words on him. 'So what do you think, is it worth more than just a try?'

'Do you really want to know?'

'Yes, of course I do.'

'Why don't you stick to weaving shawls instead of dreaming up fairy stories, Weaver?'

'I thought one could occasionally turn fairy tales into reality.'

Ranjandas smiled ruefully. 'Get real, Weaver.'

The riots and the killings lasted for five days. We should have headed back home now that things had quietened down but I was unwilling to leave without first identifying the six or seven men who had killed the pupils in my care. How was I going to face their parents? I knew then that I should have at least had the decency to die with them.

Thousands of Muslims had been displaced and there was chaos as they fled Dharmabhoomi for safer havens. It took me barely two days to locate the group that had attacked me and my students. I did not let on that I had identified them but went to see the governor with sketches of the killers. There were at least six security guards at the gate of his residence who went through my identity papers, and every one of them made it a point to feel me up, ostensibly to check if I was carrying any weapons.

What was I to make of this man? He had that look of tranquillity, of a man who had made his peace with his God and fifteen per cent of the population of the town whose licence to life he had so casually withdrawn. Their only unforgivable crime was that they were not Hindus. Nobody dared say it and yet everyone knew that he had orchestrated this bonanza of death and bloodletting. The police had been ordered not to interfere with the rampaging mobs. They had forced their way into homes, raped the women, burnt or mangled the menfolk and slammed the heads of children like washing at the dhobi ghats.

I showed my identification and gave the governor the precise addresses of the murderers and handed over the sketches I had done of the five men who had killed my pupils. He crumpled the pages without even looking at them and threw them into the litter bin and smiled sadly.

'In Spanish there's a saying, Que sera sera. It means "Whatever will be, will be." Whatever's happened has happened. Let bygones be bygones. People say these folks who are no more had had it coming for a long time. I guess they have a point. When water starts boiling, you have to let off steam. Otherwise everybody gets scalded. Can you imagine how I must have suffered?'

'Suffered? Am I to understand that you too were beaten up?'

'Suffered because I care so deeply. As the governor, I am like a father to the people of Dharmabhoomi.'

My admiration for the governor was boundless by now. With what ease this august man's bogus sentiments slithered off his tongue.

'Three of my apprentices were murdered in front of my eyes. I was to be the next victim except they noticed that I worked for His Majesty.'

'Life's a lottery,' he told me with benign resignation, 'and the luck of the draw was on your side.'

'You could have brought out the police, even the army, and stopped it.'

'Ah, the wisdom of hindsight.'

'The word is that you gave orders that the police were not to lift a finger and that's how three thousand Muslim men, women and children were massacred.'

'I would like to stress that as a committed believer in democratic principles I couldn't possibly have gone against the wishes of almost eighty-five per cent of the population of Dharmabhoomi.'

'This is the first time I have heard that mass murders are a vibrant testimony to the practice of democracy.'

'I would advise caution, my friend.' I noticed the governor never raised his voice and you had to strain to hear him. And that made him come across as even more blood-curdling. Even as he talked he pulled the bell-rope next to his seat to let his staff know that they could now usher in the next visitor.

'I wish you well, Weaver. I believe you are one of His Majesty Ramdeoji's favourites, something like a jester at his court. You were lucky to have survived the bloodbath. But one still hears of the occasional flare-up. Who knows, even when you are making your way back home, God forbid, they might waylay you . . . and you too will become history.'

I had to admit the governor had a talent for put-downs. Just then a man in uniform embellished with all kinds of medals for heroism on the battlefield was shown in. He was in a temper. 'It's a week since you banned the sale of buffalo meat along with beef. Seventy per cent of Hindu civilians eat beef and buffalo meat. Of course they also eat mutton and chicken but as you know we are not big on poultry and goat farms. Hundred per cent of the army are meat-eaters. How do you expect them to survive and defend our borders if you starve them?'

I was halfway out of the audience hall and have no idea what got into me. 'What's to complain?' I asked. 'There's plenty of meat around. Enough to feed the army and the populace. Granted that they may have to change their eating habits a wee bit, that's all. Till last night there were so many carcasses lying everywhere on the streets, the authorities had no idea what to do with them.'

The man looked at me, wondering who the hell I was and why I was bothering to answer when the questions were addressed to somebody else. The governor's cheeks had turned a hot red as he looked past me. I turned around to discover HM Ramdeo Singhji listening to my outburst. I would have liked to add a few more nasty observations but could see that the king was waiting for me to depart. What was he doing here? When I was level with him, HM spoke so softly, I could barely make out his words. 'Come to the Atithi Palace at 8 p.m.'

I knew what was in store for me. My anger had got the better of me and I was in for . . . For what? A firing? The termination of my services? A prison term? I would have to wait for the answer.

I reached the Atithi Palace a quarter of an hour early and wandered around a bit to while away at least ten minutes. Atithi Palace. What a strange name that, since HM couldn't possibly be a guest in his own palace even though it was outside the capital city of Shantipura. Dharmabhoomi was the holy of holies in the state of Panchananda. It was a sort of confluence of different faiths. Buddhists, Hindus and Jains and even Muslims had their most important and sacred sites here. Ah, it suddenly came back to me why the Maharana's residence here was called Atithi

Palace. God himself was supposed to be the host here in Dharmabhoomi and as such even HM was his guest . . . at least metaphorically.

There was, however, no mistaking the unique style that was the hallmark of all the palaces built or renovated by Ramdeo Singhji. All his residences were in an inviting low-key white. He loved terraces and balconies and every floor had a variety of them. They were placed strategically so that you got a constant flow of air from cross-ventilation. There was something unostentatious in the ambience and yet the atmosphere was never parsimonious.

HM was waiting for me in his private chambers. I knew him well by now and was fully aware that he did not carry his emotions on his sleeve. Certainly not on his face either. He was not a dashingly handsome man but he had something far more valuable, an easy gravitas and a hint of a smile that could, if the occasion demanded, float lightly around his eyes. I had often wondered whether he had trained himself in front of a mirror never to allow his face to reflect the state of his mind, however overwrought or furious he was. I had warned myself over and over again that trepidation was hardly the right frame of mind to approach my liege in. But the truth was I had been asking for trouble and I was about to get it.

Ramdeo Singhji waved away my adaabs, salaams and greetings and came straight to the point. His voice was low, but I could sense the dark, minatory clouds rolling in.

'I thought I knew you rather well after all these years but I must confess that today's performance was a revelation. Your strategy has always been to make certain that the other party loses its head and its patience and you keep your cool. So what went wrong today? I'm not sure whether your outburst this morning was spontaneous or calculated since I have no idea what preceded it. I suspect it was both. What is certain is that you were not merely egregiously offensive, you were playing with fire. I wonder if you realized that but for the fact that I turned up by sheer chance at a crucial moment, the governor could have put you behind bars then and there and no one would have heard from you ever again.'

'Your Majesty, have you heard of a dire condition called half and half? It's one of those mathematical anomalies where the two halves never add up to one.'

'I've never heard such nonsense. I see that you are indulging in one of your favourite pastimes of confounding your listener and thus escaping what's coming to you.'

How could I not note that last bit. Almighty God, what was coming to me, I wondered. 'You do me serious injustice, sire. As you are well aware, one half of me is Hindu thanks to my mother who's said to have let me float down the river for reasons beyond me, and the other half is Muslim as the parents who brought me up were followers of the Prophet. Well, when the riots broke out in Dharmabhoomi, the Hindu mob murdered three of my students and then turned on me because they believed I am what they call a lande or foreshortened one. It was sheer luck that as one of them tried to rip open my belly, my identity card stating that I worked for you fell out and I was spared.

'I was foolish enough to appeal to the governor for justice since I had managed to locate the men who murdered my pupils even though I had been warned that he was the instigator of the riots since he wanted to cleanse the state of the Islamic virus. I didn't wish to believe such absurd rumours and I put my faith in him.

'After having ensured that at least three thousand people had lost their lives, that's not counting my three disciples and the two hundred thousand who preferred to be displaced rather than face death, the governor smiled enigmatically and took a lofty tone with me. He said the will of the majority is supreme in a democracy and hence he had no option but to stand by and let the majority have its way.

'How could this man, sire, this man who was appointed governor to safeguard the people of Dharmabhoomi, with his eyes open and a functioning mind permit such atrocities on a section of his own people?'

Ramdeoji chewed on what I had said for an intolerably long time. 'I have a question for you, Weaver, a question that sits like a succubus on my neck night and day, draining me of hope and resolve. How do we put an end to this recurring cycle of violence and carnage that overtakes us every decade or decade and a half? How do I convince both Hindus and Muslims of the utter futility and madness of it all? The Hindus outnumber the others but that doesn't seem to offer them a sense of security. Nothing, it seems, neither the passage of time nor the natural atrophy of public memory will permit them to forget or forgive the indelible atrocities committed by the Muslim invaders and rulers, starting with the destruction of the Somnath temple in Gujarat.

'It's the opposite with the Muslims – they take beating after beating after beating and then suddenly they are consumed by an insatiable appetite for vengeance for crimes committed against them a year ago or a quarter- or a half-century back.'

'I'm no soothsayer, sire, but I can't say that I feel particularly optimistic. Quite the contrary, since both the communities are convinced of the righteousness of their faith. The cause, or rather the pretext, for the last instalment of the riots was the rumour that a Muslim family had slaughtered a cow and consumed beef. Let me not go into the veracity or otherwise of that statement. As you know, after the governor of Dharmabhoomi had declared that the cow was a sacred animal, you could go to jail or hang if you killed one.

'He cited the Vedas, the sacred Hindu texts as his authority. Clearly he had either not read the Vedas or he was lying, for the Vedas specifically mention that the people of ancient times ate beef. What matters though is that most Hindus believed with the governor that their culture and dharma were in peril and were only too happy to go on a rampage.'

'So you predict that these spontaneous or deliberately engineered mass murders will go on till kingdom come?' HM asked.

'I have a fundamentally different take on the matter. I believe that that animal species called mankind is incapable of grasping how absurd their first principles are.'

The Maharana looked at me warily.

'I'm afraid I've lost you, Weaver.' I could feel the mercury rising. 'Are you playing mind games with me?'

'No, my liege. I have never been more earnest.'

'Well, let's hear what you have to say.'

'In ninety-nine per cent of the population, religion is nothing but an accident of birth. If you were born in a Hindu family, you would very likely remain a Hindu even though you did not choose your faith but had inherited it. And of course if you happened to be a fanatic, you would want to shove all the Muslims into the Arabian Sea. It's no different with Islam. Those born in Islam know beyond the shadow of a doubt that their God is the only one. Does any Hindu pause for a minute and ask himself what would have happened if he had been born in the fold of the other faith? For instance in Islam? Isn't the answer obvious? He would of course have been hell-bent on annihilating Hindus and vice versa.'

HM looked bemused and stared at me as if I was trying to pull a fast one on him. I thought it best not to look him in the eye and give him the feeling that I was bent on provoking him. We were both caught up so intensely in our conversation we had not noticed the armies of black clouds gathering threateningly above the forest and the palace and the wind doing a mad dance amongst the trees. The atmosphere had suddenly turned tense and you could feel the elastic in the air being stretched to breaking point.

The thunder in the skies grew more dire with every passing moment and the lightning kept zigzagging across the sky like a python streaking past. And now the dam shattered and oceans of angry, impatient waters poured down from the sky and the terraces and the palace grounds were awash with raging waters.

'I've been trying to process what you just said. It's so obvious and logical, how come all the scholars and the simplest souls have not known it? Frankly, how come it never occurred to me?'

'You are right, sire, it is banal beyond belief. But it took me years to work that one out for the simple reason that one is brought up to equate any questioning of one's religion as blasphemy and an insult to one's God.'

Ramdeo Singhji looked out as the tempestuous monsoons tried to pulverize the earth. 'A moment's interruption, Weaver. Would you care to go out on to the terrace and get soaked to the bone?'

I didn't bother to answer HM. I opened wide the doors and both of us ran out to enjoy the fury of the monsoons. Within seconds we had both turned into waterfalls. The help in the Atithi Palace rushed out and held open umbrellas under which we could take shelter. But we had both regressed to being children and rejoiced in the sheer power of the whistling winds and the rains that came crashing on to the terrace and were already flooding it.

'Wasn't that magnificent? Let's go in now and continue our discussion about God. So what you are saying then is that the ruling principle of the universe is chance,' Ramdeo Singhji hollered at me as he led me inside into the private rooms of the palace, opened the doors of a cupboard and flung one towel at me and dried himself with the other. 'And that we humans have converted happenstance, accident, serendipity, call it what you will, into fate or destiny?'

'I never forget, Majesty, that the first and foremost lottery in the world is God. Nobody consults you about which faith you would prefer to be born in. It's entirely up to the one up there purportedly in heaven. Both Shias and Sunnis worship Allah and share the same Prophet to whom the angel Jibrael, a.k.a. Gabriel, revealed the teachings of the Quran and yet each of them believes the other is a heretic and must be annihilated for spreading a false version of the Quran.

'It's no different with the Catholics and the Protestants.

They both believe in Jesus, the Son of God, and yet they were killing each other for centuries. Somewhere at the core of one's being one is convinced that one's faith has been personally ordained by God himself. When the question of another religion crops up, it's taken as read that it's fraudulent. It is the rarest of humans who of his own free will crosses over to another creed from the one to which his parents belonged.'

'You know, Kabir, what you have to say may make eminent sense but try and tell that to any believer and he's going to put the curse of both God and Satan upon you.'

'Where do you stand, sire?'

'I suspect in some measure you could say I'm like you, half and half. Half of me clearly thinks what you said just now makes sense, eminent sense, but the other half is trapped in tradition and fearful that the divine can neither be explained nor comprehended.'

'What I am unable to understand, Majesty, is if God had been around from Day One, as every religion has dinned into our heads, He would have instilled in the subconscious of every human being that He was the sole and only possessor of divinity in the world. Then we wouldn't have had so many claimants to Godhood and, even more important, we would not have been killing in the name of one God or the other since the beginning of time.

'What we rarely want to admit is that over many millennia different prophets, gurus, saviours, gods and sons of god have turned up in different parts of the planet and have become all-powerful satraps in their own territory. Over a period of time their disciples and followers have spread the word to other countries and continents and generated incredibly bloody internecine conflicts. The oddest thing is that each faith willy-nilly first divides into two and then into four and then there's no stopping the fissiparous divisiveness.'

'That's exactly what my science teacher had taught me,' suddenly HM's face lit up and he interrupted the Weaver. 'But that was in the context of the very first cell and its simplistic method of multiplying. Do you think, Weaver, that over the next few centuries or millennia many new faiths will spring up and keep subdividing?'

'Good question, but I don't have an answer. The problem is that no believer's ever willing to ask whether God Almighty is then a human creation. The people of the book had most likely not heard of Hinduism, another ancient religion with its own pantheon, but even if they had, it's doubtful that it would have had any impact on their own beliefs. And let's not forget, the gods too come with an expiry date. Who worships Varun, Agni, Indra amongst the Hindus today? Or Zeus, Aphrodite or Apollo whom Alexander and his people prayed to? Of the Hindu trinity, Brahma too seems to have fallen by the wayside. It's amazing how reluctant we are to acknowledge the many popular Dravidian folk deities who were assimilated into the Aryan family of gods.'

'You know, Kabir, I have often asked myself if religion is infectious. How else does one explain the fact that people are willing to betray their original faith and convert to a new theology?'

Kabir paused for a bit before answering. 'The problem is that the believers have no interest in the complex relationship between geography and religion. If the Son of God was born in Bethlehem, five miles from Jerusalem, how was someone thousands of miles away in India to have known about it except when the apostle landed on the shores of Kerala? Buddhism travelled rapidly not just to Sri Lanka and China but all the way to Japan, while Hinduism didn't get any purchase in these countries though it did find a permanent home in Bali and for many centuries in Thailand and Indonesia till they were taken over by Buddhism and Islam. Each faith is convinced that it is the one and only chosen one. Not just that, we are convinced that ours is the one and only one to have been divinely revealed.

'As you pointed out a few minutes ago, sire, one would think that conversion from one faith to another under duress would ensure that its victims wouldn't forget their original religion, but all it takes is a generation or two on the outside for the new faith to become the revealed gospel. As we all know, switching faiths is very often a matter of economics and sheer survival. There's never any question of humankind understanding that religion is nothing but a matter of inheritance, an automatic gift of your faith to the next generation.

'It's incredible how many great minds have written tome after tome about metaphysical issues. The depth and scope of their wisdom is undeniable but let's understand once and for all that religion is not open to reason. However much of a tautology it may be, faith is taken on faith.'

Dinner was served and I had my first home-cooked meal in more than a fortnight, and that too a meal worthy of kings. I could see that the crisis regarding my unfortunate outburst had passed and I was truly grateful. It was late and

I tried to take HM's leave but he insisted that I spend the night in the Atithi Palace.

I laughed and said, 'My liege, I have rented a room in a hotel which took an advance payment from me.'

'Well, never mind, Weaver. You've been through some horrific days and not slept for I don't know how many nights. Go to bed now and get up whenever you feel like it.'

'Sire, that's very kind of you but I don't have any night clothes. So I will take your leave.'

'Stop fussing. No one's going to come into your room.' He smiled and added, 'Unless you want to be entertained by the ladies of the night.'

I laughed. 'I'll take a rain check on that offer, sire.'

'So go ahead and sleep without a stitch on you. We'll head back home tomorrow. Goodnight.'

I don't know why but I had the feeling that he was keeping something from me and was not going to allow me out of his sight. Truth to tell I was relieved that I didn't have to head back to the hotel for there was still no stopping the dazzling array of lightning and the vengeance of thunderclaps and the incessant waterfalls from the sky.

HM turned to leave and then turned around again. 'The Samadhanpur trip is still on. I know that all the fabrics in the fair have been burnt down but I haven't changed my mind about giving Her Majesty a whole season of clothes from the fashion house of Kabir.'

I could barely manage to say goodnight and fell asleep even as I was brushing my teeth.

I must have been tired, very tired, for it was nine by the time I woke up. I had a quick bath and a heavy breakfast with Ramdeo Singhji. It was decided that I should wait for him at the border post of Dharmabhoomi at 11 a.m. Not much time left so I hurriedly went to pick up my newly bought clothes from the boarding house where I had stayed. There was a crowd outside. The pupil who was not too badly hurt rushed towards me.

'Where were you?' He sounded anxious and tense.

'With HM in the Atithi Palace. What's going on here?'

'Someone slipped into your room in the middle of the night and stabbed you at least eleven times. Apparently a member of His Majesty's intelligence service had been waiting for the murderer in your room and had arranged a few cushions and the quilt in such a fashion that the murderer thought it was you. The culprit's now in custody and being interrogated.'

'I've arranged for a carriage to take you and our patient back to Shantipura. I will see you at the workshop directly. We will have to go into overdrive now that Mission Dharmabhoomi has been a damp squib.'

I no longer remember how many years I have been Weaver to the royal family. They've always treated me fair and square but then that's the way they behave with everyone who is in their service. Politeness and courtesy are never a put-on for them. It's been, if I may misuse a scientific term, part of their genetic coding. Let me not overdo the modesty bit but happily confess that HM is fond of my poetry and often quotes my verses in the durbar. There have been many occasions when we have sat and discussed philosophical issues and I can remember at least three or four times when we have not seen eye-to-eye or, to put it bluntly, disagreed severely.

But the prospect of travelling together today on a seven-plus-hour journey back to Shantipura made me uneasy. Metaphorical distance is what nurtures a solid relationship. Familiarity, on the other hand, is a tricky slope and can land you in quicksand from which you may never be able to extricate yourself. Seven hours, God have mercy on me. Or should I say on HM?

Ah, the joys of travelling by royal carriage. My arse had never had it so good. Superb leather seats with so much springy padding that I was floating on air. Tea, coffee, snacks, ask and thou shall be given. Let me rephrase that: Don't ask and it shall still be given.

After I had settled down in the royal carriage and we had travelled a few miles I broached the subject that had been on my mind for some time now. 'I don't know how to thank you, Majesty, for saving my life.'

'I had seen the governor's face when you lost your temper last morning. We've known each other for many years and I had a hunch that he may want to settle scores with you in a hurry.'

We must have talked about all manner of things but then I could not hold back the one question which had been continually needling me.

'I owe you my life, Majesty. So what I am about to ask will seem like an unforgivable act of ingratitude. And yet ask I must, whatever the price I may have to pay.'

HM was silent for a few moments and then said, 'I'm waiting for the unforgivable question.'

'When I saw you last morning at the governor's audience hall, I thought you had come for the final reckoning of the governor's complicity in the massacres, rapes, and the appalling atrocities over the past few days. But then I heard that all you had to say to the governor for the uncontrolled rampage in Dharmabhoomi was that his conduct was unbecoming of rajneeti or the ethical principles of the state.'

I looked out of the window at the rapidly passing countryside but apart from the dense green grass which seemed to have sprung up overnight, nothing registered. And now we were at the border of one of the main trade centres of the kingdom, and before we knew it there were hordes of people lined up to see and greet their king. How did they know that Ramdeo Singhji was about to show up? HM, as was his wont, leaned out of the window and greeted his subjects.

When he settled back in his seat I picked up from where I had left off. 'The Maharana Ramdeo I know was the one who persisted for nearly ten years to establish peace with Panchananda's greatest enemy, Samadhanpur. It was an enmity that went back twelve or thirteen decades. Your arch-enemy, the ruler of Samadhanpur, would not acquiesce in your unrelenting pursuit of a permanent peace treaty. But you did not give up. How then am I to explain or understand the fact that all you had to say to the governor was that he had failed to live by the ethical principles of statecraft?'

'I gather you found that critique vapid and wanting.'

'The efficacy of a pallid state ethics in the face of a planned genocide, sire, is somewhat questionable to say the least. It might sound like a worn-out platitude but nevertheless I must repeat it: the life of every human being is precious, regardless of his religion. What was undeniable was that your own subjects were being butchered. Justice itself was at stake. It's well known that the governor was busy egging on the Hindus to wipe out as much of the

Muslim population of the city as possible. But let me grant that until the facts are established in a court of law, he was but a mute witness to the mass murders. But wouldn't you agree that even if he was nothing but a silent witness, he needed to be instantly removed from office and tried under the most stringent laws of the state for not taking immediate and severe action?'

'May I remind you that Dharmabhoomi is officially under the governor's rule and it's advisable not to interfere with his jurisdiction and actions there.'

'A neat argument, Majesty but . . . little more than a quibble.'

'I may be the final authority in our land but it's always wise for the king never to test the full extent of his power.'

We had reached the royal palace in the capital and were still arguing.

'One murder and the culprit goes to jail and then the law hangs him. Ten murders, same punishment since a criminal has only one life to lose. But kill a thousand or two or a million or more and you are above the law. And before you know it, amnesia sets in and the mass murderer is hailed as a hero, a saviour of the people. You are the conscience of this vast empire, Majesty, and the ethical exemplar for your people.'

Ramdeo Singhji eyed me warily. 'I wear the crown, Kabir. Which means I must be a politician and statesman first and last. My primary objective will always be peace and goodwill amongst my people.'

'Yes sire, that is indeed the oath Your Majesty took.'

'Why do I keep getting the feeling that behind that acquiescent demeanour, you are castigating me? All these years you've maintained that you are neither Hindu nor Muslim. So now you've appointed me your deputy and made me responsible for every denizen in the kingdom.'

'Sire, as you will recall there is an unwritten contract between a liege and his subjects. Your subjects owe you and the Constitution total loyalty. The flip side of that contract is the paramount duty of the head of the state to safeguard the life of each one of his subjects.'

'You are getting on my nerves with your highfalutin talk of responsibility.' He got down from the carriage and hollered, 'Is anybody there?'

A guard came running and took orders. 'Put this man in the black hole. No food, no water and no light till further instructions, which may never come.'

I had no idea how many hours had passed since I had been shackled in that dungeon but one thing I was sure of. I was here for good. Do you know why they lock you in a tiny underground cell and leave you there without natural light, a candle or the time of day or night? Because even a clock that shows the wrong time is hope. Timelessness or the absence of time is nothing but living death. I had no idea whether I had been in the dungeon for ten hours or a full day or more. There was no sensation in my legs or hands and I was so thirsty I could not even manage a whisper.

I suddenly knew he was there with me. Yes, none other than His Majesty himself. Do you know that if I've woven the cloth, I can tell its presence by the sheer aura of it? He was on his own without a single guard as an escort. All he had was a lamp to guide him and the key to remove the handcuffs and the shackles at the ankles. He had to support me for at least ten minutes before I could stand on my own.

Finally we walked out without exchanging a word. There was a carriage parked outside the prison. He helped me up next to the driver's seat and flicked the whip in the air and we were off, followed by the royal guard at a distance. Within a quarter of an hour we were on the banks of the Tarangini river. We had not exchanged a word yet. He threw some clothes at me, undressed and ran into the water. I tore off whatever I had been wearing and plunged behind him.

Some think of water as sacred, a blessing from none other than God. If it is Gangajal then it's purported to cleanse all your sins. Still others think of it as the medium for a baptism. For me it is nothing less than a rebirth. We were in the Tarangini for a long, long time, all of it devoid of conversation. By the time we got out of the water and dried ourselves, the guards had laid out a meal for two on the sands. The aroma ascended surreptitiously into my nose and I was suddenly very, very hungry. Ramdeo Singhji watched me eat like a fiend.

'No hard feelings on the silver plate, Weaver. Just a leg of chicken and fresh curds.'

It was such a ludicrous comment, I laughed heartily. I was happy to be with him, with no malice or antipathy dividing us. We talked about all kinds of stuff, mostly inconsequential, but I knew something was weighing on his mind.

'I've been asking myself why I went all the way to Dharmabhoomi and yet not confront the governor for his unpardonable crimes? Somewhere at the back of my mind was this ridiculous thought that I personally had no concrete evidence of his misdeeds. And so when I saw the barely controlled rage in his eyes when you spoke so ironically about replacing beef and other meats with human flesh, I wondered what his reaction would be. Fortunately, my sixth sense proved right and my soldiers took the man sent to murder you into custody. We now have his confession saying that he was sent by the governor.

'But I too have a terrible confession to make. Since I was digging deep into my possible motives for not taking any action against the appalling atrocities, I suddenly realized that I was not very different from the governor. I suspect there must be something like an archetypal, utterly irrational prejudice amongst us Hindus against Muslims that has come down for centuries, for while I told myself that I must put a stop to the carnage and take the governor into custody, when it came right down to it, I just couldn't do it. I came up with one excuse after another. I can justify my inaction by telling you that it was our Muslim neighbours who killed my paternal uncle Bhanwar Singh when I was an impressionable seven-year-old, and skinned my cousin alive when he was barely three, but I have to perforce also confess that all this occurred after the Hindu population had killed thousands of them, or perhaps even more.

'I realize that for all my talk of universal justice, I have to be doubly on my guard about a deep-seated stereotype. Like it or not, it's in the air we breathe and none of us is immune to it, just as our Muslim brethren too have to be wary of the stories about the purported deceitfulness and inhumanity of all Hindus.

'You tell me time and again that I am the conscience of my people. But the reason I cannot stand the sight of you occasionally is that none other than you are my conscience. Now before I pass a judgement on the governor of Dharmabhoomi, you'll have to come to a decision about my failing to do my duty.'

So much for my high-mindedness. Me as His Majesty's conscience, how about that? Shall I order HM Ramdeoji to resign from the kingship, hand him a life sentence and crown myself top honcho? Or maybe just declare a public holiday and order him hanged in the Shunya Bhed Bhav Gardens? How in the good Lord's name was I going to wash my hands of this awful quandary that I had got myself into?

All I wanted now was to be back home and let my body and mind heal after such tumultuous life-and-death events. Kashmira was staying with her parents while I was away. It was nearly early morning when I reached my house. But there was no home to return to. The mullah had taken possession of it and kept a posse of men to throw me out because I had Hindu blood that was polluting the purity of Islam and of the mosque where I occasionally went to pray.

I have to admit something which I realized rather late in life. If you happen to be half and half or a religious androgyne or eunuch, neither the Hindus nor Muslims have room for you. I wonder if it will be any different in the afterlife.

I was standing undecided about where I could find a room in the capital to knock off for the remaining part of the night when a security guard from the palace handed me a note. What now, I asked myself irritably.

Dear Kabir,

You must be wondering why I let you out of the prison. The reason should be obvious. While the majority of the courtiers and ministers of Panchananda are fawning and self-serving lackeys, you are an incessant, pesky troublemaker, but you still have some uses. You may have conveniently taken it for granted that since the National Fabric Fair was a dead loss and I had not mentioned the subject of the new selection of clothes for HM Anagha Devi and Prince Satyanam while we swam in the Tarangini river and then had our high-minded conversation about crime and punishment during dinner, the visit to Samadhanpur must have been dropped.

I am sorry to disappoint you. The subject of this dubious visit was your suggestion. It may have been very bad advice but I made the blunder of committing myself to it with HM Anagha Devi.

So kindly get on with the job instead of procrastinating as is your wont.

Goodnight.

HM

PS: As you may have learnt by now, working for HM is not a cakewalk. We are scheduled to leave within twenty-four days. Have a good day.

It was close to a month after the last missive when I received a letter from Samadhanpur.

Dear Weaver,

I'm thinking of extending my visit by three, maybe four days. Imagine having a honeymoon five years after getting married. I really should be wary of taking your advice in the future. Thanks to you, I am now neglecting my royal duties at home.

Enough ribbing. Thank you, Kabir, for dinning some sense into HM.

Warmest regards,

Ramdeo Singh

Bura jo dekhan main chala,
Toh bura na miliya koi,
Jo man khoja aapna,
Toh mujhsey bura na koi.

In my quest to spot the evil ones,
I found none who were evil,
On delving deep into myself,
I found none more evil than me.

13

Alan was by far the most sensitive, make it oversensitive, apprentice that the Weaver had had from the time he had set up his workshop. If that was not bad enough, he was also unfailingly gullible. Which meant that he was the butt of endless practical jokes. Fortunately, he was good-humoured and forgot rather than forgave his tormentors. Kabir was protective of the lad most of the time but every once in a while he too succumbed to the temptation to say something a little piquant.

Right now the Master and student were having a muted altercation about the One up there in that place which cannot be reached except by Jacob's ladder.

'Tell me something, Alan,' Kabir said in his most fake-earnest manner, 'all of us refer to the Creator as Him. The Christians certainly believe that God is a male and had a son. But as you perhaps know, it takes a woman to beget a child. So you may have guessed that this deed had to take place without any physical contact or to put it baldly without physical intercourse. I take it that the Holy Spirit alone could have pulled off this rather difficult sleight of hand: keep Mother Mary a virgin while she bore and delivered the

Saviour. Things, however, become a little more complicated if you factor in the rider that post-Jesus, Mary became the mother of four more sons.

'The Bible of course prefers to ignore the fact that there's enough material here for a full-blown, overheated melodrama about favouritism and murderous jealousy. In any other family this would have caused the scandal of the century, nay, the scandal of the millennium. Can you imagine the torrid soap that must have developed in the family since Jesus hogged all the attention and the other siblings almost ceased to exist as far as the Bible was concerned? Surely the good Lord, or maybe it was the apostles, must have scotched all possibility of the story becoming a colossal embarrassment.'

Alan was too polite and gentle a soul to reveal his disgust with the Weaver's scurrilous reflections but he felt compelled to put an end to them. 'Do you have any idea how much it hurts a believer that you are so disrespectful of God? Why are you always picking on Him and blaspheming?'

'You are right to censure me, dear Alan, and I do apologize for hurting your feelings. But surely you will grant that the Almighty is brother, father, mother, friend and lover to all the Bhakti and Sufi devotees. You can only tease and needle and pick on someone who is family and you love more than anybody else and has a sense of humour. Ambivalence towards Him – or is it Her? – is part and parcel of an intense relationship.

'It's taken for granted that we humans will sulk and even bad-mouth Him. For all you know He might be doing the same though we will never know about it. But bear in mind that the joke's on us. He must surely have created mankind to shower love on us and have a laugh at our follies, and forgive us for believing that we are all-knowing, and priding ourselves on being the crowning glory of creation, and pretending to be civilized when we are anything but. For all you know he may be laughing at us for inventing and worshipping him instead of Satan. All right, all right, I take that back. Just thought I might get a rise out of you. Don't forget, for the nonce, and that's a nonce that has lasted at least hundreds of thousands of years, God is nothing more than hearsay or a rumour.

'Let me get back to the subject of the gender of God – earlier civilizations preferred to see divinity as a female. But do you see what's going on here? Our endeavour has always been to reduce God to human dimensions and attributes. If it seems absurd to impose a gender on God, would it have made better sense to make him sexless or, to put it bluntly, a eunuch?'

'Are you done, Master, with your heresies and your problems with God's gender?'

'I'm sorry to disappoint you, Alan,' there was a twinkle in Kabir's eyes as he spoke, 'but I intend to go on since I've got such an attentive audience. But seriously, Alan, we call him omnipotent, omniscient and omnipresent. If he's all-seeing, how come he's blind to the rapes, torture and killings of children, all of them committed in the name of religion? How come he doesn't annihilate all those who invent one deadly gas after another to wipe out entire peoples? How come he doesn't banish all religions once and for all since they are the cause of the greatest number of murders and massacres? How come he keeps inventing new plagues every few years?

'If He's omnipotent how come the caste system or deadly racial prejudices have not been scotched out yet? How come he doesn't din some sense into all those who deny the terminal climate crisis which is playing havoc with the planet and will destroy mankind unless we take drastic measures to ban fossil fuels? How come, how come, how come the world is so unfair?

'No one has ever seen him and yet we are singing his praises night and day and keep egging him on to look kindly upon us and shower presents on him. Indeed we can't stop building temples and mosques and cathedrals for him. Is he an accident of fate, a genetic code imprinted on human memory or just a figment of our imagination?

'Frankly, what a colossal bore eternity must be if to be divine means that God is perpetually fated to be right. Time and again the holy books tell us that the righteous will inherit the earth. What they prefer not to mention is that the self-righteous with their superior airs, their overweening self-importance and their utter lack of humour will turn even paradise into hell.'

Dukh mein sumiran sab karey,
Sukh mein kare na koye,
Jo Sukh mein sumiran karey,
To dukh kahe ko hoye,

We invariably remember Him when we are disconsolate,
No one, however, thinks of Him when one is happy,
But if you remember Him when the times are good,
Why would the bad times bother you?

14

This was the worst year of the drought. It had not rained the last seven years but the country had managed to survive because of the series of interconnected lakes and the system of rainwater harvesting in the villages which ensured that the underground water table was richly replenished. Now the lakes were dry and so was the water-table which supplied water to the wells. The drought had killed thousands of people and every day saw the numbers climb. The skeletons of dead cattle were strewn all over the countryside. The vultures watched from atop the bare and barren trees and swooped down the moment a cow, bull or buffalo gave up the ghost and tore into its innards. They did the same if by chance a human being fell dead on the road or the field. And yet hordes of people from the hinterland kept coming over to the towns and cities in the hope of finding water and work.

The priests in the temples and the mullahs in the mosques were in great demand since they were supposed to have a direct line to the Almighty. Night and day they prayed for the rains on behalf of the farmers, the populace and the Maharana. The rich and the super-rich sought to bribe God with all kind of gifts and promises. But to no avail. Who knows, the drought may have cut off the lines of communication with God or, worse, it may have killed him too.

A few more years passed without a drop of rain and then it was winter. The kingdom of Panchananda had lost half its population and you hardly saw anybody in the countryside. The capital Shantipura didn't look so abandoned because whoever was still alive and even slightly mobile had migrated there in the hope of finding food and employment. It was 8.24 p.m. on the 17th of December when the sky collapsed and it rained. And rained. And rained.

What does one call a ceaseless monsoon in winter? The Tarangini river, unstable at the best of times, had changed course and moved into the north of the capital. The velocity of the flooding waters was so great it swept away everything in sight and it was impossible to tell how many people lost their lives.

The Weaver and his twenty-nine apprentices and assistants were lucky even though they were in the Tarangini's new path, since they had moved to the solid terrace of the workshop. On the seventh day the rains took a turn for the worse and became a tornado. Before the Weaver and his team realized what was happening, two members of his workshop had wound up in the whirling funnel and flown to celestial heights and dropped.

It was four days later that the rains finally stopped and the sun made a fleeting appearance. And now a million and a quarter stars were out and scintillating. The Weaver's team, Hindus, Jains, Christians and Muslims, spontaneously went down on their knees and each one sang a prayer to the Almighty. Adnan, the youngest apprentice, was the last to offer a prayer in the form of a question, 'How shall we thank you, dear God, for saving us in this calamitous time?'

'Has it occurred to you,' the Weaver interjected, 'that the dead might have a rather different view of things?'

'And what would that be?'

'The survivors all claim God saved them,' the Weaver said softly, 'but the dead on the other hand would like to know who's responsible for killing all those who died in the tornado? And in the endless years of the drought? They must surely be asking why we humans are so damned afraid to give credit where it's due.'

'And pray who according to them should we give the credit to?' Adnan asked.

'Oh, I think you do know who they are referring to. The same party who according to you allowed us to survive.'

There was a shocked silence. All the pupils gave the Master a look of unvarnished disgust. It was Abhay who spoke for all of them. 'You are an insufferable ingrate, that's what you are.'

'You are probably right. But think about it, Abhay. If he's the Creator and the source of all things on Mother Earth and in the heavens, then it would be sheer perversity to zero in on anyone but God. Let me ask you a simple question: Are you terrified of speaking the truth and naming the guilty party for fear that there will be hell to pay?'

Abhay would not look the Master in the eye nor would he speak.

'It's okay. You don't have to answer me. Let me just remind you that God is by definition the very essence of truth and integrity. So I doubt if He would mind the occasional truth.' The Weaver smiled and patted Abhay's back.' Lest I forget. There are two other possibilities.'

Abhay gave the Weaver a dirty look and said witheringly, 'I'm sure there are and you are the only one who is privy to them.'

'Oh, I think we all know what the first alternative is but prefer never to refer to it.'

'Since you seem to hint that we are dealing with the unspeakable here, I suspect you alone will have the courage to tell us about it.'

'I'm sorry to disappoint you but it's no big deal frankly. Life is patently irrational and that's all there is to it.'

'And what about God?'

'What about Him? The only explanation many thinkers give is that mankind needed desperately to believe in some higher power and so posited him.'

'And the second alternative?

'It's what's known as the theory of evolution. It could perhaps be seen as a learning curve or God's baby steps to knowledge. This hypothesis holds that the origin of animate life began with the cell. For all you know mankind itself is a work in progress.'

The dead were hanging on treetops, blocking gutters, stuck head first in the window of the minaret in the mosque, impaled on the pointed spikes of the iron railings of the Alakhnanda Palace. You had to wait in long queues at the burning ghats. The stink of rotting flesh was enough to make even the dead gag. The Weaver had gone over to the palace and mooted the idea of mass cremations to His Majesty, but like the rest of the populace, King Ramdeo Singhji was revolted by the suggestion. On the second day, as the waters of the Tarangini began to recede, the deadly odour reached the palace and HM had a change of heart. He was now willing to cremate not just the dead but also all those who had survived.

'Do something, Weaver. Get rid of that ghastly smell. This instant. I can't take it any more.'

'Sire, if you recall when I had broached the subject in the durbar hall in front of the people's assembly yesterday, you had forbidden me to even utter the words "mass cremations". You had quoted the holy books and told me the shastras insisted that the priests say individual prayers and perform rituals for each soul separately.'

'Don't be so damned self-righteous and throw what I said back at me. Just do it. Make sure that all the dead, Hindu, Muslim, Jain, Buddhist, Christian or from any other faith you may have invented in the last minute and a half, are cremated together.'

I had no choice but to get down to business. I let it slip to the palace gossip that four cases of the new plague ebola had been discovered. Come evening there was an incessant clamour for mass incineration of the dead. By next morning the troops in the capital had dug a huge pit seven miles north of the city limits and the roads were clogged with the living carting their dead and dumping them in the excavated hollow in the earth.

It would take years, four or five decades at the very least, for the economy to recover and life to come back to normal. Thousands of families which had become homeless pitched tents in the fields or were now being accommodated in dharamshalas and temporary lodgings. Slowly, almost imperceptibly, the capital was once again discovering a heartbeat and the desire and drive to be a living city. While new houses were coming up desultorily in place of the old ones, the most dynamic sign of life in the city was the building of a mosque five times the size of the original one which had been nearly razed to the ground by the tornado.

The new expansion plans for the mosque gave a mighty shock to the priestly communities of the other religions. If the Muslims who were barely fifteen per cent of the populace could finance their holy enterprise on such a large scale, why couldn't the Hindu priests tap into the resources of their community, which was four times larger? Damn it, this was nothing less than a matter of the prestige of the Hindu faith itself. Make no mistake, the Hindus would build a brand-new eye-poppingly magnificent nine-storeyed temple on Gaurishankar Hill that would house thirty-five hundred of the most important gods and goddesses in the Hindu pantheon.

The Jains were barely five per cent of the population but money was their trade and their capital. They had been financing the royals not just of Panchananda and Samadhanpur but of every kingdom on the subcontinent for centuries. They would now show the world what real love and dedication to their divine spiritual heritage meant. They would build the most exquisite marble temple in the world.

Never forget, God, whichever creed He belongs to, is an extremely competitive guy. He has to be one up on all the other impostors who claim to be Him. So your guess is as good mine when it comes to picking the right God.

Yes, the times were bad and millions of families were way below the poverty line, surviving on a single meal on the lucky days. But drought or no drought, the rich were never short of cash.

In the latter half of the drought followed by the floods and the tornado, the Weaver had heard murmurs from people of various faiths about God having gone deaf and what was the point of praying night and day to the Almighty and sacrificing buffaloes, cocks and goats if He didn't give a damn whether the peak of his creation perished or survived.

The priestly class was in imminent danger of losing its profession and livelihood. But now the spiritual scenario had undergone a change of a hundred and eighty degrees, and no prizes for guessing who was behind the machinations. The new gospel according to the priests in every community was that the climatic disasters were not caused by the rampant exploitation of Mother Earth and the use of fossil fuels, but due to the fact that mankind had forgotten God and had become ardent followers of none other than Satan. And so now God was back with a vengeance in every single community in Panchananda.

HM Ramdeo Singhji accosted me even before I had time to greet him. 'How do you explain why these same people who donate hundreds of thousands to build the most elaborate new temples, and spend hundreds of millions on their children's marriages, are so loath to pay taxes? What is the rationale in forking out all that money to house a God who is supposed to be omnipresent in each strand of our hair, not to mention within each of our sperms, but refusing to put down a little money to help build housing for all those unfortunates who have lost their homes?'

'Forgive me, sire, but you are missing the point. The notion of philanthropy is beyond Hindus and their Jain brothers. They will gift 24-carat gold crowns encrusted with the most expensive diamonds, rubies and emeralds and every variety of jewellery to images of the gods, but suggest charity and they'll ask "What's that?"

'There's rarely anything spontaneous or generous about their gifts to the gods either. It's a quid pro quo business relationship. God has to either deliver in advance and then he gets rewarded. Or on other occasions God has to be bribed first and then he just might deliver that longed-for contract, job, son, or recovery from terminal illness.

'But it does raise some puzzling questions: Are the gods and goddesses also as besotted with jewellery as we humans are? What exactly are the biggies in the Hindu pantheon supposed to do with the hundreds of crowns they have been getting over the last few millennia? Wear one on top of the other?

'Are the goddesses as conscious of their looks as our women, mistresses and courtesans are? Since the gods and goddesses can't really wear the crowns, do the priests plonk them on their own heads after the doors of the temples are closed and seduce their wives?

'All this I'm afraid doesn't really reflect well on God, for what's impossible to deny is that God must indeed be the most insatiably avaricious and wealth-obsessed entity in the universe, thanks to His supra-affluent devotees.

'But let's for a minute talk about the babas and gurus. Not the bogus fraudster godmen-industrialists who amass crores in their lifetimes, but the truly anonymous saintly ones who spurn money and fame and live a life of penury and work ceaselessly for the amelioration of the poor and the destitute. Or take the Son of God, Jesus Christ himself.

He loved children and the poor and went all out to help them. The first few centuries after his death he stayed poor, as did the true saints of all faiths. But never forget that even if you are Jesus Christ, the Son of God, and penurious, you have to be super-rich to be acceptable to mankind once your fame spreads far and wide. That's why while the Church nails Jesus to the cross and sticks a crown of thorns on his head, by the time he returns to Heaven, he's wearing a crown of gold and so is his mother. As Queen of Heaven she wears the most expensive of silks and holds the sceptre in her hand. The sad irony is that once the truly-pure-of-heart Bhakti, Sufi or Christian saints make it to the big time and get the godmen treatment, they too cannot escape becoming obscenely rich.'

'But do you know, Weaver, the most intriguing folks in our society are the Jains.' HM Ramdeoji spoke as if he was trying to sort out a puzzle that had been bothering him for a long time. 'Both their sects, the Digambaris and the Shwetambaris, share a creed of extreme non-violence and rock-bottom, absolute selflessness. As you know they are totally invested in the idea of never, but never, doing any harm to a living creature, be it an ant, cow, goat, serpent or a human being. Any spilling of blood then is an unforgivable sin. And yet this small community is moneylender to every small, medium and big potentate, king and emperor in the country. So while technically Jains can never be accused of participating in wars, they are the ones who finance all of us kings and are obliquely responsible for the killing of hundreds of thousands of men and warriors.

'Not just that, while they swear by non-violence, they are some of the most intolerant folks in the world. Forget

Muslims, they will not permit even meat-eating Hindus to live in the same environs as they do.'

'My liege, this is indeed where jurisprudence must fail miserably. As you pointed out years ago when you asked me to try my hand at parsing the most complex issues in ethics and law, two plus two does not always make four. There's another intriguing facet of the Jain faith. I'm sure you are familiar with the fact that in some of their temples the very first prayers and rituals dedicated to their great enlightened souls, the Tirthankars, are auctioned to the highest bidder every day at 5 a.m. Thus whoever coughs up the most money earns all kinds of wondrous merit.

'What does that tell us about us, that species called mankind? We speak of God in the loftiest terms. He's Creator, virtue incarnate and metaphysical perfection. He is omniscient, omnipresent and omnipotent. And yet when seeking favours from him our sycophancy is so transparently flatulent and over the top, it must surely make him cringe. We see him as a reflection of ourselves and our basest instincts and blithely assume he is on the take and bribe him.

'And what does this tell us about God? Does anybody care to know the truth? Here it is: we know absolutely nothing about Him, starting from whether we made him up. He is after all the greatest mystery in the universe and will always stay that way.'

Bada hua toh kya hua,
Jaise par khajur.
Panthi ki chhaaya nahin,
Phal lagey ati door.

Granted you are tall, so what's the big deal?
The date palm's tall,
But it offers no shade to the traveller.
And its fruits are beyond reach.

15

It was the Master's sixtieth birthday in November that year and HM Ramdeo Singhji had declared the 5th of November a national holiday in the kingdom of Panchananda. Many other neighbouring states had followed suit. Tributes and congratulations and gifts and kudos had already begun to pour in from all over the country. Indeed, from abroad too. Thousands of people from every corner of the subcontinent were expected to visit Shantipura, the capital of Panchananda, to get a darshan of the great man and receive his blessings. They would of course stay over to celebrate this most auspicious of occasions and spend a few more days visiting the monuments and historical sites in the capital.

About a month and a half before the big day, the Master sought an urgent appointment with Ramdeoji. A letter addressed to the Weaver arrived by courier in the evening.

> Dear Kabir,
>
> I am leaving for Basera tomorrow morning to oversee how the work on the Jamuna dam is progressing. It will take me about a fortnight to return and then I will be completely

caught up for the next few weeks in the preparations for your grand birthday celebrations. We must warn you not to turn up at the court on that auspicious day in your shabbiest clothes as is your wont when you visit me, to try and insinuate that I pay you a pittance to dress me and my family in beautiful fabrics with the most unique designs and scenes and thus embarrass me. Incidentally, Kabir, how does one put a price on something as exquisite and yet robust as the scenes you weave for us?

So see you now on your birthday, unless there's something desperately urgent about which you want to see me.

Warmest regards,

Ramdeo Singh

Even before he had finished reading the last line of the letter, the Weaver was on his way to HM's Palace.

'What?' Ramdeoji was obviously in a jovial ribbing mood. 'You here when I thought I wouldn't have to see your face for the next five weeks?' Then he saw the dejected look on the Weaver's face. 'What's wrong, Kabir?'

'Majesty, you are going to think I am the most ungrateful creature on earth . . .'

'That you undoubtedly are, Weaver, but what's bothering you?'

'Sire, I don't know how to say this but will you please cancel the celebrations honouring me?'

'Why? Are you unwell?'

'Nothing the matter with me, Majesty. All I know is I don't deserve this honour.'

'Oh for God's sake, Weaver, spare me this modesty trip.

I take the decisions here. Some of the most important dignitaries in the subcontinent will be travelling all the way to Shantipura, our capital, to felicitate you, and you want me to cancel all the functions we've lined up and that too at the last minute?'

'Still five weeks left, Majesty.' The Weaver's voice was less than a whisper.

There was such despair in Kabir's voice, Ramdeoji got up from the throne, held the Weaver by the shoulders and looked into his eyes with apprehension. 'What ails you, Weaver? Speak your mind.'

'I was so taken aback and deliriously happy when you announced that my birthday would from this year on be a national holiday and none other than you would launch the latest collection of my poetry, I mean the dohas and the book of my meditations on any and every conceivable subject, but then with every advancing day I realized that somewhere deep inside me I was becoming more and more disenchanted.'

'And why was that?'

'All my life I've exposed those frauds called godmen and I'm now in grievous danger of becoming one myself. It is one thing to believe in oneself despite enormous self-doubts and disparaging comments by critics and one's near and dear ones, but on the other hand hero worship saps and corrodes the critical faculty and destroys one's internal sight and instincts. It's like smog, it blurs everything. Clarity is its first victim. You can no longer tell the difference between a haze and a halo.

'Its vehicle is emotion and that precludes rigour. It's a rot that also eats into your soul and yet you can never have enough of it. Sadly, it is an intoxicant whose demands are insatiable. God help you if you start to believe your fan mail and buy into the hoax that you really are a godman. In the beginning you don't take the hero worship seriously, but flattery has an insidious way of slipping under the skin and soon you not only take it as your due but resent it when someone forgets to tell you what a wonderful artist, scholar, historian, thinker you are, or as in my case, what an extraordinary metaphysical poet I am.

'Soon you are convinced that you are the cat's whiskers and you can breathe easy only when your admirers turn up the volume and keep inflating the fawning. But here's the awful paradox: even as you hunger for more and more fulsome praise, you have nothing but contempt for your adoring fans who you believe are sorely lacking in discernment. You are on a perpetual see-saw. You yearn for an intense critique and a demanding readership that keeps you on your toes in those who read your work or discuss metaphysical issues with you, and yet you are constantly seeking reaffirmation of your genius. But there is a far–'

'And so you would rather,' HM Ramdeoji interrupted the Weaver, 'that we dropped the idea of celebrating your ability to put even the most abstruse and philosophical ideas into playful verse?'

'I'm truly beholden to you, but yes, Your Majesty, I fear for my ego.'

'In that case if I've understood you correctly, I too should not celebrate my ascension to the throne or the day when we managed to seal the peace pact since the majority of my subjects cannot stop singing paean after paean in praise of me with or more likely without reason.'

'Sire, I would not have dared to reveal my innermost thoughts and contradictions if I did not believe that you were one of the rare sovereigns with whom one could debate ideas. When confronted with those royals or dignitaries who cannot tolerate dissent or a contrary opinion and have closed minds – you can do that, of course, so long as you are conscious of the fact that exile, or the charge of sedition awaits you, or better still, the noose is hanging around the corner for you.

'But permit me to complete what I started out to say. My problem is self-loathing. How come, I keep asking myself, that despite my belief that all human beings are equal, I too am a victim of a bogus superiority?'

'Weaver, why do I get the feeling that while you are excoriating yourself, you are really talking about me?'

'Si . . . Si . . . Si, Sire, that was the last thing on my mind.'

'The man protests too much.'

That was when Kabir saw the devilishly mischievous smile on Ramdeoji's face and cracked up. 'If the cap fits, Majesty . . .'

'I suspect it's a common disease.'

'If I have to pick a bone with anyone it is with the so-called intellectuals. They have a fixed opaque but high-sounding vocabulary which they use to effectively stymie an opponent. It's a closed coterie or club which nominates and patronizes the flavour-of-the-season artist's book or painting.'

'I've a suggestion, Kabir. This country suffers from a surfeit of monster egos. Let's celebrate your birthday every year as the National Festival of Ego-busting Comedy. How about that? We'll celebrate the doubters, the questioners, the sceptics and pull everyone down a notch or two, starting with you and me.'

Pani keraa budbudda,
Us maanas ki jaath.
Dekhat hi chhip jaayega,
Jyon taara parbaat.

Human life is as short.
As a water bubble.
It vanishes the moment you see it,
Like stars at dawn.

16

'When you are gone, Master–'

To say that Shabbir Khan doted on the Weaver would have been a bit of an understatement. He thought that not just the Master's words but his pauses, his temper tantrums, his excessive politeness when he was setting someone up for a dressing-down, his banalities, his misfired barbs, his ego trips, his preening and his cock-of-the-walk number when an attractive damsel turned up to order an odhani that would cover part of her face and yet make her even more seductive and irresistible, indeed every gesture of the Master was a metaphysical gift to mankind.

'I regret to tell you I'm not going anywhere, Shabbir,' the Master interrupted his pupil before he was able to complete whatever he had set out to say.

'I was speaking of your migrating to an altogether different universe where the good Lord would welcome you with open arms.'

'More likely it would be the antithesis of the good Lord who has been waiting eagerly to fry me in his 24/7 fires. But let me enlighten you about a simple fact. I may have lost more teeth than I was born with but I have no intention of dying. I leave that to other mortals.'

'Ah sire, surely you will reconsider what you just claimed for whilst your heart is bound to cease one of these days and your flesh turn to dust, I assure you that you will be immortalized in innumerable ways. You are the wisest teacher and guru the world has ever seen. Every utterance of yours is full of pearls of wisdom. You are the ray of light which brings succour to all of mankind. Your pupils are truly blessed. You are the most revered Weaver in the world, not merely because of the exquisite fabrics you weave but because you alone can unravel the mystery at the heart of the Almighty.

'I give you my word that I will, with the help and generosity of other admirers and followers including His Majesty Ramdeoji, build the greatest and most imperishable mausoleum known to mankind in honour of you, something far grander than anything Shah Jahan or the Lodis have built for themselves and their ancestors.'

'Dear Shabbir, I am touched by your regard for me. But what is a mausoleum if not a coffin? Yes, it may be a thousand, if not a hundred thousand, times larger receptacle for a dead body than an airless coffin, but a coffin nevertheless. The same holds for a casket made of perfumed sandalwood and lined with the most luxurious silk. But let's never forget that there's no greater disrespect for the dead, be it a parent, a beloved or a wife, a brother, sister, child, or a very dear friend, than trying to imprison in a claustrophobic box that most mysterious of birds, the soul of the dead person which has already flown the coop.

'It has always foxed me that in some faiths like Christianity, the people closest to the one who's no more actually pay to commit the extreme sacrilege of embalming the body of the departed soul. To eviscerate the body of a loved one and treat it with deadly chemicals and then paint it with make-up as if it were a mannequin, with the sole purpose of making it presentable, is sheer profanation. In fairness to the ancient Egyptians, they actually believed that the pharaohs would be born again and live in the afterlife in the same way as they did on earth, and so made ample arrangements to ensure that they enjoyed the same status, amenities and lifestyle in the next life.

'There's no gainsaying the fact that while a mausoleum, a pyramid or a statue can be awe-inspiring, its primary objective is to assert that mine is bigger than yours and everyone else's. It is an exercise in grandiloquence. And while it pretends to memorialize the departed, it's really a monument to the power of the surviving heirs, and to self-aggrandizement. Sadly, it has little to do with the intense loss experienced by those genuinely bereaved.

'Not that a family vault is any different. The idea seems to be to bung the dead body in and then all he or she can do is to wait for every member of the clan to pop it and to live happily together ever after again. But even if we were to grant that it is indeed a symbol of the love and longing for the dead, the grief-stricken party needs to be reminded that the only one occupying the vault is the nothingness of death.

'The Trappist monks seem to know how to deal with death far more sensibly. They bury their own in a simple grave, wrapped in a cloth, and after a period of time they collect the bones and put them in a common grave. Perhaps the Zoroastrians have an even better idea. The dead help to keep vultures and other birds of prey well fed and happy.

'There is only one amazing link which keeps the contact and the soul of the departed alive. It is that wondrous gift called memory. That is the shrine which will keep your near and dear one who is no more fully alive.'

Kaal chakra chakki chaley,
Bahut diwas aur raat.
Agun sagun doi paatlaa,
Ja mey jeev pisaath.

The grinding stone of death,
Carries on day and night.
The form and formless are its two grinding wheels,
Every one of us is being ground in between.

17

It was the marriage season, and barring the lunch break, the working hours often stretched from seven in the morning till eleven at night, with barely a half-hour break for lunch and forty-five minutes for dinner. There was no ban on conversation but even a novice apprentice realized early on that the Weaver was a master of deception. It would be a grievous mistake to think of him as someone who played wonderful games with geometric designs. He was first and last a painter, an artist of such subtlety that unless you were on your guard constantly, you would be in serious trouble while translating the work into a woven picture on the looms.

Take just a simple instance. All these years it was common knowledge that there were seven primary colours and a few dozen shades in between. The Master, however, had taken the liberty to add a few hundred more. As if that did not complicate matters enough, he came up with new ones any time the particular job he was working on demanded it. How to translate these painterly transmutations into the weave required not only an extraordinary nuanced sense of colour but immense concentration.

What other highly talented weavers often failed to grasp was that while the Master's work looked so simple, it was nothing short of being an extremely complex mix of maths and art.

The Weaver took a walk around the workshop every couple of hours to check the progress on each loom. If you were distracted for a split second and made one wrong move on the warp or woof, you would land up in a bloody mess and would sometimes have to undo a whole day's work.

Come the lunch or dinner break, and a tsunami of simultaneous conversations would flood the workshop. Everybody, including the odd stray dog passing by, felt compelled to add his two-bit. It was as if they needed to reassure themselves that they still had a voice box and it was actually functioning. Perhaps that was the reason why the Weaver failed to notice the rumpus that noon till it got out of hand.

It was his habit to close his eyes when he got a free moment and whisper the words of the doha or ulti-bani he was working on over and over again. That way he could get the feel of the sound and rhythm of the poem and change a word or sentence. At other times he would decide to reject the stanza or rework it, and occasionally even dump the whole poem itself.

He recalled seeing the apprentices and old hands just a few minutes earlier, back slapping and conversing with each other as they chomped on chapattis or rice, vegetables and dals, and shoved red-hot pickles into their maws, but now suddenly the half-eaten lunches had been abandoned and there was nobody around. What was unmistakable, though, was the intensity and volume of a major altercation outside the workshop.

What was going on? How had a feisty meal, the Weaver wondered as he walked down the length of the workshop, turned into an ugly brawl? The glare of the afternoon sun hit his eyes as he reached the door and all he could make out was the backs of the people from the workshop watching some kind of game where a few folks seemed to be kicking a big ball around. It took a little time for him to shade his eyes with his hand and focus. No ball that, it was a crumpled human being. And then the blood in his veins froze. It was Bhushan Pawar, his pupil from one of the communities that fell outside the caste system.

Why was he mincing his words, using such elaborate circumlocutions when the plain truth was that the young man was an untouchable. The day the Weaver had accepted him as an apprentice, the entire staff and the student community had called a strike and given him an ultimatum: throw Bhushan Pawar out or they would all leave instantly.

They should have known the Master better by now. He was perverse; a man who rejoiced in being contra-suggestible.

'It's been wonderful knowing all of you but as you know, all good things, hopefully bad ones too, must come to an end. I wish you all the very best. Goodbye.'

That was it. He turned around and went back to work. Well, they would teach him a lesson he would never forget and bring him to his knees. How the hell was he going to carry on with just one assistant? They would start their own businesses. Or perhaps they would form a conglomerate and take over all the orders and force the Master to close shop. Ha ha, hee hee.

There was just one problem. He was Weaver to the Maharana, HM Ramdeo Singhji. Which meant that most of the wealthy aristocrats and businessmen too preferred to patronize him, even though they had to often wait for months to get their orders fulfilled. There was one other minor problem. There was no one as good as him in the business. It took over two weeks, but they came back to work.

'Enough.' Kabir heard a voice tell the men who had been raising Cain. Thank God someone had the sense to put a stop to this insane brutality. Bhushan would be safe now.

'So you think I've brought up my one and only daughter so that she can elope with low-caste scum like you, get her pregnant and force me to allow her to marry you, do you?' Kabir could see the moustachioed elder who had ordered the mob to cease their violence pick up the battered and bloodied Bhushan and talk to him through the interstices of the men from the workshop.

'Just because you've got a job with that no good, half-breed, troublemaker Kabir, you think you are entitled to a young woman way above your station? Well, my friend, let me give you a piece of advice.

'Attempt to see her once more, just once more, and I, Narottam Swamidas, assure you that is the last your family and the world will see of you. You got that? I . . .'

'I doubt if poor Bhushan has got your message, Narottamji' the Weaver interrupted the father of the girl – 'since your folks have beaten him unconscious, but I have a rather naïve question for you. You do realize that there will be consequences, don't you? For instance, if you were to carry out your threat, you would be swinging from a rather high noose for the whole world to see you.'

'Oh my God, oh please, your honour, I had no idea that such a terrible fate would await me.' Narottamji went overboard with his breathless melodramatics. He fell on his knees and grovelled at the Weaver's feet. 'Forgive me, oh please forgive me. I give you my word, once I kill that shameless son of a bitch I will never kill him again.'

He stopped then and looked sardonically at Kabir as the whole crowd including the members of the workshop went into peels of laughter and clapped their hands.

'You think I give a fart about being hanged and quartered in the public square? There is nothing more valuable for me than my honour. All I care about is my reputation in my community.'

'Ah,' the Weaver said after the guffawing and backslapping had subsided. 'I'm grateful to you for bringing up the subject of the community. Perhaps you will do me a favour and enlighten me about a few things. Am I right to think that you are from the same community as my colleague Bhushan here?'

'Of course not. How dare you equate him with me and my people? He and his people are nobodies, they belong to the lowest rung of the caste system.'

'My apologies if I have in any way hurt your sentiments. I had no intention to lower your standing in society. Correct me if I am wrong, but the Brahmins claim that your people and Bhushan's do not belong amongst caste Hindus and hence are the same.'

'What utter crap. There's a world of difference between

us and them. But even if I were to grant what you say, how does that alter the fact that that disciple of yours would pollute our very essence and dishonour us?'

'And what about your own daughter? Does she not have the first and last say in who will be her lifelong companion in her marriage?'

'That may be so in your case, Weaver. We all know how your wife threw you out on the road and made you the laughing stock of the town. But I am my daughter's father and the patriarch of the family. And I and I alone take the decisions in my family.'

'For millennia now you and your people have rightly blamed Manu and his tome, the Manusmruti, for institutionalizing the curse of the caste system and thus making you outcastes or untouchables. And yet you take that very construct as your exemplar and recreate the same caste paradigm which has been the source of every conceivable injustice known to man amongst the people of the outcastes.'

'Hey preacher and holier-than-everybody-else, for your information I didn't pinch that structure and slip it into our system. I certainly don't know who did. But it's there for the whole world to see and all your lofty talk is not going to change a damn thing.'

'Change, as you know,' the Weaver interrupted him, 'can only begin on an individual level. Indeed you could set a precedent. It's up to you and your untouchable brothers and sisters to show two fingers to the caste system within your fold and put an end to it.'

'Are you done, Weaver? As you would know better than I, the Muslims in this country too adhere to it and so do the Christians in Goa. You are both Muslim and Hindu. Why don't you try your hand at it?'

'I just did.'

'And failed miserably. Get real, Weaver. I trust you will have learnt your lesson by now.'

There it was, that two-word sentence that the Weaver had heard more often than any other. 'Get real.' Sound advice perhaps, but he had always felt that if he ever did take it, then the status quo could never be altered and it would amount to giving up on life itself.

Kal karey so aaj kar,
Aaj karey so ab.
Pal mein pralaya hoyegi,
Bahuri karogey kab.

What was scheduled for tomorrow, do it today,
What you planned for today, do it right now.
Who knows there may be a deluge the next minute,
Delay a moment and all may be lost.

18

Not even fifteen minutes from our workshop was the Hastinapur animal sanctuary. While there were no tigers or cheetahs in these dense jungles, it was home to rhinos, water buffaloes, hyenas, foxes, jackals, boars, blackbucks, barasingas, deer and every variety of beast. But the numero uno here was the tribe of elephants. No royal could match their easy majesty. You should have seen them as they walked to the Amrutsagar lake early in the mornings for a dip and frolic in the waters with wives and children. Sometimes even as they were returning, they would hear Indra Dhanush singing and they would come to a halt just a few feet away from where he sat. This may sound absurd but there were no two ways about it. They were lost in the music. Every now and then when Indra plunged into the depths of the raga or explored its ethereal realms, the elders swung their trunks into the air, following the arc of his voice. What was unreal was the reaction of the toddlers. They folded their knees and sat down with their eyes closed and slipped into a reverie. When the impromptu concert was over, often one of the adults would lift Indra into the air, do a little jig and softly bring him back to earth.

Must have been five in the morning when I woke up with a start. I sat upright on the mattress in the dark, unable to decide whether I was having a bad dream or whether the jerky keening was something real and close enough for me to be startled by it. There it was again, that spastic sound which could neither be wholly released nor tamped down. I placed the palm of my right hand on Kashmira's mouth as I shook her gently awake. My wife looked around puzzled but was unable to utter a word. She looked askance at me as she pushed my hand away irritably, but by now she too had heard the choked scream.

'It's–' I jumped out of bed and was grabbing my kurta off the wooden hook – 'it's Indra Dhanush.'

Kashmira and I were outside the house now but the young apprentice was nowhere in sight. The only thing to do was to follow the trail of the voice. We were both running now but came to a sudden halt as we neared the banks of Amrutsagar lake. No. No. NO. NO. I knew I was being hyper-melodramatic but I couldn't help thinking I would rather be blind than look at what we were staring at uncomprehendingly. What we were seeing was a massacre. The sand had turned a bloody red and you could still see bubbles popping up and bursting in it. There were thirty-one elephants lying on the sand, their feet tied up with two-inch-thick ropes. They had been butchered, stabbed and gored multiple times. And every one of them had huge gaping holes on either side of their trunks. The whole lot had been de-tusked, while four little elephant babies were trying to nudge their parents awake.

Indra Dhanush was kneeling over the big tusker and trying to hold his head in his arms and kiss him over and over again, but since it was still bleeding, he was a red mess. He looked around unseeing and picked up a butcher's knife from among the axes, spears, scythes and heavy hammers and began to slash himself with such speed, the blood was spraying like a bath shower. I tried to grab the knife from him, only to find Indra was screaming dementedly at me. 'Don't you dare come near me.'

'Give me the axe,' I said quietly and tried to get a grip on the handle but Indra Dhanush swung the axe at himself in a wide arc and nicked me across the chest. I stepped back instinctively but my kurta was already turning a flaming scarlet.

'Shedding more blood is not going to bring the elephants to life,' I tried to reason with him.

'Leave me alone.' However emphatic the words, there was an urgency to the cry that would not brook any delay.

Kashmira signalled to me to move away and walked unhurriedly towards Indra Dhanush. The young man kept shaking his head but collapsed in her arms and sobbed without let. 'Why, why would anyone want to kill them? What harm had they ever done to anybody?'

'No tit for tat here, Dhanush.' Kashmira Mai spoke softly. 'Just greed. Insatiable greed. The tusks fetch far more than gold.'

I tapped my wife's shoulder. 'Will you look after him?'

'Where are you going?'

'To inform HM. I suspect the robbers came from across the border from the state of Akhand.'

'How would you know?'

'The blade of the axe Dhanush was trying to kill

himself with had the name Tej Singh. That's a well-known manufacturer from Akhand.'

'Choke your wound with cotton,' Kashmira instructed me. 'I'm sure it's not deep but best not to take chances. And don't forget to change your clothes. Or Dhanush will be in trouble for trying to stab you.'

'Why so?'

Kashmira looked at me impatiently, unable to believe that I could be so dumb. 'Because he cut you up while getting at himself. And that would get him into more trouble than he already is in.'

My wife was right. I can be opaque and drive even the most patient soul up the wall. I went home, bandaged the wound, wore a brand-new kurta and left for the palace.

It was not even 7 a.m. yet and the head of security, Pratap Singh, was loath to wake up the Maharana. 'Not a good idea, Master. He went to bed late last night and is bound to give me a dressing-down.'

'Better to get a firing,' I told him as I got off my horse, 'than be fired from your job for ignoring an emergency.'

The head of security was right. HM came down from the palace in a dudgeon.

'Can't a working man get even a night's rest? What's so bloody urgent that you presumed to wake me up at such an unearthly hour, Weaver?'

'Majesty, you decide whether I did the right thing or not after you accompany me to the Amrutsagar.'

'Amrutsagar?' HM asked petulantly. 'Why would you want me to take a bath in the lake when I can have it . . .? What's that red spreading on your kurta?' Ramdeoji was fully awake now. 'What's wrong? You are bleeding, Weaver.'

'It's nothing, sire. I'm fine. We have a bit of a crisis on our hands. It's urgent and will become clear as soon as we get to the lake. Time is of the essence.'

'I don't like mysteries. This had better be something damn serious.' He climbed onto his horse and gave a slight pat to the steed's flank and we were on our way. As always when HM stepped out, his ADC Jagdev Singh and his two assistants followed at a distance.

Hordes of vultures took off as Ramdeo Singhji and I approached the lake which was supposed to be the repository of ambrosia while Jagdev Singh and his two assistants stayed some distance away. HM's face had gone a dead grey as he stood looking at the mangled carcasses lying helter-skelter on the beach. There were long queues of red ants and other creatures entering every crevice and opening in the scattered dead. I wondered if I had made a blunder insisting on bringing Ramdeo Singhji to this graveyard where the bodies had not even been buried yet. The Maharana's deathly silence had begun to worry me. I was even tempted to say, 'A penny for your thoughts,' merely to quieten my own nerves. Ramdeo Singhji's eyes were fixed forever, it seemed, on the ascending sun now.

There was only one tiny sign that he was alive. From the edge of my left eye, I could see a single swollen vein in His Majesty's forehead pulsating furiously from time to time. Then the Maharana did something so unexpected, I rushed over and collided with him, thinking he was about to faint. What I saw then was a sight I would never forget. Ramdeo Singhji knelt down in front of the seniormost mother elephant and untied the rope around her feet. He then laid his head on them and recited a Sanskrit shloka from the great philosophical text called the Brihadaranyaka Upanishad.

Asato maa sadgamaya;
Tamaso maa jyotirgamaya;
Mrytor maa amritgaamaya.
Om shanti, shanti, shanti.

From ignorance, lead me to truth;
From darkness, lead me to light;
From death, lead me to immortality.
Om. May peace descend upon all of us.
Peace, peace, peace.

'Did you know that my father was of the opinion that unlike human beings, animals were more honorable creatures and made far better friends?' I thought he was talking to me but I was wrong, he was conversing with the mother elephant.

'He believed that big and small cats, fish, lizards, foxes and hyenas, rhinos, the tiny creatures and the birds in the sky, each and every one of them had strict ethical codes. I often thought that when he went to temples on festival days it was to worship not the resident deities but to doff his crown to the peacocks, eagles and tigers who were said to be the vehicles of particular gods. But his all-time favourites were the big tuskers who could carry the whole of mankind on their backs. Believe it or not, he imported sixty pairs of elephants from Mozambique since unlike the females here, African ones too grow wonderfully long tusks. The journey must have been hell but once you arrived, you were treated as royal guests. In time your numbers grew and there were herds of African elephants all over our jungles.

'How shall I ask for your forgiveness, Maa Shantini, when I failed to protect you and your children and grandchildren? What I will promise you is that I will attempt to catch the men who murdered you and your family. I will punish them, but that will not bring you and the rest of your dear and near ones back. This is a black day in the history of Panchananda and a black stain that will be forever on my soul.'

But HM was not done yet. He was in no hurry for he knelt down at the feet of each of the remaining thirty-one dead elephants, and untied their feet. He knew their names and spoke to them in a soft whisper and then bid them a final goodbye. When he finally got up, he would still not look at me.

'Do you have any idea who did this?' HM's voice was barely audible.

I showed him the steel blade of the axe with the name of the smithy on it.

'Some marauders from Akhand?' Ramdeo Singhji queried.

'I can't vouch for that as solid proof but it's likely.'

'How long do you think since they left?'

'Forty minutes. An hour at the most.'

He turned his head to me and asked, 'How come there are no baby elephants around?'

'There were four. They were distraught and trying to get a response from their dead parents without success. I think my wife Kashmira must have taken them home.'

'Did you know this was my family?' HM asked me.

I was grateful that he was not looking at me for I had no idea what the hell he was talking about. Which family was he referring to?

'Sometimes I was convinced that I was closer to them than to my parents.'

Now I really was lost. Who could have been closer to Prince Ramdeoji than the Maharana and Maharani?

'My mother told me that I was six months old when she had taken me for a walk in the palace gardens in my royal pram.' HM was obviously in a reminiscent mood. 'As usual dozens of people instantly turned up to greet the queen. Apparently that was the time when the royal mahout was just returning after giving Shantini a bath. Her Majesty must have been talking animatedly to her subjects for she didn't notice that Shantini had picked me up with her trunk and swung me high up in the air as she stood on her two rear feet. There I was whizzing past, east to south and north to west and every other direction known or unknown to man. I guess I had never had such a rollicking time and couldn't stop screaming my head off with joy. Mother was convinced that I was in grievous danger and was snapping at the mahout, reminding him that I was the heir apparent and if I wasn't handed over to her the next instant, he would discover that his head had been detached from his body.

'The poor man did Her Majesty's bidding but that was when all hell broke loose. Or rather, I went berserk. I'm told Father rushed out from the durbar which was in session. My mother gave me every toy she could lay her hands on, took me to sit with her on the swing, gave me her breast to suckle at, sang me lullaby after lullaby, but I refused to be pacified.

'The royal physician was called and came rushing. He

put me on one of the marble benches in the palace garden to take my pulse and check my limbs for a broken bone and feel my belly for a ruptured liver. Apparently Shantini who had been watching my antics, then picked me up again and swung her trunk every which way and His Highness, none other than yours truly, was transported to the ninth heaven or maybe it was the seventeenth one. I was burbling, laughing, and within minutes fast asleep.'

I was surprised to find the fifty-strong emergency squad slowly streaming in and taking position at the back. I didn't recall HM asking his ADC to summon the emergency troops but obviously Jagdev Singh was a better mind-reader than I and understood the gravity of the situation.

'I've known Maa Shantini almost since the time I was born. Every now and then she would disappear to deliver a baby, look after her husband or go into the jungles to restore her peace of mind. Over the years I came to know her children and grandchildren and they were indeed my closest family. If she was in Panchananda, I spent time with her first thing in the morning and often went for a ride with her. This is bound to sound ludicrous but we communed with each other in a language that needed no words.'

What neither Jagdev Singh nor I had grasped was the fact that even though the horses were standing way back amongst the trees at the very edge of the forest and couldn't possibly have seen the carcasses of the elephants, they were neighing madly by now, stamping and rearing up on their hind legs in protest and terror and creating a violent sandstorm. Another couple of minutes and they had already thrown two of the soldiers to the ground.

'Thank you for bringing over the crisis team, Jagdev,'

HM said softly. 'As you can see, horses are far more sensitive than us human beings.' HM paused as if he had been struck by a new thought. 'Come to think of it, even when dealing with my father whom I loved and respected enormously, there was almost always an unarticulated hidden agenda. My constant endeavour was to live up to his expectations. I wanted him to think that I was worthy of not just his love but also of being his successor. At the same time, while it's true that the father figure expects you to be the image of him, there's always a dark corner in him which fears that you will outperform him. Or worse still, usurp his job or throne. What Shantini and her family taught me, not by setting out to do any such thing but by sheer example, is that love is sufficient unto itself. It is bereft of any ulterior motive.'

'We should leave right away,' HM told Jagdev Singh, 'unless we want a stampede on our hands and heads and be trampled by our own horses. But there's an even more urgent reason for us to act, and act swiftly, for if these vicious murderers cross the border to Akhand, we'll never be able to catch them. Let's ride for a few minutes till we reach a clearing where we can decide on a plan of action.'

Twenty minutes later the Maharana raised his hand and everybody came to a halt.

'Have you heard the phrase "hell-bent for leather"?' Ramdeo Singhji asked the fifty-strong squadron. 'I have no idea how that phrase came about but let me misconstrue it and tell you we are going to that place called "leather" without a break. There will be zero conversation from now on. My hands will do the talking.

'I raise my hand and we halt. I poke my finger at the sky and the best tree climber amongst you will go up to the top of the tallest tree and take a 360-degree-look-see. I suspect the tree-climber or one of his colleagues will have to do this at least three or four times since the people we are looking for have had a head start of at least an hour before us. Maybe even more. If and when the tree climber catches sight of a gang of murderers carrying elephant tusks, he will take his bearings and slither down as fast as he can. We will work out a plan and immediately translate it into action.

'Good luck to all of us. Let's go.'

'Your Majesty,' I said hurriedly as HM and the troops nudged their steeds, 'with your permission, may I take your leave now and head home?'

'Of course, Weaver. Thank you for grasping the crucial importance of this tragedy and informing us. See you when we get back.'

I bid goodbye to Ramdeo Singhji and wished him all the best on this bizarre expedition and was already on my way home when I got the feeling someone was chasing me and calling my name.

It was HM. 'Would it be demanding too much of you if I asked you to accompany us, Kabir?'

'Me, Majesty? You know very well I am just a weaver and no more. I'll merely be a nuisance and a drag.'

'You may be right, but I have an uneasy feeling about this whole thing. I have no idea how you could help but let me just say I would feel better if you accompanied me.'

I have always had the highest regard for Ramdeo Singhji, but even more than that I like the man and the way he doesn't permit the idea of royalty to sit on the tip of his nose so that he's never open to a genuine exchange of ideas and differences of opinion. But a confrontation with these vicious marauders was just not my cup of tea. What if I got a panic attack and messed up the mission? What if I passed out and the troops noticed it or worse still I peed in my pants and HM discovered the wetlands below my waist? For how many years have I claimed that I am a man of peace and now suddenly . . .

I had to come up with a plausible excuse to not go on this raid on the spur of the moment and all I could think of telling him was that Kashmira would go out of her mind with anxiety, but before I could say a word, HM patted me on my back and said, 'Don't worry, I will send a message to Kashmira Mai so she knows you are with me.'

This was the fourth time HM had pointed his index finger at the sky and the little monkey of a man had once again sped up the tree, but there was no denying that he was slowing down. He took a long time up there as he scanned the horizon and the adjoining area and descended to the ground.

'Are you sure you still haven't seen the dacoits? Our one and only advantage is that we are not the ones carrying the heavy tusks and so should have overtaken them by now. We've been travelling for the last four and a half hours at breakneck speed and before we know it we'll be at our border with Akhand. Do you think we might have missed them somewhere at the back?'

'No, my liege,' the climbing whizz said softly, but there was no mistaking the understated certainty in his voice.

Another twenty-five minutes when the tree climber stopped without a signal from HM and put his ear to the ground, and now he was already halfway up the palm tree.

'Forty-seven men resting and feeding the horses about a

mile away,' he wrote on the floor of the forest with a broken tree branch. 'They are heavily armed.'

'I think we know that.' Ramdeo Singhji smiled wryly and whispered a question, 'How else would they have hacked and butchered so many elephants?'

He got off his horse and sat down on a rock and closed his eyes, as was his wont when he was in company and wanted some privacy to think things over.

Just then something squishy dropped on my head and I passed my hand over it, only to discover that some bird had shat on my head. I looked up and there it was, the bloody parrot dropping a little more wet stuff into my eyes. It was a very tall jackfruit tree and I suddenly felt very hungry since I hadn't had even a cup of tea since morning. Before I knew what I was doing I was halfway up the tree, plucking the monster misshapen fruit and dropping them to the ground. The troops rushed to pick up the jackfruits. I ventured further up and waved to the people down on the ground to move away from the tree. I plucked a dozen more and saw their innards open up as they landed. Time to go down. I hoped at least one of the soldiers would have the decency to let me have a quarter of a jackfruit.

I must have gone down barely a few feet when some quicksilver suddenly blinded me. What was that? This was bizarre, I couldn't spot it any more. I climbed up again and the quicksilver slit my eyes. Best to go up a notch or two to avoid the reflection. There was a body of water, a long python of a river really, none other than the Shankari. What an apt name, for Shiv always has a snake wrapped around his blue throat to keep it cool after he had swallowed the lethal poison Halahal.

As I landed on the ground, I saw that HM had drawn a map of how the attack would take place in three phases, and the troops were listening intently even as they and HM chewed on the cloyingly sweet chunks of the fruit. When Ramdeo Singhji had finished giving instructions and all the doubts raised had been clarified, I asked HM whether I could have a moment alone with him. He looked at me completely baffled.

'What have you gone and done, Kabir?'

Not sure why he was annoyed with me, I asked hesitantly 'Done what, Majesty?'

Oh no, I shouldn't have climbed that tree. Grazing against the bark of the jackfruit tree had reopened the gash Indra had given me.

'You are dripping blood. I had seen the stain on your kurta this morning but in all that chaos forgot about it. What happened?'

'Oh nothing, sire, I was cutting some overgrown branches of the apple tree outside the workshop when the axe slipped and I got a shallow gash.'

'You are such a bad liar, Kabir.' He shook his head, as if giving up on me. 'I hope it was not Kashmira Mai who was disciplining you. Well, never mind, I will get Jagdev Singh to bring the army surgeon who accompanies the emergency squad to take care of you.'

'May I first share something of import with you, Majesty?'

He undid his turban and tied it around my lower ribs and belly. 'Now talk. The surgeon will do the rest.'

We had our tête-à-tête and the Maharana summoned the crisis team together again. 'Change of plan . . . We are now headed for the Shankari river via a slight detour so that we don't alert these murdering highway robbers who are bound to land up there on the way to their home in Akhand. I will take the headman of the Shankari village into confidence and all of you will play second fiddle to the real boatmen. Don't forget we're still on our own territory, and like good hosts you will help the murderers across the Shankari with all their heavy luggage. Needless to say, for a price.'

Perhaps for the first time that day he smiled. 'Are you with me? I trust you will do the good-neighbour bit to perfection.'

Once the Maharana had conferred with the village elders, our first priority was to locate fishermen's clothes for the twelve soldiers who would assist the six boatmen to transport the Akhand lot and their loot across the river. Never before had old torn clothes fetched such high prices.

Normally the boats were capacious enough to carry thirty passengers but had now been ordered to carry only six each along with their horses and outsize cargo. As expected, the moment the thugs got off the boats with their gunny sacks, they tied their mounts and headed straight for the crumbling liquor den. This was perhaps the only time in their lives they would get a free drink and that too without ordering it. As the phrase goes, they would never know what hit them. From there on the action shifted almost entirely to our troops positioned inside the hut.

By the time I got back home it was close to daybreak. Our place had been turned into a nursing home. Indra Dhanush was lying all bandaged up in the guest bedroom while Kashmira was in our double bed with the four elephant babes.

My wife had just two questions for me.

'Did you get the killers?'

I nodded my head since I didn't wish to wake up the little ones.

'Will you ask HM whether he will permit a woman to hang each and every member of the gang?'

I thought she was joking. She wasn't.

Apparently none of the four elephant babes had drunk any milk or eaten anything, though she had tried all day long to feed them. Kashmira was not one to give up, but by the fourth day she had begun to fear for her babies. She was untiringly patient and persuasive and every once in a while the young ones would give in and drink milk or chew on sugarcane, fruits, roots and grasses, but there was no sign of an appetite or recovery. Ramdeo Singhji took to dropping by at least once a day and cuddled the little ones, but he too had begun to lose hope.

Luckily Indra Dhanush was recovering steadily. What I missed most was his singing. Like Kashmira Mai he too spent every free moment with the orphans. He had even begun to report for work though he wouldn't look me in the eye or speak with me. I took him aside one evening, sat him down and told him he had no reason to feel any guilt towards me since that nick was accidental, and anyway I was a tough old codger and you could barely see the cut any more. He smiled and said, 'You are my guru and I raised my hand against you. Why did I not do the same when the little ones lost their parents and uncles and aunts?'

'But you were not witness to their murder. Truth to tell, I am grateful that you were not around when the slaughter took place for they would have killed you too.'

'If only they had.'

I had no answer to that.

On the ninth morning the littlest one did not wake up. He never would.

Kashmira clammed up. Ramdeoji rode down the moment he heard about it and hugged Kashmira and me but would not say a word. Indra Dhanush's voice cracked and he broke into a nameless raga that spoke of sorrow and loss and the quandary and contradictions that human life is.

That night Kashmira called Dhanush over and told him, 'From tomorrow you will be responsible for the three babies. I loved your song but it was about you, me, HM and the Master and our sorrow. From now on bring joy to my little ones. Give them the gift of amnesia. And an irresistible hunger for life. I cannot bear to see them so bereft and hopeless.'

There was no celebration after the Akhand gang was brought to the capital. Since HM himself had been a witness to every turn and twist of events except the murder of the elephants, he was the main witness in the trial along with Indra Dhanush, Kashmira Mai and me. Along with five judges of the supreme court, Ramdeoji had removed the death penalty from the laws of Panchananda in the very first year of his reign. It took three and a half weeks for the highest court in the country to, after due process, award life sentences of rigorous labour to all the culprits who were captured on the banks of the Shankari.

'I owe you a big one, Kabir,' HM Ramdeo Singhji told me after the verdict was delivered. 'This is the first time, yes, the very first time, that the crisis team has achieved its goal without losing a single member. And that too against some of the most ruthless and despicable men on earth.'

'I'm grateful to you, Majesty, for the praise you heap on me but I have to confess that it was by sheer chance that I saw the glinting Shankari from the treetop.'

'My dear Kabir,' His Majesty chided me, 'you should know by now that that particular treetop is what we call luck.'

Can the human voice and the songs it sings really make a difference, the difference between hope and despair? Between life and death? Between drawing the curtain on the past and facing the reality of the present, whatever it's implications? Your guess is as good as mine. All I can say is that Indra Dhanush sang and our three little ones took heart and survived.

It took barely two months after my last meeting with Ramdeo Singhji for me to come face to face with that 'treetop' again. What I should have remembered is that Lady Luck is two-faced and has a forked tongue. Raja Shaktimaan of Nirmana attacked us on the 17th of October, just five days after it came to light that his eldest son Zorawar Singh had planned and personally led the vicious de-tusking attack on our elephants.

Talk about an interesting, or rather intriguing, relationship. It was the same Zorawar Singh who had breached the first principle of kinship: loyalty. He had suborned the nine-thousand-strong elite Zinda-dil brigade to rebel against his father, the Raja himself, in an attempt to usurp the Nirmana throne.

The heir apparent who no doubt had been in a tearing rush to crown himself had made one miscalculation: the rest of the troops had not forgotten their allegiance to the king. The different companies and divisions had come together in a strong show of unity and Raja Shaktimaan had chased Zorawar right out of the kingdom. Since Nirmana and Akhand had been sworn enemies from almost the beginning of time, it was hardly surprising that Zorawar was so warmly welcomed by his father's enemy.

Seven years had gone by but father and son had still not made up. So it came as something of a shock when Raja Shaktimaan wrote a furious letter to HM Ramdeo Singhji, asking him how dare he take the heir apparent Zorawar prisoner. Not just that, he demanded that the prince be released immediately. To this day I am not sure whether this was the blood-is-thicker-than-water syndrome or was Shaktimaanji being devious and aiming to finally apprehend the son who had revolted against him but had never been caught.

One would have expected my liege to have responded to the arrogant royal of Nirmana with the same degree of hauteur and contempt, but then you don't know HM. Nothing would persuade Ramdeo Singhji to abandon good breeding and politesse.

> Dear HM Shaktimaanji,
> Greetings and here's wishing you a very happy and long life.
>
> I was truly sorry that your son Zorawar Singh had brought such grief and dishonour to Nirmana by seeking to revolt against the throne. Since I am a father myself, my heart went out to you. While it's marvellous to be young, youth is a condition that is sometimes fraught

with immaturity and volatility. But your oldest son is a mature man now and hence I am at a loss to understand how you can blame me and my people for Zorawar Singh and his gang of marauders surreptitiously stealing into Panchananda and butchering three-quarters of our most prized and loved herd of African elephants.

Let me also clarify that we were totally ignorant of the fact that your eldest son was not just part of this band of thugs but also its leader and brains till the trial of these culprits started. Your Highness, kindly bear in mind that the highest justices in Panchananda have, after due deliberation, condemned him and his companions to life imprisonment. So I'm afraid the question of handing him over to you does not arise.

Yours sincerely,
Ramdeo Singh

The very next week Raja Shaktimaan crossed over to Panchananda. Give or take a few days, the war lasted intermittently for five years. That's about 1,725 days. The casualties and deaths on the Nirmana side were far greater than on ours but that did not make it any the less gruesome or pointless. Unlike his Rajput ancestors, including his own father, for whom war was the greatest validation of their lives (perhaps the French phrase raison d'être sums it up more aptly), HM Ramdeoji believed there was nothing more barren than war. As to the notion of bravery, especially the Rajput glorification of the idea and ideal of death-rather-than-defeat, he thought this was the biggest humbug created by his tribe. As he put it, its only justification was to entice folks to enrol in the military and seek death and glory.

Since perversity has been one of my favourite ploys, I asked HM, 'And yet, sire, where would Panchananda have been without a highly trained and ready-to-die army?'

He looked at me with narrowed eyes. 'Do you know, Weaver, one of your most irritating habits is playing the devil's advocate. I've often wondered why I haven't locked you in the stocks and thrown the keys away. But the damned problem is that however much I might hate your cheeky questions, you force me to rethink. I suspect this is the quintessential paradox of the human condition. One might be in the right and yet one is often forced to choose the wrong option to survive.'

Throughout his grown-up years, HM Ramdeo Singhji had committed all his energies to the pursuit of peace. There's no denying that by the end of this utterly insane carnage he was a highly disillusioned man. While it's true that most of the time Panchananda got the better of the enemy forces, perhaps HM may have been relieved to find that we were not responsible for the defeat of the enemy or rather, the end of hostilities. As if it needed reiteration, it once again turned out that no one has as many shabby tricks up his sleeve as fate.

Raja Shaktimaan was playing with his favourite dog (believe it or not, it was called Naseeb a.k.a. Luck) when it bit him. He thought it was a friendly peck and paid no attention to it till it was diagnosed as rabies, but by that time it was too late. Within six days, the Raja was no more. Perhaps this is what is often mistaken for justice.

One could say that Ramdeo Singhji had the last word. He said, 'Now we will have to wait fourteen years for Shaktimaan, Jr, to take up the battle from where his father left off.'

Dheerey dheerey re mana,
Dheerey sab kuchh hoye.
Maali seenchey so ghara,
Ritu aaye phal hoye.

Slow and steady, oh mind,
Everything will come about in good time.
The gardener may pour lots of water,
But the fruit will only arrive in its own season.

19

Master, Master . . .' Yashpal, the supervisor of the workshop, rushed into the studio and called out to the Weaver, 'where are you?'

'Right behind you, Yashpal,' the Weaver answered.

'Would you know whether God is instantly available when there is an emergency?' Yashpal was close to tears.

'What seems to be the problem, Yash? '

Yashpal was having trouble breathing. 'My wife's gone missing.'

'Take it easy, Yash, or you will get a heart attack. It's really quite simple. All you've got to do is report the matter to the police and they'll get her right back.'

'Really, Master?' Yashpal looked witheringly at the Weaver and asked, 'How about this, both the Police Commissioner and she are missing.'

'Oh?' It took a full minute for the meaning of that statement to register. 'Oh oh.'

'I suspect she's been carrying on with him behind my back for at least a year. Maybe more. I was desperate for help and rang the bells in the central temple frantically and then went to every small and big temple in Shantipura. Yes,

I rang every bell I could locate but there was no response. What's the point of worshipping the Lord every day of my life if he won't even answer my urgent call?'

The Weaver looked uneasily at Yashpal. 'You mean to say you don't know?'

'Know what?'

'That God has gone deaf.'

'You've got to be joking. God doesn't age.'

'It's been decades since he declared that he had decided to break all contact with the world.'

'How can that be? Mankind is the peak of his creation.'

'Before he switched off he said he couldn't take it any more.'

'Take what?'

'Oh, a whole host of things. For instance the bells in our temples. He said they drove him up the wall. The ones in the churches are ear-splittingly loud but they are at least sonorous. The ones in our temples, on the other hand, make such a racket, and that too at all hours of the day and night. D-H-A-N-G, D-H-A-N-G, D-H-A-N-G, D-H-A-N-G, D-H-A-N-G, D-H-A-N-G, D-H-A-N-G, D-H-AN-G, D-H-A-N-G.' It's never enough to ring one bell and that too just once. The idea is to ring as many as you can. After all, what if the Lord's asleep? Maybe he's in the toilet. Who knows, there might be lightning and thunder where He dwells. Best not to take a chance. Every worshipper feels compelled to inform God that there's not a day when he doesn't think of him. Not just that. Dhang, dhang, dhang, dhang, dhang, you got that, Almighty?'

'Hold it, Weaver, how else is one supposed to register one's presence? Besides, don't forget, I was calling for help.

After all, she's not just my wife, she's the mother of my children.'

'So are a few million others sending SOSs every minute. Do you expect him to take care of all the calls simultaneously? If it's sequential as in a queue system, then it might take a few years for him to get back to you. But God insisted there was something much worse than the maddening bells.'

'What was that?'

'He couldn't take the flagrantly bogus flattery, the bloated hyperbole, the extravagant adoration that is spouted by rote morning, noon and night. "You are the greatest, the most merciful, the most generous, the one who removes all obstacles and substitutes them with spectacular largess. You are the purest, the wisest, the kindest, the most forgiving," and on and on and on. Do they really think God of all people couldn't see through this fake hyper-adulation? It got on his nerves. He claimed he had borne this same crap for ages, but no more. He had had enough.

'The last time he spoke he said, "I could puke listening to human beings because unlike all the other creatures on the planet, humans alone almost always had an ulterior motive. I want, I want, I want. Sahil has a bungalow even though he has no children; I have nine and I live in a tiny, rented room. What I need is nothing less than a skyscraper. Will you please oblige and do the needful? I promise I'll buy you a diamond-studded crown. Mohan has a hundred thousand acres of land, I have only fifty thousand. That's double mine. Is there no justice in this world? Give me two hundred thousand acres and I'll turn my nose up at Mohan and I will build a marble temple for you. That philanderer

Surtaj is carrying on with fifteen women while I have to make do with just two mistresses and a wife with a runny tongue that never stops, not even for breath. Please get rid of her. Do that and I will take you out once a year in a golden carriage studded with rubies and emeralds.

'"Can you imagine," God asked in a towering dudgeon, "the gall of trying to bribe the Almighty? The animal kingdom, the fish in the sea, the birds in the sky and all the big and small creatures roaming the earth leave me alone and demand nothing from me. They do their thing and I do mine. But when it comes to men, women and children, what can one say? A pox on them, their demands are endless and they are never, never, ever satisfied.

'"Even after such ingratitude and truly offensive bargaining," He said, "I can forgive the whole lot. What I cannot stomach, what I loath are the tribe of priests, they call them Pandas I think in Benares, those middlemen who have a memory bank of all the devotees from your family who have been to a particular temple and have only one mission in life: how to insert themselves between me and my ardent followers and milk them for all their worth. As touts, or rather pimps, they stand outside temples and swarm around every person or group that turns up. Their intention is always the same: they hawk me, yes, no less than their God, as if I was a whore being offered to the highest bidder.

'"Their brothers, the temple priests who are supposed to conduct the various rituals purported to pump me up with the same Sanskrit claptrap every single day, are of course very much in charge of all the ceremonies inside the sanctum sanctorum. Come five in the morning, they are already waking me up with their horrible, tuneless chanting and singing. What comes next though is sheer torture. They start to bathe me in what is supposed to be the height of luxury. Milk. Oh, how I hate to have that damned milk poured all over me. Have any of those holy intermediaries ever been subjected to a dip in that ghastly, cloyingly sticky white fluid? Your whole body revolts and starts to go sour and stink. Have these folks never heard of water, the purest and most transparent of liquids? Now here's the paradox. I am supposed to be Almighty, the Ultimate and the Last Resort but I have no say in choosing what I would like or want to do.

'"How come the priests assigned to me, the highest of the high, are the filthiest lot in the country? Their dhotis have this fetid, musty smell and they stink of grease and oil. I have no idea why the premises I'm housed in are always kept in semi-darkness with one or two oil lamps and the suffocating scent of flowers that makes me gasp. Oh, what would I not give for a breath of fresh air and light and the blue sky and the playful breeze.

'"I have a question to ask. Just one. Has it ever occurred to any of you from your planet earth to ask me whether I have had a single night's rest in the millions of years I have been on call? Have you ever asked God whether He needs anything?"

'That was the last we heard from him.'Some say He plugged his ears with cement after that. Others think he got his eardrums perforated. Many believe he sound-proofed the whole of heaven.'

'I came to you for help–' Yashpal finally managed to interrupt the Master's tirade– 'and all you've been doing is raving and ranting as if you were holding a brief for God, but how about getting my wife back?'

The Weaver looked a bit shamefaced and finally answered, 'Ahem, if your wife's taken off with the Police Commissioner, I'm afraid even God can't do a thing about it.'

Jaisey til mein tel hai,
Jyon chakamak mein aag.
Tera sai tujh mein hai,
Tu jaag sakey to jaag.

Just as the sesame seed contains oil,
As the spark is present in the flintstone.
The divine is within you,
Comprehend this if possible.

20

Abhay was one of the Weaver's brightest students but he could be so persistent once he was on one of his 'tell me why-where-how-when' binges, he often got on the Master's nerves. As always after dinner in winter, all the pupils and assistants were sitting around a campfire under the banyan tree when the Master discovered that Abhay had a new bee in his bonnet.

'You claim you come from a small town, a village really, called Rupadi which even the late Maharana Ramdeoji had not heard of. Then how come you moved to Shantipura, no less a city than the capital of Panchananda, and were appointed Weaver to the royal family?'

The Weaver had been asked that same question for over thirty years and he had always had the same answer. 'You see, our ancestors had the good sense to move about naked till the priests and that fiction called religion turned up and declared that all mankind had to be clothed or God would close his eyes.

'Well, that's how I became a weaver and clothier. I need hardly add that I was a smart cookie and noticed that the royals needed more clothes than common folk. As I've always said I like butter on one side of a slice of bread and jam on the other. So I fawned and flattered and became the Royal Weaver. There, you have your answer.' When the Weaver wished to short-circuit an explanation or avoid confessing to some embarrassing fact about himself, he would fall back on an old ploy: indulge in some phoney but funny exaggerations or put-downs of himself.

But today the Weaver was in a reminiscent frame of mind. 'Both Maharana Ramdeo Singhji and Maharani Anagha Devi have been dead for some years. I feel that if I do not speak now, there will be an unforgivable hiatus in history.

'Ramdeoji was a man of great wisdom. He had the kind of courage that is far greater than the stereotype of bravery and bloodletting that we in this country adore and revere. We will never admit that war is death and devastation. We've always treated retreat as cowardice and defeat. And we've sacrificed thousands upon thousands of lives when it would have made far better sense to put our tails between our legs and come up with a stratagem whereby you live to fight and win on another day. There's no end to our hero worship, never mind how foolish and bloody our commanders' decisions may turn out to be. We glorify anybody who plunges into the thick of battle and comes out dead and defeated.

'The heroism of HM was of a totally different order. You have no idea against what odds and how hard and indefatigably he fought for peace. Never forget, the gift of peace is life and dignity. I played a very tiny part in that endeavour, but I am beholden to Ramdeoji for letting a small-time weaver stand beside him and see a great mind at work.

'Just one word of caution. It's a long story with almost endless twists and turns. So if you are feeling tired and sleepy, we will leave it for another day.'

'No, no, no, no, no, no, no.' All the students and supervisors hollered together. 'We've waited all these years for that story. We want it now.'

'Don't say afterwards that I didn't warn you. Let me try and summarize what this chapter of my life is about.'

> It's about youth and high jinks, about thoughtlessness and sudden maturing, about intrigue and betrayal, and the deadly – I use the word advisedly – problems and dilemmas that may confront you in the pursuit of high ideals. But most of all it is about right and wrong and the complexity of delivering justice. As Ramdeoji himself put it, 'Most of the time in the name of justice we end up doing nothing but injustice. The issues involved in disbursing justice are occasionally as clear-cut as light and darkness. But more often than not what you get is a dense fog and all you see is shadows. You may have been a judge of the highest court for years and yet the pursuit of justice can leave you baffled and often you may end up fearing that what you mete out is the exact opposite of justice.'
>
> It was my twenty-fourth birthday and I was facing the most serious crisis of my life. I was bored, bored out of my wits. My parents were getting old. And while there was enough business to keep body and soul together, it was relentlessly repetitive work. After all, we lived in Rupadi, a small town albeit just ten minutes from the main highway to Shantipura, the capital of our kingdom, Panchananda. All that the local women wanted from me was a pair

of halfway decent salwar kameezes, and one with a few interwoven motifs like deer or a pair of lovebirds to wear on festive days.

Once in a while someone would place an order for a bedcover, and then there was the odd customer who wanted a gruff thick woollen shawl. The only time there was a bit of excitement was when there were a few weddings in the more affluent families. But even in those two or three families, the height of fashion, or risqué adventure, never went beyond depicting two pairs of feet woven across the pallu of the sari taking the seven steps of the saptapadi which sanctified a Hindu marriage.

Correction. There was one other instance. A bride's hand and arm dripping with gold jewellery writing the name of her husband-to-be for the seven hundredth time on the full length of the sari with a reed. Weaving 'Amarnath' seven hundred times was no easy task and I was worried that from then on every bride would want her future husband's name written as many times on her bridal wear.

As luck would have it, Amarnath lost his temper on his wedding night because his bride fell asleep and wouldn't acquiesce to her husband's urgent entreaties to allow him to exercise his conjugal rights. As a result he attempted to outdo his wife's record and stabbed her, the rumour goes, six hundred and ninety-nine times, and then he too gave up the ghost. The brides-to-be, or perhaps it was their parents, took the decision to play it safe and never again tempt fate by getting the groom's name woven on wedding saris.

Amongst the four well-to-do Muslim families the height of design was a favourite verse from the Quran. If money was not a problem the odhani could feature intricate geometrical designs.

What I was looking for was a complete change of lifestyle, something that would bring excitement and tension into my life, perhaps even a touch of danger. In short, force me to live on the edge: a life full of thrills. From childhood I had had four friends. All of them had inherited family businesses but loathed the drudgery and the inescapable predictability of a nine-to-six routine. Shyamlal was a wagoner, Farhad a butcher, Musharraf a tailor, and Parikshit had a grocer's shop. We were inseparable and were known as the gang of five. We met every evening, played cards, went hunting for deer, attended the local folk theatre or drank ourselves into a stupor. No wonder my friends too suffered from the same malaise as I.

One Sunday night when all of us had gone for a swim at the Jannat lake and sat boozing on the shore, I said, 'We've been talking about a change of careers for over a year now and nothing's come of it. I've an idea. It's so radically different, you are bound to think I'm kidding or that I have gone off my rocker. From now on we are going to lead a double life. There will be no change in our daily routine, not on the face of it. But our other life will be . . .' I paused and looked at each of my four friends, leaving the sentence hanging in mid-air.

'Can we cut to the chase, please?' Parikshit interjected.

'In our parallel lives we are going to be highway robbers.'

'Give me a break, Kabir.' That was Farhad, the butcher.

'For God's sake, can we skip these bogus fantasies?' Shyamlal had had enough of my tomfoolery.

'I'm in deadly earnest. The workshop with the six handlooms will from now on be a front. I will continue to take orders each week and fulfil them, but that's just to keep up appearances. Indeed, our real life would commence only at night.'

They thought about it and came back with the same answer. 'Yes but . . .' They wanted a clean break with the past. No parents, no brothers or sisters, no children and certainly not this damned hick town where we lived. They would migrate to the city and take up the new career.

'Let's take one step at a time.' I insisted. 'Come what may we must perforce lead a double life. The only way we can take on something as exciting and dangerous as brigandry, yes, nothing less, is to have a hellishly boring job so that no one would ever associate us with such nefarious pursuits.'

Nine months went by but Pancham, as our gang of five came to be known, had little to show for itself. All five of us wore black turbans, covered our faces with black scarves so that only our eyes could be seen, and carried knives and swords. But truth to tell, not even our so-called victims took us too seriously. My partners, who dreamt big, took every opportunity to tell me we were failures. For instance, we waylaid a wedding party which claimed this was their very first encounter with dacoits and believe it or not, the bride wanted to make out with me, and invited us to the festivities and insisted we join them for the wedding dinner.

Then there was a joint family on its way to celebrate the patriarch's ninety-first birthday in Benares, but the old man said that all his life he had wanted to be a dacoit and now that finally his wish was coming true, he would bid goodbye to his near and dear ones and insist that Pancham accept him as its sixth member. No way, we said, but the old man was adamant. This was a quandary none of us had envisaged. Fortunately, the ancient kept falling off his horse and the excitement was too much for him and we brought him back to his family after we had travelled barely a mile. As if these misadventures were not enough, we ran into a group of pilgrims who were so penurious, they insisted we pay for the inn where they wanted to stay and also for their meals.

My partners, I must say, were not being altogether fair to me. It was not all bad news. We had had some successes but none of them yielding the windfalls they were counting on. Twice the butcher Farhad and the grocer Parikshit got fed up and threatened to opt out. It was clear, they said, that all we had managed to do was to chase what turned out to be petty jobs that added little or nothing to the Pancham kitty. Soon the other two members of the gang of five, Shyamlal and Musharraf, too felt that I had no game plan.

The Big One, as far as I could see, was like the horizon. The distance between man and the horizon was a fixed one. The farther you went, the farther the horizon receded. No one, but no one, could close in on it by a single millimetre. If we were to be brutally honest, we would have to admit that Pancham was not cut out for this kind of work. As if to underline our miserable failure, just the previous week the rival gang of dacoit Rathod Singh had looted a Jain banker's home and made away with not just hundreds of thousands in currency but jewellery worth crores. The next few weeks it looked as if we five friends were about to part company in sheer frustration.

But suddenly there was good news. The royal houses of Panchananda and Samadhanpur had been feuding for fourteen generations. Almost everybody had forgotten how and why the two neighbours had got into a wrangle, but every now and then there were deadly skirmishes between the two. They no longer needed a pretext. Sometimes things got so bad they even declared war and lost thousands of their soldiers. What was tragic was that peace was never an option. But Maharana Ramdeo Singh, the late ruler of Panchananda, had a mind of his own and refused to follow the hallowed traditions of mindless warmongering. He began to make overtures to Paramjeet Singhji, the ruler of Samadhanpur, but was rebuffed time and again. He did not give up despite the repeated put-downs. Ultimately, after nine years of negotiations, Ramdeo Singhji's efforts began to bear fruit. The good news was that the two royal families were not merely ending decades of bitter hostilities but Maharana Ramdeoji would very soon get married to Princess Anagha Devi of Samadhanpur. The celebrations were to last for a whole month.

It was winter and the sun had already slunk away by five-thirty in the evening. I was hurrying home along the top of the little hill adjoining the highway after delivering a shawl in the next village when I saw a dozen elite soldiers along with a loaded royal wagon carrying the insignia of Samadhanpur. They had parked their horses between the canal that brought water to the farms outside my town and the knoll on which I was standing. It didn't take a genius to put two and two together and conclude that very likely the carriage was carrying gifts for His Majesty Ramdeoji.

I got back home and had a spur-of-the-moment

powwow with my friends and told them about the possibility of a monumental heist. Within an hour we had decided on a strategy for a raid on the well-armed soldiers. We settled down just beyond the corner where the hill took a turn to the left and started practising a ribald folk song about Lord Shri Krishna coming back after a night of dalliance with a gopi when he runs into his queen Rukmini, who asks him archly if he'd been to the temple to worship Lord Vishnu. He is, to put it mildly, flabbergasted to be accosted so early in the morning by one of his senior wives who has just had a dip in the river Jamuna. 'Yes, yes,' he says, 'I stayed up the whole night praying.'

'Really?' Rukmini sounded a bit surprised. 'But as you would know better than me, the temple has been closed for repairs for the past two months.'

'Oh yes, now I remember. I must have got mixed up. You know how many gods and goddesses we have, hard to keep a count of them. Little wonder I got confused. It was Eklingji's temple I visited. You are well aware of how sensitive and touchy he is. Can't afford to alienate someone of his stature.'

'Too true, too true.' Rukmini nodded her head sagely. 'He's extremely conscious of his rank in the hierarchy of divinities. And he does have a temper, doesn't he?' Her eyes widened and she smiled sweetly but then added, sounding a bit puzzled, 'But how could you have gone into the Eklingji temple? All doors to it are closed at ten sharp.'

It was night, pitch dark and bloody cold, and we had lit a fire and were helping ourselves to a drink to warm up every now and then. Till about ten minutes earlier you could see a few lights in our village but now there were none.

'I bet she's got him this time.' A thunderous voice came over from the top of the knoll. 'And then? And then?' At least a dozen Samadhanpur soldiers came down with their leader. 'May we join you?'

Farhad, the lead singer, smiled and welcomed them with a gesture of his hand and continued to sing. 'Yes, you are spot on. I apologized to Eklingji and said I will come and pay my respects to him in daylight and moved on to the temple of the goddess of learning and knowledge. It's always a pleasure to learn about all the wonders of the world at her feet.'

Parikshit got up and served the soldiers drinks and their leader whispered, 'Just leave the bottles in the middle so we can help ourselves and you don't have to get up time and again to fill our glasses.'

Curiously enough, it turned out there were enough drinks for everybody. Or rather two sets of drinks, one that was laced heavily with opium, and the other which was nothing but water mixed with jaggery and ripe tamarind paste to look like wine for me and the other gang members. Quite simply it was a set-up. The song of course went on for some more time, for after all, as Shri Krishna himself had said, there were countless gods and goddesses, and the soldiers joined the Pancham team vociferously. As usual by the time the song ended, Shri Krishna had turned the tables on his wife and said, 'Shame on you, Rukmini, that you don't even remember that I was with you all night since you are the only goddess whom I worship.'

The soldiers had been out for the count for the past half-hour and each one had been tied hand and foot and their mouths plugged with kerchiefs of soft cloth. Pancham, the gang of five, had overnight made the grade as the most daring highway robbers in the country. We unpacked every single gem and jewel, necklace, bangle, anklet, ring and earring, and kummerband, and feasted our eyes on this treasure. Finally we got around to looking at the clothes His Majesty Paramjeet Singhji of Samadhanpur had got his personal tailor to make for Ramdeo Singhji for the sangeet celebrations when everybody would be dancing to lilting music. Even I had to admit that I had rarely seen a kurta, sherwani and leg-hugging salwar as finely cut and fitted as the ones we were looking at. The golden kurta and salwar and the dark wine-coloured sherwani were all made of the most exquisite silk shot through with threads of real gold. But what was even more enchanting was the perfume emanating from all the clothes.

Farhad and Shyamlal, the two connoisseurs of this ethereal art connected so intimately with the nose, could not stop feeling the cloth and arguing about the possible agents that went into the making of this divine scent. They kept telling me to feel it but for some reason I was loath to touch the fabric.

'What's the problem?' they asked me. 'You know cloth better than any of us.'

I shook my head since I was trying to concentrate and tap into my memory for some clues.

'At least sniff the scent and tell us how the cloth can retain the perfume for so long.'

I inhaled the perfume five, maybe six or seven times, and then once again. Suddenly I was alert and fearful and spoke softly but there was no mistaking the urgency in my voice. 'Move away from the clothes, now, this very instant and do exactly as I tell you.'

I poured the jaggery water we'd been drinking on the ground and mixed the earth into it, making a soggy mess of it. 'Plunge your fingers in it and rub them as fiercely as you can with the soft earth.'

Shyamlal's face was twisted. Tears were rolling down his cheeks as he shoved both his hands in the mud.

'I can't bear it. My fingers are on fire.' Farhad was screaming blue murder while rubbing the muddy goo all the way to his elbows.

'Go.' I herded the two sick men together. 'Go quickly and jump into the canal while we pack up everything.'

By the time they got back, Shyamlal and Farhad had fingers as red as beetroot.

'First of all, we are taking the soldiers to your house, Musharraf, since you live alone, and we'll lock them up. Farhad and Shyamlal, make sure you take the mud treatment every two hours for the next twenty-four hours. One other thing, do not breathe a word about what happened tonight to the two of you.'

'What about you?' Musharraf asked me.

'I have an urgent mission to carry out. I'm taking the jewellery and the clothes all the way to the capital, Shantipura, to see His Majesty.'

'You've got to be joking.' Parikshit spoke up even before Musharraf could retort. He had a butcher's knife in his hands.

'Like hell you are going to the capital or anywhere else, Kabir.' Parikshit had the knife thrust against my throat. 'Do you really think we took such risks for you to suddenly turn holier-than-thou and hand over everything to the king who has a thousand times more treasures, I bet, than this little pile of jewellery?'

Musharraf's eyes suddenly lit up and he laughed bitterly. 'Going to see the king? Good try, Kabir, but I'm on to your tall stories. The man's an outrageous liar. He thinks he can fool us and disappear with the loot.'

I looked my four comrades in the eye for a long minute. 'For nearly ten years His Majesty Ramdeo Singhji has pursued just one goal – peace and friendship with Samadhanpur after endless decades of enmity. The curious thing is that instead of the older royal being the wiser it was our Ramdeo Singhji who is the visionary. He swore he would not marry until he had realized his aim. Ramdeoji is under the impression that peace is finally Panchananda's as much as Samadhanpur's. But his in-laws-to-be have other plans. Under the guise of sending a set of clothes for Ramdeoji's wedding celebrations, they have delivered a death warrant for our king. That perfume in which the clothes have been soaked will kill anyone who wears them within eleven minutes on the outside. More likely within nine minutes.

'The choice before us is simple. Would you rather that Maharana Ramdeo Singhji died and Panchananda became a colony of Samadhanpur and all of us second- or third-class citizens with no rights or, to put it more bluntly, slaves? You know I'm no martyr.' I laughed sardonically. 'Quite the contrary. I so wanted to hit the big time as a brigand. But whatever the consequences for me now, HM must be warned of the diabolical treachery of Paramjeet Singhji who led him to believe that enduring peace would settle upon both the kingdoms even as his daughter was to marry our liege.'

'And what about the consequences for us? Your going over is bound to cost all four of us here extreme torture and the death penalty.'

'I'm aware of that. But I give you my word, come what may, I will not reveal your names.'

'More easily said than done.'

'True. Then you would be well advised to do away with me right now.'

We had been thick as thieves, simile unintended. Perhaps that's the only reason I could get away, but I also understood that very likely this was the end of our friendship.

One of my students, Amrut, looked at me and sniggered. 'As expected, no one can tell a lie with as much honesty and conviction as you, Master. I'm sure you pulled a fast one on your four inseparable companions, right?'

'Dear Amrut, I always knew that you are sharp and can see through me. But why not hang in there for just a couple of minutes before you find out what comes next.'

I was on my way. I had never met a Maharana before. I smiled at my presumption. What was I trying to suggest? That I was on familiar terms with slightly less august beings, like rajas and rawats? Well, never mind. Was it any wonder that I was a trifle nervous? Ha, what delicate phrasing, trifle nervous. I had taken my razor and two sets of my best clothes. I rode all night but stopped outside a village a few miles short of the capital and slept in the Samadhanpur royal carriage.

I was up by seven. I shaved and bathed in the river and had breakfast at a roadside dhaba.

Within an hour I was at the gates of the palace and showing the papers I had stolen from the chief of the elite corps of Samadhanpur to the head of palace security.

'Please tell His Majesty I have an important missive from Maharana Paramjeet Singhji of Samadhanpur and would be grateful if he saw me rather urgently.'

The man was back within ten minutes. 'His Majesty Ramdeo Singhji will see you now.'

'May I ask for another favour? There are all kinds of gifts for Ramdeo Singhji and his family in the royal carriage. Since it is my duty to explain the significance of some of the unusual items, would you please arrange to have them delivered even as I present myself to HM?'

This was, I found, an unusual king to say the least: instead of keeping me waiting, Ramdeoji was waiting for me. Was this because I was purported to be the ambassador of his newest allies, Samadhanpur? Or was HM in a hurry because he had various other engagements lined up? Or was this a ruler who did not believe that his status depended on how long he made people wait? I had quite a few moments to form first impressions as I walked a good four hundred feet till I reached close to the throne, bent low and did an adaab. The Maharana was said to be barely thirty-one years old, but though he looked young, his face also conveyed the sense of a man who had seen more than his share of life and would not suffer fools.

'Any representative of Paramjeet Singhji of Samadhanpur,' Ramdeo Singhji said, 'is a guest of honour in Panchananda.'

Too bad I was going to disappoint HM in a few minutes.

'Majesty, here is the letter Maharana Paramjeet Singhji has sent for you.' Ramdeoji reached for a paper-cutting knife on a silver plate next to the throne, cut open the sealed envelope and read the letter. Almost simultaneously, five guards along with the chief of security brought all the various jewellery boxes and parcels and the elaborately wrapped clothes and placed them on four tables.

There was a smile on HM's face as he put down the letter and looked at the spread of gifts and opened them one by one.

'Please tell Paramjeet Singhji that if I am going to get such magnificent wedding presents, then I will be considering remarrying his daughter every alternate week.'

The security guards had left by now, and having gone through the stunning variety of jewellery, HM was about to move over to the clothes.

'Majesty, let me display the clothes specially made for you. They have to be seen from a little distance to appreciate the artistry of the cloth and the cut.'

I had covered my hands with a very thick set of gloves and opened each garment with a flourish.

'I know nothing about fancy silks and brocades or tailoring but I must admit they look rather spiffy.'

'I'll come closer so you can see if there's anything else that you find striking, Majesty.'

The king shrugged his shoulders as if he would rather

be done with this elaborate presentation, but then suddenly his eyes lit up. 'I have a blocked nose which is why I suspect I did not smell the perfume right away but I have never come across anything even remotely as spellbinding as this scent. HM must have spent a fortune on these incredibly expensive and memorable gifts. But enough talk. Come and join me for lunch now. Please stay the night with us, and tomorrow morning I will write a note of thanks to HM and tell him that I am not sure I am worthy of such fine gifts, especially the clothes.'

'Majesty, will you please sit down? I have something important to share with you.'

'I can stand and listen to whatever you have in mind.'

'I beg you, sire. It's going to take quite a bit of explaining.'

His Majesty looked puzzled but went and sat on his throne. 'All right, let's have it.'

'My liege, I am not an emissary from His Majesty Paramjeet Singhji of Samadhanpur. I am one of your subjects.'

The king smiled. 'How can that be? If that was the case you couldn't have brought all these presents from Samadhanpur.' Then his eyes clouded. 'Unless you stole them from . . . Did you?' HM Ramdeo Singhji looked horrified and then shook his head slowly. 'But that doesn't make any sense. For if that was the case, why would you come to see me, knowing fully well that you would very likely be immediately imprisoned for a life of unremitting hard labour?'

'You are right, sire. I would have to be out of my mind to come here if I had stolen the goods. But before we sort that out, may I draw your attention to something far more urgent? Look at the set of clothes you are to wear for the sangeet and dance evening prior to the wedding.'

'I'm afraid I'm at a loss to understand what you are implying.'

'Wear these beautiful clothes, sire, and you will be dead within nine to eleven minutes. Perhaps even less time than that.'

'You don't really expect me to believe such hokum, do you?' Ramdeo Singhji looked at me with growing suspicion and unease. 'Why would my future father-in-law, Paramjeet Singhji, want to kill his daughter's husband-to-be after spending years negotiating a very difficult peace?'

A new thought struck HM and he rounded on me. 'I think I understand the diabolic scheme: our jealous neighbours have conspired to destroy the new-found friendship between Samadhanpur and Panchananda.' He laughed then. 'Besides, how would a wedding wardrobe put paid to my life?'

'It's an old trick, Majesty. I am a weaver but very few of us in the profession know this lethal stratagem. Let me show you how it works. But before that, would you mind asking for a basin of cold water? In the meantime I'll bring those rose pots over here. We will pour the water in them to make a mud broth as a safety measure.'

HM was fast losing his composure. 'Don't try my patience. I have a lot of urgent work to take care of instead of watching these stupid games.'

'Life and death games, my liege. If I am lying, I'll deserve whatever punishment you think fit.'

He looked at me with growing annoyance but rang the bell and asked for a bucket of cold water and a basin.

'Watch me now. I am going to gently rub the silk kurta with my left hand for a minute at the most.'

Before even three-quarters of a minute was over, my hand had lost its epidermis and now even the dermis was peeling and the hand was an angry red. I held my hand out. His Majesty scoffed at the sight of the swelling, bloody hand.

'Whatever hanky-panky you are up to I'll expose your little trick in no time. Nothing's going to happen to me.' HM ran his fingers back and forth over the sherwani. 'See, my hand is absolutely fine.' Within the next thirty seconds his demeanour had changed and he had jerked his hand back and was wincing and knocking his fist against his forehead.

I pulled Ramdeo Singhji's hand away from his forehead and plunged it into the soft mud. 'Not near your eyes, Majesty, unless you want to lose your eyesight.'

'Will I lose my hand, Weaver?' HM Ramdeo Singhji asked as he rubbed his hand with the sticky mud and then plunged it in the basin of cold water along with me.

'No harm will come to you, my liege, while I am here.'

'How long will it take for the hand to heal?'

'If you soak your hand in the soft mud every couple of hours, I think your hand will get its dermis and epidermis back within three days at the most.'

HM had shoved his hand into the mud again. 'What if I keep it in the soft clay throughout the day?'

'It might expedite the healing. However, Majesty,

perhaps you might not want anyone else to know that you have burnt your fingers.'

HM looked at me with a new-found sense of curiosity. 'Good advice. But it's obvious by now that you did steal the precious gifts and the clothes. Am I right?'

'Yes, sire, I did along with my friends.'

'What made you change your mind, Weaver? You could have stolen the jewellery and walked away.'

'My first thought and my last one too was to take the jewellery and run. It would also have upgraded our reputation from bumbling robbers to highly successful and dangerous brigands. My four gang members and I went by the name Pancham. We knew we'd never get such an opportunity again. After all, I was the one who had spotted the eleven soldiers from the Samadhanpur elite corps. Our group of five dacoits conned them by singing folk songs and getting them drunk. Even after I discovered the terrible ignominy of Samadhanpur's intended betrayal, I kept trying to persuade myself that I was reading far too much into the wedding clothes, that this was beyond my ken, that there was bound to be some larger vision or plan that you and your would-be in-laws had hatched.

'But at the same time, at the back of my mind there was a clarity I could not escape. I was suffused with a kind of light. I realized that a decision had already been taken somewhere in the depths of my, what shall I call it, mind? Soul? I was suddenly aware of something much greater than myself. Is it possible to mature within a matter of minutes and discover how utterly foolish and self-absorbed one had been?'

'You mentioned a kind of clarity or light. What did it mean?'

'It had a finality to it. While Samadhanpur and Panchananda had been enemies for far more than a century, you had a very different vision for the entire region and chose peace over war.

'But there was something else, Majesty. My father was sending me to buy dyes from the city of Dharmabhoomi. It was my birthday within a week and my mother had given me strict instructions that, come what may, I was to be back home by the 17th of the month. "Why, Ammijaan, what's so important that I must come back within a week?" I asked my mother.

'My mother knew very well that I was deliberately playing the ignoramus and getting her to tell me what she was planning to give me for my birthday. Ammi had a terrific sense of humour and we loved ribbing each other.

'"Oh my son, didn't you know?" she queried me. "We are getting you married to a lovely young woman from the village of Satnam. Her name is Padmavati. She's a little squint-eyed and is hunchbacked and slow-witted but she has a heart of gold. And she's bringing a huge dowry. Aren't you excited, my son? A bride plus the windfall of money?"

'"I'm so excited," I told her, "I think I am about to have a heart attack. I think it will be best if I don't return. And Abbajaan takes her as his second wife."

'"Getting your father a second bride, is it?" She brought the broom out and chased me around the house.

'It was the last time I saw my Ammijaan and Abba. The Samadhanpur troops ransacked our little town of Rupadi two days before I returned. My folks were lying dead on the floor, their heads severed from their bodies. Now I really was an orphan.

'Despite having agreed to the covenant of peace, the perfumed wedding garments offered indubitable proof of Paramjeet Singhji's treacherous game plan. He clearly intended to use the covenant to murder you and take over Panchananda. As luck would have it, I was the only one in the Pancham group who understood the significance of that perfume on the clothes. I had no choice but to let my gang members down and come to warn you.'

HM was pensive for a long time. 'Weaver, I want to sort things out by myself. I shall meet you after two hours in my private rooms for lunch. Now that peace is out of the question, far too many decisions need to be taken in a very short time.'

The lunch was tense. HM was preoccupied with his own thoughts and did not look at me. I knew from the start that I had no business having a meal with him and yet there was no way I could have said no.

'What's our next move?' HM asked me suddenly.

Time to run for my life. What game was Ramdeo Singhji playing with me? They say the earth swallowed Sita. How about coming to my rescue, dear Mother Earth?

I was dumbstruck. 'Sire, you must discuss these matters with your Prime Minister and the minister of defence.'

'Don't tell me what to do, Weaver. For the time being this sorry tale must stay between us. But I am curious, or rather foxed, by why Paramjeet Singhji would prefer war to peace. You won't believe this, but my own ministers were opposed to my peace forays for the longest time.'

'I am no statesman or reader of minds, Majesty, but my uneducated guess is that the likes of Paramjeet Singhji and all those in power prefer wars because they can dictate terms, obviously humiliating terms, to the enemy and get to attach not just significant territories but also exact substantial annual monetary tributes. I need hardly add that's if they win the war. You are that rarest of exceptions, a king who's in search of peace. I imagine kingdoms mirror zamindaris on a macrocosmic scale. In our villages we have seen how it suits the big guys to attack the small ones so that they can swallow them whole.'

'Let's get back to what do we do now.'

How did HM guess, I wondered, that I had spent the whole night and even the time I was left alone in the palace putting myself in his terribly difficult position and trying to figure out how to deal with the immediate future.

'Let's get the soldiers whom the Pancham gang ambushed and kidnapped to Panchananda first,' I blurted out, 'and then send an effusive missive to your sambandhi, Paramjeet Singhji, thanking him for the exceptionally beautiful gifts and also telling him that we are keeping his elite soldiers behind to help out during the wedding celebrations.'

'Yes, I must make a note of that,' HM replied. 'Now let me clarify where we stand as of now. Whatever devious fate Paramjeetji had in mind for us should be reversed and played back a hundred per cent. You are the expert on clothing and poison. So here's what I expect of you. Devise a two-part strategy that will shake him to his hair roots. Throw him off balance. Let him quake with suspicion and fear, thinking that we are about to poison him one way or the other. I will leave it to you to decide by what method you will terminate him.

'In the meantime I will have to take care of urgent military matters. The corollary to bumping me off must surely be to take over Panchananda. Which means I have to set myself a dual task. Paramjeet Singhji had informed me that he was bringing along his senior military commanders to work out joint defence strategies between the two armies. I had thought his proposal made good sense at that time but of course I see it in a different light now.

'By now I'm certain his troops too will be quietly moving in to encircle us. Within a day or two our spies will have a clear idea about their locations and I will announce my wedding day as a holiday along with an official notice that since we are celebrating the real and metaphorical marriage between Samadhanpur and Panchananda, all weapons will be collected and kept in storage to mark that day of peace and goodwill between our nations. Simultaneously, two-thirds of our army will occupy and take over Samadhanpur.'

It was something of a mystery to me why the king would share his military plans with me till I realized that he felt he owed it to me to keep me informed about what was going on in his mind and the steps he was taking to safeguard the state since I was the one who first warned him about the dire threat not just to him but to the kingdom itself.

'I can see that a whole lot of you are about to start snoring,' I told my students. 'Best that I take a break and we continue some other time.'

'Don't you dare try your bogus stunts on us today.' A chorus of vehement objections and threats followed my plea to retire. 'You are not leaving till the full story is told, even if it takes till next morning.'

I let out a deep sigh. 'I give in. Do I have a choice? I'm beginning to understand who is Master here and who the obedient slave.'

I was given a suite of rooms in the same wing as HM but in the attic. A steward was to attend to all my needs and to accompany me into town to buy whatever I needed: looms, threads, needles, whatever. The only condition was that I was not to socialize with anyone. Two weeks later I was still sewing the border of the sherwani the Maharana of Samadhanpur would wear at the sangeet ceremony when there was a tap on my door.

'They'll be here in an hour's time,' HM told me. 'Are all the clothes ready?'

I shook my head. 'The ones for the visitors are done. But I'm still working on yours.'

The next evening, which was the first day of the wedding celebrations, was the sangeet. My work was done and I would have hawked my soul to get just a few hours of rest, but that was out of the question since HM had decided that I was to be in charge of tracking Paramjeet Singhji's and his wife's reactions.

Come four in the afternoon the next day, it was Panchananda's turn to give gifts to the guests from Samadhanpur in the durbar hall.

'Your Majesty, we loved the exceptionally fine jewellery and the clothes you specially made for us for this evening's revelry, but we at Panchananda too have a surprise for you. We are a tit-for-tat people and wanted to show off our skills and have made some exquisite clothes for you. Clothes to die for.' I watched my king with new respect. He was a superb actor and his choice of words, though a trifle obvious, was lethal. Paramjeet Singhji's face was a rictus of a laboured smile and fear.

'This evening we will see whose tailor is the better designer and of course who is the better-looking king.' Ramdeo Singhji guffawed theatrically at his own humour and handed over the set of clothes I had designed and tailored for the Samadhanpur royal. 'We'll have a panel of three of Samadhanpur's top dressers and three of ours who will be the judges.'

Paramjeet Singhji's hands were shaking as he received the package and the next moment it was on the floor. HM laughed as he bent down and handed the wrapped parcel back to its new owner. 'Am I to understand that you admit defeat even before you have seen the suit?'

The visiting king smiled wanly and answered, 'We prefer to win rather than brag and lose.'

'See you at 7 p.m. sharp in the open air Tribhuvan mandap. Don't forget our sangeet's not just fabulous music but also full of lilting rhythms to which even dead men wouldn't be able to resist dancing. For every song and dance item there will be a prize. As you know it is the unique tradition of Panchananda to invite every single denizen of the city for the wedding celebrations. All the royals, aristocrats and commoners will dance and sing together till after midnight. So come prepared.'

Four courtiers were sent to pick up HM Paramjeet Singhji, Maharani Ameera Devi and the shy and bewitching bride-to-be, Rajkumari Anagha Devi, and the heir apparent, the six-year-old Prince Sumer Singh, who was more than a handful for the sangeet. As Paramjeet Singhji turned the corner of the palace and stepped into the beautifully lit and decorated grounds, Ramdeo Singhji came forward to greet him. The ruler of Samadhanpur froze in his tracks and couldn't take his eyes off the clothes I had replicated with such meticulous care.

I knew exactly what was passing through his mind. How long had His Majesty Ramdeo Singh been wearing them? Even if he had got into them just before leaving the palace, it would still have taken at least fifteen minutes to come down five flights of the staircase and walk all the way to the Tribhuvan mandap. I don't think Paramjeetji was even conscious of what he was up to as he leaned over and ran his fingers through the silk of Ramdeoji's sherwani.

'I see that you are in shock and it's obvious that I have already won the prize for the best-dressed man today,' Maharana Ramdeoji told his counterpart.

There was a wan smile on the Samadhanpur royal's face but he seemed unable to move. Maharani Ameera Devi came to her husband's rescue. 'No way. Look at the superb cut and stitching of his entire ensemble. It is perfection itself. And I must admit that your weaver and tailor have done my husband proud. I was, as a matter of fact, scheming to steal both of them if you would only tell me their names.'

'Maharani Sahiba, let me tell you that you are welcome to spend as much time as you want in Panchananda and get all the clothes you want stitched right here, but if you walk away with the weaver and tailor whose names I will not reveal, I will indeed go to war with Samadhanpur.' Both Maharani Ameera Devi and Ramdeo Singhji burst into laughter just as Maharana Paramjeetji bent down and tried to smell the fabric of the sherwani meant for him.

'What are you looking for?' Ameera Devi pulled her husband back in embarrassment.

'Nothing,' her husband said shamefacedly, 'just wondered what perfume His Majesty uses.'

There was enough tension now for the air to be zinging and Maharani Ameera Devi was both bemused and furious with her husband. Just then the court singer, Sadanandji, appeared on the stage, and broke into one of our most popular folk songs. 'Oh please, oh please, all I want is a bride. Is that asking for too much? I'm not fussy. I will be more than happy if you'll find me a gorgeous woman. Anyone between nineteen and ninety will do.

'Hey, I grant you that I am not the handsomest man around but I am dapper, bright as sunlight, and I can whip up a storm of love that will fly you to heaven.'

The whole crowd of four or five thousand clapped lustily and sang the lines of the chorus. HM was the first to break into a dance. He pulled a three-year-old away from her parents, put her squarely on his shoulders and danced with her mother. That was it. It looked as if even the lame and halt could not sit still. I was on the dais by now since I was about to launch into a wedding-night song full of double meaning and could see Paramjeetji refusing to join the dancing. He was fidgety and restless, shifting uneasily inside the kurta and knee-length sherwani I had stitched for him. It was really cold by now but he had taken off his jacket and was unbuttoning his kurta.

Oh, how I sympathized with the royal guest. He was not only convinced that his attempt to poison Ramdeo Singhji had been discovered but that we were returning the favour and any moment he would drop dead. Even from this distance I could see the Maharani trying to calm him down. I must have got caught up in my song for I did not even see them leave.

It was only after two in the morning when the last song had been sung and the throbbing drumbeats had died down that His Majesty signalled to me to join him upstairs in his private rooms.

'Congratulations, Weaver. You obviously understand human nature far better than I or most others do. You hadn't used a drop of poison and yet HM had got the willies. Truly the mind can poison and destroy a human being far more effectively than a deadly poison. I danced with his daughter, my purported wife-to-be, and was about to ask the Maharani to join me when the royal couple left without even saying goodbye to me. I bet the moment they went back to their suite of rooms he got rid of the set of clothes you had sewn with such care and attention for him.

'But let's move to more urgent matters. I take it you have already arranged for the blanket on his bed to do the needful.'

'Yes, sire, I did that even before the sangeet started.'

'I owe you my life, Weaver. Some debts can never be repaid. Go to bed, now. We have another hectic day tomorrow. The marriage will have to be cancelled and the royal funeral arranged for.'

'Goodnight, sire. Barely four hours before sunrise. Make the most of the . . .'

There was a soft knock on the door just then despite the fact that it was open. Bad news. Maharani Ameera was standing in the passage along with Paramjeet Singhji. Almighty God, what was that truism about the best-laid plans?

'May we come in, Majesty?'

Ramdeo Singhji was immediately alert and stood up to greet the guests, his face full of foreboding.

'Please do. Is everything all right?'

'No. But I am here at this ungodly hour in the hope of making things all right.'

'Majesty, may I take your leave now?' I asked softly.

'No, you may not,' Ramdeoji shot back at me. 'I may need you yet.'

Maharani Ameera looked at me suspiciously for a brief second and then addressed Ramdeoji. 'I don't know where to begin. So without any further ado, I will dump the entire burden of what I have to say on you, Majesty.'

Paramjeet Singhji's eyes were stuck to the floor.

'I'm all ears, Maharaniji. But first make yourself comfortable.' Ramdeoji was the soul of politeness.

'That is not possible. Tonight is the worst night of my life. I have never been so humiliated.'

'Has anyone from my staff insulted you or not done your bidding?' His Majesty seemed genuinely upset.

'Your staff has been courteous throughout and bent over backwards to do our bidding. There is no greater source of humiliation in life, Majesty, than one's own family. I do believe you know why I am here. You came to my husband with the most priceless offer possible for our two kingdoms: the offer of peace. My husband Paramjeet Singhji hemmed and hawed for nine years, his rationale, or rather excuse, being that you were unreliable and insincere. Every time you two met to negotiate the peace agreement, he came up with new objections. Finally you offered to sanctify the peace covenant by marrying our daughter.

'I don't normally interfere in state matters but I lost my patience and warned my husband that if he didn't sign the treaty we would be caught in another war and rivers of blood would flow once again in both of our lands. I could not, nay, I would not, be party to that. At last both of you agreed to sign a permanent peace treaty at the same time as the marriage. I have no idea how you learnt that he had decided to eliminate you by poisoning the set of wedding clothes we sent for you. Unfortunately I came to know of this double-cross only today when my husband realized that you had discovered his diabolical plan and he was certain he was going to be bumped off.'

Ramdeoji was silent for a long time and his voice was a whisper when he spoke. 'Thank you, Maharani, for coming clean. But where do we go from here?'

'I wish I knew, sire. How does one retrieve a situation that is beyond salvaging? I have no option but to ask your advice. I have only one thought, Majesty. There will always be a doubt in your mind whether I was in the know of my husband's heinous intentions. But you will grant that my daughter who is to be your bride is innocent. Totally innocent.'

'How can I believe you since the marriage, as I learnt just a few days ago, was never meant to take place.'

'I understand your reservations and doubts after what has happened. Unfortunately I've no idea how to induce you to believe me when I say I will make up for my husband's deceit and betrayal in whichever manner you want to me to.'

'Please sit down both of you.' Ramdeo Singhji looked at me and said, 'Do go across and get one of the attendants to bring some fresh fruit juice for all of us. And please ask my attendant why my bed has not been made yet.'

If the king needed a drink, all he had to do was click his fingers. But I'd got the message, he was stalling for time. I went in, asked one of the servants to bring the drinks, and then ran like a man possessed to the suite of our royal guests, pulled off both the blankets and the bed sheets and replaced them with two others from the linen cupboard. I ran back and dumped the blankets in HM's hamaam and joined the three again.

'Let me put it this way' – Ramdeoji was in the midst of a conversation with our royal guests – 'I don't wish to say anything which I will regret later on.' The watermelon juice was served and there was a pause. 'I am conscious of the fact that the ball is in my court. Let me try and sleep over this matter. Maybe something genuinely worthwhile may strike me. Who knows you too may have some ideas by the morning. Let's hope we find a way out of this awful quandary.'

After they left, HM asked me, 'What do you think?'

I shook my head. 'Sire, you will be far better advised by

the Prime Minister and your cabinet members since this is way beyond my limited experience.'

'Are you trying to suggest that this is something of a daily occurrence in my life?'

'Hardly, Your Majesty, but you are the king . . .'

'And that gives me the liberty to make as many blunders as I can?'

I shook my head foolishly and said, 'I don't know, Majesty. I'm inclined to believe the queen but not a hundred per cent. Was she party to the original plan to kill you but is now seeking to get her husband alone to take the rap? At the moment, however, the only question is what does one do with His Majesty Paramjeet Singhji? Just because he was caught red-handed before accomplishing his objectives doesn't make him any less a murderer. I guess we don't really have the option of hanging him or putting him behind bars for life. But let him go scot-free and very likely he will be even more vindictive because his betrayal was exposed.'

'How true. I must bear that in mind when I consult the Prime Minister and a couple of my ministers tomorrow first thing in the morning and decide what our course of action should be.'

'May I take your leave now, Majesty? You have a long and difficult day ahead of you.'

'Goodnight, Weaver. Thank you for all your help.'

I wished His Majesty goodnight and retired to my room. Oh, what a relief it was to get back. I barely managed to empty my bladder and dropped dead on the bed. As far as I could see, my work at the palace was done. So it was something of a puzzle why I woke up with a start at five past ten when I could have slept for the next week or two. To this day I am not sure why I took a rushed bath, and that too with freezing cold water to wake me up, and ran to His Majesty's suite.

The Prime Minister and two cabinet members who belonged to HM's inner circle were leaving by the time I reached.

His Majesty was sitting red-eyed on the swing, more dead than alive.

'Morning, Weaver. After endless arguing and tallying the pros and cons, we've finally come to the conclusion that we will ask Her Majesty Queen Ameera to leave the heir apparent of Samadhanpur, Prince Sumer Singh, in Panchananda and allow us the privilege of bringing him up. That will certainly prevent HM Paramjeet Singhji from trying anything funny.'

'Oh? Oh, I see.'

'You don't look too happy with the solution we've come up with.'

'Majesty, I was merely digesting what you told me.'

'Stop pussyfooting, Weaver. I know that despite all your pretence of ignorance, you are constantly putting yourself in the decision-maker's corner and trying to come to grips with problems that tend to be almost impossible to resolve.'

I could see he was very tired and not just physically. I began to wonder if it would have been much better if we had not chosen to frighten the daylights out of Paramjeet Singhji but had made certain he had worn the poisoned garments and called it a day.

'Majesty, forgive me if what I say sounds presumptuous, but even if both Paramjeet Singhji and his queen were to acquiesce to your suggestion, you will not only alienate them but, far worse, the citizenry of Samadhanpur, who will wonder why the king and queen would want to part with the heir apparent. However, the one I would worry about the most is Prince Sumer Singh.'

'On what grounds? We intend to treat him as if he were our very own son.'

'I'm sure you will. And that's precisely why he will wonder why he's no longer the most favoured when the real heir apparent of Panchananda is born and, worse, learns that you deprived him of his own parents who happened to be the rulers of Samadhanpur. That's when he'll ask why his parents parted with him and begin to hate you. The end result will be that your endeavour to establish peace between the two kingdoms will prove to be a chimera, and the coming generations in the two countries will be even more antagonistic and vengeful.'

'I can't gainsay anything that you've just told me, though neither my advisers nor I had analysed the problem as you have, Weaver. But where does that leave me? I still have to meet both Their Majesties to discuss just what conditions I will set to sign the peace agreement and marry their daughter.'

'Majesty, I have only one suggestion to make. You and your team will obviously have to decide how effective or useless it's likely to be.'

'Well, let's first hear your proposal.'

'My proposal is that you draw up a statement describing the initiative you took seeking an end to the multi-generational feud between Samadhanpur and Panchananda. The text should describe briefly how long it took you to overcome the resistance and objections that His Majesty Paramjeet Singhji raised, and finally convince him of the enormous economic, agricultural, military, maritime, scientific and cultural benefits that would accrue from a permanent peace agreement.

'To vouchsafe the integrity of your intentions, you went further and proposed to sanctify the peace negotiations by marrying Princess Anagha Devi, the daughter of Their Majesties Paramjeet Singhji and Ameera Devi of Samadhanpur. The marriage was to coincide with the signing of the peace agreement. But it was by a sheer stroke of luck that you discovered HM Paramjeetji's diabolical plan to murder you through the gift of a set of wedding clothes steeped in poison that would kill you within eleven minutes of contact with your skin.

'The last paragraph will state that it is your solemn promise never to breathe a word of this to anyone except if either HM Paramjeet Singh or HM Ameera Devi renege on their promise to honour the peace agreement. When both the Maharana and Maharani have gone over the full document, and are willing to sign it, please make sure that their signatures are underwritten with the seal of the kingdom of Samadhanpur.'

The king eyed me with apprehension and relief. 'You are a tricky customer, Kabir. I should appoint you my adviser, but I warn myself every minute to beware of you.' His Majesty was silent for a long time and then asked one of his factotums to fetch the Prime Minister and the two advisers back post-haste.

'Majesty, my work here is done. May I with your permission go home now? I will, I assure you, return after your marriage when, as you had warned me right at the beginning, you will pass judgement on my stint as a brigand.'

'We'll certainly do that but I'm afraid I can't let you go. I was under the impression that the wedding would not take place thanks to you. Now that I am most likely to be married in another ten days from today – I've decided to postpone the wedding ceremony – I need some really fine clothes to make my bride proud of her husband.' Believe it or not, he winked at me then. 'I know that you will have time to only weave the cloth, but at least do the cutting and supervise the tailoring of my wedding outfit.'

Five days later I called him for a fitting.

'What, you . . . you must have worked day and night and maybe you borrowed some hours from the god of time himself. Oh, the birds, the birds flying in the blue, blue sky into the sunrise. I can't possibly wear such an exquisite sherwani. It should be preserved as an heirloom for posterity.' Then His Majesty smiled and added, 'Maybe I will wear it. My bride-to-be, Anagha Devi, might fall in love with, if not me, then the sherwani and will tolerate me.'

He slid his right arm into the right sleeve and then the other and I buttoned him up. He stared at his image in the mirror. 'You're a miracle man, Weaver, I have never looked so good, I who couldn't bear to look at myself in the looking glass. Thank you, Kabir.'

He was about to leave the room when he changed his mind and sat down on a chair. 'The last time we were together, you spoke of the punishment due to you. I'll come to it one of these days, but in the meantime I want to ask you to parse the sequence not only of the events that occurred but more importantly track the path of decisions that led you to become a dacoit, albeit a minor one, and then the raid on the Samadhanpur troops, the discovery of the jewellery and the set of wedding clothes. You had finally made it big and at that very moment you decided to give it all up and deliver not only all the goods but yourself into the hands of the one man who would punish you with a death sentence. As you perhaps know, my cabinet and I abolished capital punishment in the first year after I was crowned except in one instance, treason. But it didn't end there, did it? There were many more quicksilver changes before you were able to not only save your king's life but the peace process also.'

It was a month, maybe more, before HM called me to his office late one night. 'Sit,' he said. 'Okay. No more postponement. Parse.'

What was I still doing in the palace, you may well ask me. Maharani Sahiba Anagha Devi had decided that HM's entire wardrobe had to be redone from scratch.

'Sire, this is bound to take a long time, all night for all I know.'

'Well, I have all the time in the world.'

'I'm a weaver, sire. I weave cloth. I put it together thread by thread. As I grew up and became confident, I undertook more and more complex themes. That's how I put together that flight of birds for your wedding sherwani. Incidentally, it was my seamstress mother who insisted that if I was going to be a weaver of highly complex motifs, then it would make far better sense for me to learn to cut cloth and tailor it instead of leaving it to someone who didn't understand the chemistry between the woven fabric and the seamstress's art. And now you ask me to do exactly the opposite of my vocation, that is, unweave a whole series of the most extraordinary concatenation of events.

'The whole sequence you asked me to analyse is so interwoven and complicated, it has to be unravelled thread by thread. For instance, forgive my saying so, but you would not be here today if my friends and I had not been bored with the mindless work we did for a living in that small town of ours. I knew that we were not cut out to be brigands, but when I broached the subject and insisted on pursuing it, it added an edge to our lives, a thrill of excitement. Sometimes I've wondered whether all life's about cause and consequence, blind acts and the ripples and repercussions that ensue from them.'

'Fair enough. So let's go through the entire series.'

'I must warn you, it did not end after I revealed the fiendish plan of HM of Samadhanpur to you.'

'I know that too well. For instance, if my advisers and I had not at the very last moment ditched our own consensual plan to ask for Prince Sumer Singh as hostage, I would not be a married man today, and for all I know not merely Paramjeet Singhji but Maharani Ameera Devi would have been planning to overthrow me and grab Panchananda. So go ahead. I am all ears.'

The first half of our session went on till 4 a.m. And then HM Ramdeoji took over. 'Do you realize what a quandary you have placed me in? Thanks to you I am on a perpetual see-saw. It's because of all your thefts and wrongdoings that I was saved from being murdered by the very people whom I had spent over nine years wooing. How's that for an equation? Should I send you to jail for a lifetime for being a bandit and a threat to society? Or should I felicitate you and award you the highest honour in the nation for saving my life? Should I issue an order to hang you tomorrow morning in the public square of the capital for having the temerity to steal the jewels meant as a gift for our wedding celebrations? Or should I gift you fifty thousand acres of the most fertile land in the state for coming up with the wisest and least dangerous solution to keep HM Paramjeet Singhji on a tight leash without alienating him or Queen Ameera Devi?

'I could go on but I believe you've got the drift. I would not wish this series of dilemmas on my worst enemy. Well, I am exhausted now, as I am sure you are too. An odd time to go to bed as the sun cracks the black sky and a tentative ray of light steals through. Goodnight or should I say good morning, Weaver?'

HM had almost crossed the threshold into his private wing in the palace when I stopped him.

'Sire, you still haven't told me my punishment.'

'Oh, yes, how could I have forgotten that? Well, you will be weaver and tailor to the royal house of Panchananda. Not just for me but also for Maharani Sahiba.'

'What of the punishment, my liege?'

'Don't be so impatient, I'm coming to it. I am appointing you chief adviser to the highest judiciary in the country. That's mostly me.' He stepped back into the room and sat down again.

A bitter laugh escaped me. 'You've had your fun, Majesty. I've been waiting for months to be told what punishment is my due for my brief stint as a brigand.'

'But Weaver, I am in earnest. I had that job and every minute of my life I'd been looking for a likely candidate. Now that I've found you, that horrible burden is off my head.'

'You can't be serious about this, sire. I have no idea about the law. How could I possibly be appointed chief adviser to the highest judiciary?'

He laughed. 'Because, as I have told you once before, I have noted time and again that you always put yourself in the position first of the criminal and do your best to understand what motivated him along with all the factors weighing upon him. Your next move is to step into the mind of the justices. As a consequence, since you've grasped all the factors operating upon the criminal, you have a three- dimensional picture of the whole case and will work towards the right shade of judgement.

'Do you know what I hated the most in children's stories, even the liveliest, funniest and most enchanting ones?' Ramdeoji continued. 'The point where the narrator asks, "And children, do you know what the moral of the story is?"

'But the reverse holds true when you grow up. By that time you are not looking for a moral. Confronted by a tricky and convoluted problem, most folks will take one step back at the most, to find the facts of the case and pronounce judgement, just like the textbooks prescribe. But as you know from your own personal experience, in the most complex cases every single factor is a riddle. It's a play of light and shade and the chiaroscuro keeps shifting, making it almost impossible to get a true picture, the three-dimensional one. Which is why you have to keep digging not merely for the verifiable facts but for the deeper psychological aspects which have been at play. You have to keep at it till you can separate fact from fiction and yet never lose sight of the one simple truth – that you are dealing with the most precious and complex entity on earth, a human life and mind.

'I wish you luck, Weaver, at your deadly serious part-time job. Incidentally, this is a confidential appointment. No one but you and I will be privy to it.'

'Sire, one last question. What about my companions from Pancham, the gang that stole from Paramjeet Singhji's royal wagon?'

'I am waiting for you to give me their names.'

'They let me take the clothes and the jewellery and allowed me to reveal the plot against you only after I promised on pain of death that I will not reveal their names.'

'In that case let me see if I can recall the names of the four. Parikshit, the grocer; the wagoner Shyamlal; the butcher Farhad; and Musharraf, the tailor? Did I get that right?'

My mouth must have fallen open, for Ramdeoji was placing one of his royal rings on my tongue. 'That's the signature ring for the post of chief legal adviser in Panchananda.'

'My liege, how did you find out the names of my companions?'

'Just in case you have forgotten, I am the Maharana of Panchananda. It is my duty to keep an eye on my citizens and protect them.'

'So now you know how I met HM Ramdeo Singhji and was made to pay for my stint as a brigand by being appointed adviser to the highest judiciary in the country.'

Sayee itna deejiye,
Ja main kutumb samaye.
Main bhi bhookha na rahoon,
Sadhu na bhookha jaye.

Give me only so much, God,
It ensures that my family is fed.
I should not starve,
Nor should the holy man go hungry.

21

The Kabir Diaries

There's much talk of late in scientific circles of something called dark matter in space. But when will the great minds and visionaries begin to throw light on the dark matter in each one of us? The believers, whether they be Muslims, Hindus, Buddhists or Christians, talk all the time about God and yet keep company with Satan by choosing silence or going deaf when confronted by the suffering of others. Why does hate come so much more easily to us than love? How come each one of us humans has that highest judiciary in the world, that indefinable thing called 'conscience', and yet we so blithely ignore its diktats on the pretext of one's faith, or justify our criminal actions by telling ourselves that we are doing it for the greater good of society?

Where does the evil in us come from? Why is it that when all our needs are satisfied, we still cannot control our inexhaustible greed? Why is it that the less fortunate amongst us, the starving millions, the helpless children, the refugees fleeing their homes under the threat of death, do not find succour in our hearts? We know the difference between justice and injustice, between right and wrong, good and evil, and yet when a Hitler turns up we are more than happy to benumb our consciences and let him indulge in holocausts. How come we will not stand up and force our feckless leaders to take a stand?

Mother Earth has witnessed so many radical upheavals and changes in the billions of years she has been around. The ice age, the age of the great predators like dinosaurs. They disappeared because of factors beyond their control. Then humankind turned up. Compared to all the other ages, mankind has been around for a very short time. No other species has so wilfully set about killing its own. We had to invent new words every hundred years or so to encompass the magnitude of the death that our leaders and dictators visited upon hundreds and thousands, and then on hundreds of thousands, and on to annihilating millions of innocents who were perceived as their enemies even when many a time they were their own people. From massacres and mass murders we moved to genocides. But that still did not achieve our subconscious death-wish for mankind.

We have now entered a new age. We finally have the capacity and the will to put an end to the human species. And here's the intriguing part. Even those world leaders who understand the deadly implications of climate change and the urgency of immediate and drastic action, keep playing the game known in India as 'Pehle aap' or 'You first'. As to the masterminds who are hell-bent on making mankind extinct, all that is demanded of these universal murderers is denial and inaction. Denial of the vast incontestable, scientific evidence about the effects of fossil fuels and the refusal to take action when alternative and utterly harmless sources of energy are universally available.

I've left out the other great threat to mankind, the nuclear button. The last time we were on the brink of the doomsday clock, we were just two minutes from midnight. Given mankind's race for the 'finish line' or samapti, the once and forever end, as they call it in Sanskrit, what will it take to cover the last one hundred and and twenty seconds?

The fact is you don't need to look into space and infinity for dark matter. Look into the mirror and you will see it. We know the ailment and the cause of it, but we won't rise and unseat these monster leaders and send them into oblivion.

I keep wondering what will happen when finally mankind achieves extinction. How many millions of years will have to pass before the next creatures turn up on earth? What will they look like? Will they be far more advanced than us? Will they survive unlike us on carbon dioxide and plastic? And will they too ultimately ensure their own annihilation?

Akath kahani prem ki,
Kuchh kaha na jaye.
Goongey ker sarkara,
Baithey muskaye.

The story of love seals the lips,
It's akin to the mute
Who's tasted a marvellous sweet,
But can only register a smile.

22

Jesus Christ, the son of God, did not sit under a tree nor did the Prophet Muhammad. Nor did Zoroaster, nor Vyas who is supposed to have written the Bhagavad Gita, nor Moses who got the stone tablets enumerating the Ten Commandments from the God of the Old Testament. The Buddha alone did. He sat under the tree which came to be known as the Bodhi tree.

But for the murderous instincts of mankind, the great trees like the banyan and the peepul would live for over five hundred to five thousand years. The Buddha was the only one who understood that a tree is the memory bank of our planet.

Have we ever had the grace to acknowledge how deeply indebted we are to the trees around us? We owe our very breath to them. Quite simply, we are alive because they generate oxygen. All they know is to give and keep giving without let, but never ask for anything back.

And what is our response to their incredible generosity? We hack, axe, saw, slash, chop, lop off and fell millions of trees every year. Can you imagine the pain and the agony we inflict upon them? Gratitude is not something which comes naturally to us. We like to think nature and God owe us for being around. All we like is taking, grabbing, possessing non-stop as if it's our due. There is no creature more ungrateful than us humans.

I love the sheer exuberance of creepers and trees when they flower. It's as if there's no tomorrow. They'll pour their hearts and souls into every flower and petal. Come spring, God descends from his heavenly abode, scoops up bushels of colour and flings them any which way. Ah, the breezy, wild extravagance of Mother Earth. And yet His sense of design is inimitable. You want to see perfection, take a look at a flower, any flower. Nothing, but nothing, is as wildly generous and untamed as nature. Don't tell me how commonplace a shrub like bougainvillea is. Its flowers come in every damn colour known and unknown to mankind. It's an incredible sexual come-on and come-hither. Oh yes, I lie with every bonanza of flowers. And then there is cherry pink and apple blossom white. Indeed, I am breathless with the ravishment of nature.

Over the centuries, thousands of miles of forests have been razed but have you ever heard a whimper or a sob of acute agony from a single tree or even a branch of a tree?

Never forget that if there is such a thing as a manifestation of God on earth, it is the trees.

I owe the gift of trees to my mother. When I was a child of two and took my first unsteady steps, my mother picked me up and took me to a sapling she had planted on the day I was born. It was about as tall as I was.

'Kabir,' she said, 'this is your brother, the Rain Tree. His name is Dildaar, the generous one. He was born on the same day that you were. Give him a big hug every morning when you get up, my beloved son. Kiss as many leaves as you can and they will kiss you back.'

I did what I was told and the little leaves brushed against my cheek and gave me goose pimples.

'We humans are so egotistic we like to think that we alone can speak. How delusive can we be? Birds talk, fish talk, and animals are constantly courting each other and exchanging information about the weather or any approaching danger. Trees were the first creatures on earth who discovered speech.

'Dildaar'll talk to you in tree-speak and just as you're learning your mother tongue, you will become fluent in tree-speak and will be able to converse with Dildaar fluently.

'And there will be one other surprise. I am not going to tell you what it is but give you just one hint. Every friend of Dildaar will be your friend, and you cannot imagine what joy and happiness they will bring you.'

On another day when I was digging up the hard soil around Dildaar and packing it with fresh soft manure to let his roots breathe more easily and eat well, Ammijaan came over and asked me, 'Do you know why Dildaar is called a rain tree?'

I shook my head and she said, 'The answer is simple, because it's the harbinger of rain. As the rains approach, its leaves seem to shrink into themselves. No wonder all the farmers love this little brother of yours madly.'

It didn't take me long to pick up tree-lingo and soon Dildaar and I had long conversations. Over the next few months Ammijaan spoke to me often about my brother. 'Remember to your dying day that Dildaar's and every living thing's life is as precious as yours. So come what may, don't ever forget to look after him. Confide in him every day, my beloved son. Share your deepest sorrows and joys with him. Like every tree on this planet he never judges but loves unceasingly.'

Did I understand or appreciate what my mother told me in my childhood? I doubt it, but the echo of her words has stayed with me all these years. But one thing is certain. Even as a child I instinctively knew that trees were my closest friends though it would take years for me to understand that they are the emissaries of God. As to my brother, any time my mother or father ticked me off or scolded me, I would run to him and complain bitterly. He would pick me up and let me sit on one of his branches and calm me down. I don't know how he did it but it would soon percolate into my conscience that despite my huge tantrums, more often than not my parents were innocent and I was the guilty party.

Naturally when my friends and I were playing hide-and-seek, I would disappear into the upper branches of Dildaar which were a perfect hideout. And yet by and by I came to realize one strange irony: What is the point of playing hide-and-seek if there is no one to seek you?

You must be wondering what happened to the surprises that my mother promised me. What can I say except that Dildaar had something delightful for me every single day. I had been away for a week at Abbajaan's brother Uncle Shaheen's place to celebrate the birth of his daughter. When I got back I tried to make up for lost time. I was busy that morning working on the loom when I suddenly saw little parasitical grasses along with aggressive prickly twigs trying to take over the territory around Dildaar. I stepped out of the workshop and began to pull out the obstinate grasses and the thorny twigs.

From the corner of my left eye, I saw a little flutter and thought it must be a bee but then I heard a tweet and found a parrot sitting on my shoulder. I cannot begin to describe the thrill that swept through my entire being. I bent over to kiss Dildaar and thank him, when the parrot's mate flew in and sat on my head. That was it. All my brother's bird friends – egrets, sparrows, waders, swallows, crows, hawks and god alone knows who else – chirped and tweeted non-stop from that day on as they flew in and found purchase on my nose, shoulders, head, ears, forearms, elbows, hands and even feet.

In time Dildaar grew so tall and large, he could reach out and touch the sky. The entire population of our town Rupadi could take shelter under him when there were floods. You have no idea how fast a rain tree can grow. By the time I was fifteen he was already the tallest tree in our small town. My mother had told me to confide in him, tell him all my secrets and joys. It did not take me too long to realize that he was singularly intuitive and a mind reader. He always knew. When my mother died, he was my father's and my solace and would sing lullabies to us. Then my father too joined my mother and I began to spend almost all my nights with my brother.

The years passed and then suddenly I got a job at the Palace and became a resident of Shantipura, but I missed my brother so much that I would often go into a terrible depression. The only cure was to land up in Rupadi and hug my brother and hear his voice. I remember telling him, 'If only I could take you with me,' and he would smile and pat my back and shower me with beautiful rain tree flowers. 'Kabir, my beloved brother, I am with you now and always. Don't forget we are conjoined twins even when you and I are separated.'

Come to think of it, I am surprised that I have not so far mentioned that the company of trees invariably is one of the most calming medicines you will ever come across. Make no mistake, I am in deadly earnest. I am surprised that none of the psychologists in the world have so far discovered this incredible cure for acute mental illnesses.

One Sunday, I was about to set out for Rupadi when a man with a long white beard and a syce's uniform accosted me.

'Where are you off to, Kabir, and that too on a Sunday morning?'

I looked at the man with ill-concealed hostility and was about to ask him how was it any of his business when I noticed the horse he was riding. I knew that horse and by now I realized who was riding it.

'I'm going to visit my twin brother who lives in Rupadi, Majesty.'

'Can we cut out the honorifics please, Weaver? If you don't mind I'm supposed to be doing my rounds of the city and environs incognito.' He looked a trifle puzzled then. 'I didn't know you had a brother. May I join you? That way I can see your home town and get to know your family.'

Rupadi is a good hour and a quarter's ride from the capital and by the time we got to my old house I forgot that I was the host and slipped off my horse and rushed to embrace my brother.

'Kabir,' my brother whispered a couple of minutes later, 'I

think, your guest is waiting for you to introduce me to him.'

'Oops.' I disentangled myself as quickly as possible and walked over to HM. He had tied both our horses to the gate and was waiting for me. 'Would you like to meet my brother, Majesty?'

'Why else am I here, Weaver?'

'Majesty, this is Dildaar, my judwa bhaiyya. We were born on the same day.'

'Kabir has spoken so often about you,' I translated my brother's words for Ramdeo Singhji, 'and how you forgave him for his youthful, what shall I call them, misadventures.'

'I owe him my life, Dildaar. And now I owe him perhaps the greatest surprise of my life.'

I had known HM for over two years now but had never seen him so much at a loss for words. 'All my youthful years I have craved for a brother,' he finally blurted out. 'You are a very lucky man, Kabir, to have such a remarkable brother.'

Dildaar laughed and said, 'Now I've a question for you, Ramdeo Singhji.' You could hear the tinkle of laughter in his voice. 'May I ask what's preventing you from acquiring a blood brother today?'

'Dumb me.' HM smiled and hugged Dildaar. I can never forget what followed then. A white peacock landed on HM's shoulder, stepped on to his head, and HM's mouth fell open and stayed open. We spent the whole day together with Dildaar and left late in the evening for Shantipura. Neither of us spoke on the way back.

I was about to wish HM goodnight when out of the blue he hugged me tightly for a long time. 'How shall I thank you, Kabir, for finding my lost brother.' He smiled then and looked at me mischievously and said, 'There are unfortunately some disadvantages that are linked to the discovery of Dildaar. I now find that I don't have one brother but two.' Ramdeo Singhji guffawed loudly and added, 'If you are Dildaar's brother, I guess you will be mine too. Welcome, brother Kabir.

'I want you to take charge of the crown prince and his sister and take them to see their Uncle the next time you visit Rupadi. They will also plant one sapling each and learn tree-speak. Not just them, two months from today under your guidance every child in Panchananda will have a tree-brother of his own by royal decree. I promise you I will try to get trees from all over the world planted in Panchananda.'

And so it came to be that Panchananda became the greenest kingdom in the whole of India. Not just that, over the years the crime rate as well as mental illnesses came down radically.

When I think back to those times I keep wondering how come my illiterate mother was such an incredibly wise person. How did she know that trees were really the only creatures on earth with a clean conscience? And but for the killer instincts of human beings, trees from the time of the Buddha or even earlier would have been with us.

As you must have gathered by now, HM was a man who took family duties to heart and often he would accompany me to Rupadi, incognito of course, or even go on his own to visit Dildaar. It was the month of July and thanks to the incessant rains and floods I had skipped visiting Rupadi for two weeks, but when the rains showed no signs of easing up, I decided to go across. Right from the start I had the feeling that I had made a blunder setting forth, for both my horse Bindhaas and I would sink deep into the muck every now and then and at times it was almost impossible to find a purchase on firm ground. If only the mad rains had done the job they had set out to do . . .

There was an impenetrable darkness all around by the time we got to Rupadi. For a full five minutes I could not locate Dildaar. I was in full panic mode till I finally saw him. He was strewn for hundreds of yards all over the squelchy mud floor. No, it was not the rains which had done away with him. My brother had been butchered, hacked, bludgeoned, battered, clobbered, buggered, dismembered, mutilated and massacred to death. No thesaurus could cope with the violence done to my brother. It must have taken days to break every branch and limb of his.

I had two overpowering impulses. I needed to undo the person who had done this. And I had to run all the way till I reached the end of the world and could sit down and eviscerate my innards and thus be united with my brother and find peace.

There was no way I could ride Bindhaas. That poor animal was beyond exhaustion. I patted him on the back and asked him to forgive me for there was nothing to eat there except the horrible soggy, dead leaves of the rain tree which was no longer my brother Dildaar. Before I could start running, there was one important thing I had to do. It took all my strength to break a branch from my fallen brother.

Did I say I had to run to the end of the world? I gave up almost before I started, for every step I took meant that the next one would make my foot sink at least a foot and a half.

There was no postponing meeting my brother. It was now or never. I held the broken branch with both my hands and plunged it hard into my innards. It was then that I heard my brother speak to me. 'I thought you loved me, Kabir, and would never take the easy way out.'

That hurt more than the jab of the branch that had opened up my innards. 'You give up and they win,' Dildaar told me. 'Besides I had no idea that you were willing to abandon our brother Ramdeo.'

When I came to, HM was trying desperately to revive me. The rain had stopped and Ramdeo Singhji had pulled out the branch which was stuck in my innards. The pain was so bad, it made me pass in and out of consciousness.

'First someone kills Dildaar. And then it looks as if you too set out to ditch me, Kabir.'

I tried to speak but my voice was less than a whisper. HM bent down close to my mouth. 'I promised Dildaar, come what may I would stand by you.'

'Right now my only worry is whether the Ayurvedic medicine man will turn up on time and stop the damned bleeding. You better make it, Weaver. Otherwise I promise you I will kill you the second time because I would not know how to face Kashmira Mai.'

HM held me in his arms and rocked me gently till I passed out.

I believe it was touch and go for three months. Ramdeo Singhji had got Kashmira over and parked me in the Palace. He visited me twice a day, once in the morning and then when it was time for him to retire for the night.

One afternoon he turned up at teatime and sat on my bed.

'I've got news for you, Weaver. It's taken me two and a half months to find out who killed our brother Dildaar. It's that multi-millionaire octogenarian industrialist, Giridharlal Pahwa.

'It appears Giridharlal was taking a post-dinner walk outside his own compound when he stepped on a thorn from the babool tree. He was in severe pain for a little over a week. When he recovered he asked his gardener to pick up an axe from his own shed and ordered him to cut down the eleven-metre-high babool tree.

Just as the gardener landed the first blow, the son of an untouchable family staying in the Mahar colony behind Giridharlal's house protested, telling the old man that his schoolteacher had told the class that like every other tree, the babul too could survive for hundreds of years and it was forbidden by law to cut a tree in Panchananda.

'Giridharlal apparently turned apoplectic and roared at the boy, "How dare you little son of an untouchable shit-collector tell the wealthiest industrialist in Panchananda that it's illegal to cut down trees because they are immortal.

'"Gardener, pick up the brat and come with me, and I will show him that there is no such thing as an immortal tree. And when we have felled the biggest tree in Shantipura, I will personally cut off the cheeky bastard's tongue so that he will never have the gall to talk to a caste Hindu."

'I think you know which tree he had in mind, Kabir.' HM smiled bitterly as he spoke to me. 'Even as the gardener slammed his huge axe into the rain tree, the boy cried his heart out. Giridharlal apparently yelled out triumphantly at the boy, "You mothernevermindwhat, just you watch how an immortal tree gives up the ghost with just a few hundred strokes of the axe."

'I hear that it took three and a half days to bring the tree down and cut each and every branch of it. I need hardly add that it did not take even a minute to slice off the little boy's tongue.

'Giridharlal is in jail now and will be put on trial for murder and for cutting the boy's tongue. If I had a choice I would have liked to cut the millionaire-industrialist into as many pieces as his gardener cut Dildaar but I am afraid the law would not look favourably on that.'

It took four more months for the Panchananda parliament to declare that Rupadi would now host the largest forest on the subcontinent and it would be named the Dildaar Woodlands of Immortals. Anyone, but anyone, who dared cut a branch, uproot or hack a tree would face a life term in prison.

What is the point of playing hide-and-seek, my brother, if you are never going to be found? Not even if there are hundreds of thousands of your namesakes, Dildaar?

Kabira garv na keejiye,
Uncha dekh aavaas.
Kaal pairon punyah letna,
Uper jamsi ghaas.

Kabir, don't be so haughty,
Living in your mansion.
Tomorrow you will be lying six feet under,
With grass growing on top.

23

Every ten days or so when the day's work was done, the novice apprentices and the older pupils, the senior weavers, and the supervisors, would crowd around the Weaver and not let him go till they had forced him to tell them a story. Sometimes he was in the mood and instead of one, enchanted them with tale after tale. At other times he could be perverse and refuse to say a word. Today was not a good day. Both the parties had dug in. The more the youngsters screamed and shouted, the more recalcitrant the Master turned and his language became more and more provocative and insulting.

'You think I am a story-vending machine? All right then, cough up the money. A hundred gold coins, nothing less, for the greatest story of all time.'

The students guffawed. 'Sure, when we start dropping gold turds, we'll collect them for you.'

Just then Kashmira Mai threw the doors of the house open and called out her husband's name. 'Kabir. Where are you, Kabir?'

That put paid to all the filth instantly and the pupils began to go over to Mai who was mother, confidante, and adviser to each of them, and one by one they touched her feet. The Master's tune too altered.

'Right here, my dear. Just having a quiet tête-à-tête with all my friends at the workshop.'

'Do you remember the time you were courting me, Kabir, and would woo me with the most enchanting stories?'

'How could I forget those mad, love-crazed days, my love.'

'Will you woo me again today?'

'Why, my dear, not just today,' the Master's voice had switched to a velveteen softness, 'I'll be wooing you even after . . .'

Kashmira smiled and cut her husband short. 'Not an airy-fairy story, Kabir. Something so rooted in the earth, it will give us pause and make us rethink both the here and now and the forever.'

'The story I'm about to tell occurred at the beginning of time, when the gods and demons inhabited the earth. This was indeed the rarest of occasions when both these sworn, eternal enemies were gathered on the shores of Kshirsagar, the ocean of milk. They were here for one purpose and one purpose alone.

'After endless years of searching they had finally located ambrosia, the elixir of eternal life. There was, however, a slight hitch. It was at the bottom of the ocean of milk. Both the demons and the gods wanted to lay their hands on the amrita which would ensure the gift of immortality. At any other time they would have been more than willing to indulge shamelessly in chicanery and deceit to drink of it without sharing it with the other party. But this was one time they realized that their chances of getting at the amrita would be far better if they stood together in this crucial enterprise.

'No engineering feat, no technological marvel and no submersible could withstand the pressure of miles of milk and raise the pot of ambrosia. So near and yet so out of reach. It was unfortunate that in the excitement of the moment, the chroniclers forgot to mention who ultimately resolved the problem with a stroke of genius. The gods and the demons would churn the milk with a mountain called Mandar. But what should they use as a rope? No cord, however thick and strong, could take the friction and it was then that the python Vasuki offered to be the rope.

'And so began the samudra manthan, the great churning of the ocean of milk, the gods to the right and the demons to the left. First the gods pulled their end of Vasuki as they leaned all the way back and the demons bent forward and then it was the other way round. Soon there was a perfect rhythm to the swaying. Back and forth they went and the milk began to rotate and revolve and the ripples spread wider and wider, and at the very centre, a whirlpool was forming. And now the vortex was whirring madly till it became just a blur, and it was a good thing that the python was mostly submerged in the milk for the heat generated was so great that he would surely have gone up in smoke. And then slowly, one by one, the ocean began to throw up its fourteen ratnas, not jewels really, but the most unique objects in its deepest belly. The first to come forth was Lakshmi who fell in love with Vishnu, the creator, and became his consort. Kaustubh Mani the jewel which Vishnu wears in his necklace was next. Then the flower Parijat which Krishna brought down from heaven and planted for his wife Satyabhama; the wine

Sura; Dhanvantari, the physician; Chandra, the moon, which Shiva placed atop his braided hair; Kamadhenu, the cow who could fulfill any, but any, wish; the elephant Airawat which Vishnu appropriated as his vehicle; the beauteous apsaras who became celestial dancers; Uchhai Shrava, the white horse with seven heads; the bow Sharang; the Shankh or seashell which Vishnu blows.

And yet there was no sign of the ambrosia. And the gods and the demons began to wonder if there was some foul play, for the milk had begun to boil and foam and they knew that it was a matter of minutes before the python Vasuki collapsed.

Ah finally, there it was. At first merely the rim of the pot was visible. But it was shooting up now like an impatient sun emerging from below the horizon. The gods and demons let out a triumphant cry and they stopped churning and rushed towards the pot. And then they saw it. Along with the ambrosia, the ocean of milk had thrown up Halahal, the deadliest poison known either to men or gods. It flew up and fanned out, the livid yellow-green globules, and the rays of the sun got trapped in them, and there they stood poised above the pot of ambrosia. Think about it. The elixir of immortality was within reach and it was about to turn into poison. Can you think of a more dramatic existential moment than this one?

While the droplets hung in mid-air, the gods and the demons went into an urgent huddle. For the first time they shared a common objective. What should they do? The ambrosia needed to be rescued instantly or all would be lost. Who would come forward and do the unthinkable? What a stupid question – no one, but no one, neither the gods nor the demons. And all the while the toxic liquid beads that would wipe out immortality itself were making their way downwards.

That was when Shiva stepped forward and without a word swallowed the poison. And that's how his throat went blue and he came to be known as Neelkantha.

'Are you trying to tell us,' the fiery Hemraj interrupted the Master even as he finished the last sentence, 'that the gods actually shared the ambrosia with the demons instead of asking them to go to hell?'

'Yes. After all, that was the deal,' the Weaver asnswered.

'You can't be serious, Master. Nobody in his senses would ever make a deal with the demons. And even if they did, all they had to do was not honour it. Think about it, if the gods had been smart and distributed the amrita amongst themselves, they would have got rid of the whole tribe of rakshasas within a matter of years.'

'But then how would the gods,' Kashmira Mai asked Hemraj, 'be any different from the demons? As a matter of fact, Hemraj, you too would have to be counted amongst the daityas or the devil's own.'

'Let me pause here for a brief moment.' The Master spoke softly, in almost a whisper, so that the pupils and even Kashmira Mai were forced to listen carefully. 'The story you've just heard is one the oldest ever told and one of the most memorable. And yet what is almost impossible to understand is how often we miss the hidden stories and significant insights that lurk in the interstices within the primary story.

'Even after decades of living with this story, I am still forced to shake my head in sheer wonderment. Shiva,

Vishnu, Agni, Brahma are called the devas but the shocking fact is that they too were mere mortals. The sleight of hand here is staggering. Before drinking the ambrosia they were us. You, me and the rest of mankind. The truth is, the storytellers had predetermined who were going to be the devas and who the daityas. The latter are always depicted as rakshasas with big noses, large fang-like teeth, horrid distorted features, gigantic frames and threatening postures. But understand this, they too were nevertheless human and, just as importantly, mortal. Exactly like us. Ah, my friends, they are the infamous party which is known in literary parlance as "the other".'

'The "other" represents mankind's deadly need for division: there's us and then there's them. The "other" is the villain, the spoilsport, Satan himself, the one we love to hate. Indeed, we firmly believe that but for the "other", we would all live in harmony and at peace with nature and the universe. But step across the line of division and we discover that there's a curious switching of roles. Believe it or not, they or them in inverted commas see us as the "other". They see themselves as the good guys and we are the baddies. Oh, the gall of it. It reaffirms our conviction that they are pure evil. Erase them and we would return to paradise.

'Hard to believe as it may be, we are in truth both us and them, the devas and the daityas.'

Even as the pupils were trying to digest what the Master had just said, the generally silent Rishikesh spoke up.

'Master, you mentioned that the churning of Kshirsagar threw up fourteen ratnas and then you qualified the word ratna or jewel by telling us that it was not to be taken literally but was meant to suggest some of the most precious things on earth. Have I got that right?'

'Yes, Rishikesh, you are spot on.'

'Is one then to understand that the deadly poison Halahal is one of the invaluable entities in creation?'

The Master looked a trifle bemused and then smiled. 'Why, Tanmaya, you've got me there.' He pondered over what the young disciple had pointed out. 'This is the remarkable thing about great stories. Almost always they seem to have an element of mystery. You could search for the meaning of a statement for years and come to ten different conclusions, perhaps all of them valid.

'My random guess is that the churning of the ocean of milk is deliberately coupled with death, for truly death is the one certain fact of life. Do what you may, we mortals can never escape it. Amrita and Halahal may after all be as inseparable as conjoined twins.'

It was curious, all of a sudden an uneasy silence fell on all those who had gathered there. It was as if all the apprentices and the seniors were puzzling over the business of the conjoined twins.

'I want to go back to the devas and daityas.' Kashmira Mai had a question. 'The samudra manthan story is from Hindu mythology. But oddly enough there's almost a mirror image of these two parties in the Old Testament too. The good angels and the baddies led by Satan.'

'Ah, Kashmira,' the Master said with a sigh, 'you've touched upon a very delicate and hugely problematic subject. It questions the very idea of God. God, we are told time and again, is omnipresent, omniscient and omnipotent. Mankind, we all know, was gifted with free will. But the

Biblical angels, one and all, were angels. Which meant that they were all the purest of the pure, utterly sinless and immortal. And most of all, they were wholly God's creatures.

'If that was the case, how come some of them turned into the most devious and dangerous enemies of God and mankind? What are we to understand then, did they too have free will just like all of us and chose to be either good or as evil as they wanted? Was God unaware of this? How can that be? After all God is all-knowing. Why then did he not scotch the rebellion instantly? Why did he allow Lucifer to tempt Adam and Eve and thus throw them and the rest of mankind out of paradise?

'Some of you might tell me that the idea of good and bad angels is merely a metaphor. At every step mankind must choose between the straight and narrow on the one hand and the temptation to fall for evil on the other.

'A likely story. The simple question is, is God then not all-powerful but a bogus myth and an utter failure?'

Chinta aisee dakini,
Kaat kaleja khaaye.
Vaid bichaara kya karey,
Kahaan tak dawa lagaaye.

Worry is such a pickpocket,
It keeps nibbling non-stop at your heart.
How can the poor doctor help,
When his medicine can't cure this malady?

24

For the whole of the previous week Charatram, the perpetual questioner, had withdrawn into a cocoon of anxiety, fretting and ill-temper. The curious thing was that he refused to be drawn into any discussion about the problem. Ultimately his weaving supervisor, Rehman, approached the Master and warned him that Charatram was on the verge of a nervous breakdown. On any other occasion the Weaver's instant response would have been to pooh-pooh the matter. After all, Charatram was on the brink of life-and-death issues and decisions every alternate day, but one look at his pupil's face gave Kabir pause.

The Master walked over to the loom on which Charatram was working, pulled over a wooden stool and sat down. 'Have I said something, Charat, which has hurt you?' The Weaver ran his hand gently over his overwrought apprentice's back as he spoke. 'I know that I can be thoughtless, even nasty at times in my pursuit of so-called lightness and humour. If that's the case, I sincerely apologize to you and ask for forgiveness.'

Charatram shook his head ruefully. 'You're not the problem, Master, I am. You are my teacher and guide. And you speak of God most of the time as nirguna, the formless one. But I find it difficult, if not impossible to relate to or come to grips with the nirguna Brahman. Is he for real and am I the illusion? Or perhaps delusion is the right word.

'I am trapped between the featureless, invisible all-encompassing Brahman who is unborn and undying and the idols who are said to have lived on earth and then disappeared into eternity.

'At home my parents worship saguna gods and goddesses like Shri Ram, Shri Krishna, Saraswati, Vishnu, Shiva, Lakshmi, Durga, Kali, Ganesh, Hanuman, and countless others, each with his or her own distinctive human form. Every village has its own deity. Not to mention god knows how many small and big rocks with a red splotch on them, lying by the wayside to indicate the presence of divinity. How can one keep track of this epidemic of gods and goddesses? I suspect there are as many of them as the population of the country. Or to put it even more bluntly, a god or goddess for each denizen of the subcontinent.

'Who should I worship? Who is my God, the one who will be my lifelong companion and with whom I will have a permanent relationship? Who will lead me through innumerable incarnations to moksha, the highest goal of human life, the ultimate spiritual merging with Brahman and eternal beatitude?

'I have no way of knowing whether these saguna gods are true divine beings. If they are, then are they in competition with the formless and featureless one? Sometimes I suspect the saguna divinities bring out the worst in me. With them I am always the supplicant, the perpetual seeker, not of eternal truths or divine grace but that song called "Give me, give me, give me. I want, I want, I want." On the other hand, how does one address the nirguna God? It's like perpetually groping in the dark.'

Kabir smilingly interrupted the highly agitated apprentice. 'I'm afraid your quandary is much worse than it appears, Charatram, for you've forgotten to mention most of the pantheon of gods and goddesses who ruled before the Aryans invaded the country and were gradually taken over by the conquerors. Let's not forget that many of the idols like Vithal and his wife Rakhumai of Pandharpur, the goddess Chhatushrungi from Pune and thousands of others were chiselled out of stark black stone and had unforgettable unblinking eyes that seemed to follow anyone who had seen them, every moment of their lives.

'Unless I'm mistaken the elephant-headed Ganeshji was also a god worshipped by the original inhabitants of the subcontinent. In earlier times he was considered a malevolent deity who had to be won over with intense prayers and attention. But by the time he migrated into the new camp, he had turned into one of the most lovable and caring of gods. He was the one who gifted you happiness and prevented any harm from coming to you.'

'You are the wise one, Master and I would like to follow in your footsteps but I have to confess that despite all my efforts it's far more easy for me to relate to the saguna idols and pray to them. I fear I am a hopeless case and have let you down unforgivably.'

'Relax, Charat. You are unnecessarily getting worked up. First of all Hinduism is a bipolar faith. It is happy to practise both these extremes. The great majority of Hindus are drawn to the saguna branch for the simple reason that most of mankind finds it easier to relate to a god-figure with human features. At the same time, the philosophically inclined thinkers were drawn to an abstract idea of God. Don't forget, the Jews and Muslims too have a nirgun God, though of course they don't describe him with a Sanskrit word.

'But let's examine the majoritarian view of God in India. Take the example of Vishnu who has ten avatars. Of these, the two most popular are Shri Ram and Krishna. It is said that both of these were actual historical figures. As a matter of fact, both were extremely popular kings who gained a legendary status and over a period of time began to be seen as avatars or incarnations of Vishnu.

'There was, however, one other prince who was co-opted into this select league of ten. I am of course talking about none other than the Buddha. Looking back, one is bound to wonder why a branch of Hinduism would adopt the founding father of an altogether different faith. But that's exactly what the Vaishnava Hindus did – turned him into an avatar of the god Vishnu, a mainstream idol.

'It's important to remember that there was a time when Buddhism had almost completely eclipsed its rival. The ironies, however, keep mounting. What the Buddha sought was nirvana, the end of the cycle of reincarnation which would release the seeker into everlasting enlightenment. He totally ignored theism or the notion of god. The Hinayana form of Buddhism stayed true to the Buddha's original vision. The Buddha himself was represented symbolically by a leaf or a pair of feet or some such abstraction over the next seven or eight centuries.

'Hinduism, however, succeeded in corrupting the

fundamental principles of the faith, to the extent that soon enough Mahayana Buddhism followed the Hindu saguna path and the image of the Buddha was turned into a ubiquitous icon and was surrounded by hundreds of subsidiary ones, including the Taras and Bodhisattvas invented long after the original Buddha had died.

'It would take some more time for Hinduism to make a comeback. But even as it almost totally wiped out all traces of Buddhism, Vaishnava Hinduism's next move was a shrewd one. It turned the Buddha into the ninth avatar of Vishnu. That would ensure that even if Buddhism did retrieve ground, it would only be within the Hindu fold.

'Think about it, the Egyptians, the Greeks, the Romans, the people of Mohenjo-Daro and almost every early civilization worshipped idols. In contrast, the people of the Old Testament like the Jews and Muslims were the very few monotheistic exceptions. The Jewish faith and Islam did not tolerate any idols or statues of their God in their synagogues, masjids or homes.

'But then Jesus Christ, the Son of God, was born to Mary, and the Christian faith made its appearance and the New Testament came to be. While the Christians maintain that they are not idol worshippers, soon enough Jesus, his mother Mary and the Biblical God himself began to be depicted in human form in paintings and sculptures in the temples which came to be known as churches. But what is difficult, if not impossible, to fathom is the overarching symbol of Christianity, which is the crucifixion. Is there something about extreme cruelty, sadism and suffering which we human beings find obsessively fascinating?

'Over the centuries, Christianity spread across continents

and the followers of the Son of God and his Mother Mary rose rapidly to millions. The question is, did this phenomenal growth have anything to do with the fact that unlike the faceless and featureless Old Testament God, it was infinitely easier for people to relate to a human or saguna depiction of the Son of God, not to mention his mother and father? Don't forget, Jesus was supposed to be human, which is why he didn't survive the crucifixion. It's an altogether different matter that being also divine, his father resurrected him.

'Dear Charat, despite the fact that the Indian gods resemble humans, hopefully they are not petty-minded like us. If the good Lord can tolerate all my nonsense, surely He will wink and let you into that place called swarg or that state of bliss called moksha . . . that's if such a place actually exists.'

Guru Narayan roop hai,
Guru gyan ko ghat.
Satguru gyan pratap sey,
Man key mitey uchat.

The guru is but an avatar of God,
The guru's wisdom is like a riverbank.
The Lord's light will eliminate,
The darkness of the mind.

25

Every month full moon day was when Kashmira Mai ordered food from outside. During winter the apprentices lit a bonfire and sat in a closed circle around the Master and Mai. Usually there was lots of banter and every once in a while Kashmira Mai took the lead. She had dozens of funny stories about her husband and his mad-hatter schemes to make billions and build palaces studded with pearls, rubies and emeralds and dress her in diamonds to highlight her perfect form. Yes, you got that right, nothing underneath. But the funniest stories were about how the Master wooed her and she kept pretending that she was planning to go to the Himalayas and remain a spinster all her life. Apparently the Master promised to commit suicide if she left him or insisted that he would accompany her as a naked fakir. And she would ask, 'Why wait, you could do it right now.'

But today was different. Tanmaya got up before anybody else could say a word and cornered the Master.

'It's been months since I've been asking you to tell us about the Great Betrayal. It happened when I was a mere child. I remember my father coming home one day and telling my mother in a fraught tone about something called betrayal. I have heard the same word many a time since then but as you happen to be from those times, what was he talking about?'

'You are right, Tanmaya. Over the years I have tried, I need hardly add, to suppress the memory of that event. Let me first of all clarify that the word betrayal is almost always used in the context of corruption, jealousy, backstabbing or personal gain. But it can also have terribly complex ramifications, some of them tragic beyond words.'

The Master smiled wryly, perhaps ironically, and said, 'A long, long time ago in the fabled land called Panchananda . . .' He paused and asked, 'Isn't that how all stories are supposed to start?

> It had been a hectic ten days at the workshop. We had even worked all through the past three nights and had delivered the full wardrobe for the twenty-fifth anniversary of the coronation of HM Mansinghji of Punjab. Guess who took the eleven trunks of clothes to Punjab? None other than HM Ramdeoji along with Maharani Anagha Devi who were, of course, two of the most important invitees. It was HM who had suggested that I should show him my drawings and, as usual after he had okayed them, weave the cloth and then design the clothes as Panchananda's gift to Mansinghji.
>
> Three days before he was supposed to come back, HM sent me a confidential and urgent message which was delivered to me late that night.
>
> > Dear Kabir,
> >
> > The Chief of Police, Brijmohan Shuklaji, has just informed me that he had no alternative but

to imprison Prime Minister Mubarak in a secret location for reasons of state, whatever that means. Since the matter was extremely delicate, he merely hinted very vaguely in a postscript as to why Mubarakji was taken into custody but frankly I find the explanation absurd. He added that to safeguard the Prime Minister's reputation, he has spread the word that Mubarakji has gone out of town on some personal work and so the deputy Prime Minister had to temporarily take over.

Weaver, you were appointed my judicial adviser in the most problematic legal cases. I must, however, confess I had no idea that I would land you with a case that would be considered by any measure as way beyond hyper-complicated. Right now I have two overwhelming concerns. The first is the Prime Minister's reputation.

My other fear is that however careful Shuklaji may have been in keeping the Prime Minister's incarceration a secret, what if word leaks out? Needless to say, while you have your ear to the ground and are seeking hints, clues and answers from the lowest to the highest levels of society, make sure that no one, but no one, will suspect that the country's most trusted civil servant is in trouble.

I wish you, me and the country luck.

Regards to Kashmira Mai and you,

Ramdeo Singh

What was HM talking about? Was I to understand that no less a person than the head of the cabinet, the Prime

Minister, had been imprisoned, never mind if it was in a secret location? Had I lost my mind? Was I hallucinating? Surely HM couldn't have been talking about Mubarak Sahab. For all of his fifty-three years in government service, Panchananda's Prime Minister had been a visionary. Both Ramdeoji and he had shared the unshakable belief that, come what may, they would never give up the fight for universal peace. Mubarak Sahab was compassionate, wise and accessible but, like his conscience, unbending when it came to principles. There had never been even a whisper of suspicion about him. And now the Police Commissioner Brijmohan Shuklaji had put him behind bars in a secret place.

Brijmohan Shuklaji. Now that's a subject which would give me pause in the best of circumstances. No, I am not suggesting that he was a corrupt man. So what then? Was he a dangerous man? That depends on what underhand deals you were involved in or what nefarious actions you were party to. But we are talking about the Chief of Police here, a man who many believed had eight pairs of eyes, and another eight of ears, one set for each direction. He was so soft-spoken you could hardly hear him. He had seen so much of the wrong side of life, it was shocking that he could still pretend to be a normal human being.

Anybody in the finance department would enlighten you about how Shuklaji had a leather-bound diary on every real estate magnate, mega trading family and multi-millionaire jeweller, landowner, exporter or anyone else who had a white and black account. And of course on all the folks in the government who were on the take. No and no again, I preferred to keep my distance from the

Commissioner of Police, but now HM expected me to go over to Shuklaji's office and have a tête-à-tête with him. Let me admit without beating about the bush that he was said to be a very, very sharp man whose arsenal of ways and means by which he could elicit the truth were countless and, more to the point, effective beyond your best, or should I say worst, estimate.

What was unarguable, though, was that there was no gainsaying the fact that even harmless, innocuous and innocent souls preferred to keep their distance from him. If possible a distance of a few continents and oceans. And the reason was simple: What if the rumours about his having a docket on every single citizen were true? What if he could read your thoughts? Or to take a random example, what if he knew that in your grandfather's severe puritanical patriarchy, you and your cousin Sheila had played doctor-doctor; or you had visited some of the ladies of the night when you were a little starved for sex in your late teens?

As to yours truly, no, I didn't care to run into our Chief of Police. After all, I knew beyond the shadow of a doubt that he was familiar with my past. Why am I being coy? I am talking about my stint as the leader of a gang of dacoits, not to mention that despite my questionable record HM had appointed me as his confidential judicial adviser.

I should have been flattered by HM's request to keep my ear to the ground and pick up pointers and innuendoes under the static. Instead I felt cornered. Sure, every once in a while an industrialist's eldest son may complain to me about how his father was favouring his younger step-brother, or a supplier of arms to the infantry would reveal how the secretary to the chief of staff was demanding a cut on every purchase.

But I know my failings or, if you prefer, shortcomings. I have a tin ear and invariably fail to catch verbal clues and nuances. Nor do I have a nose for carrying out clandestine investigations. Fortunately I realized that discretion would be the better part of making an ass of myself and decided to tell HM a white lie and say that there was nothing of note that I had picked up on the street. It was already past twelve and so I could call it a night.

Who was I trying to fool? My bogus bravado was getting on my nerves. Was there even a remote chance I would be able to lie to Ramdeoji? Even more to the point and just as pressing was the same question which, try as I might, I could not get rid of, 'Why was Mubarak Sahab put in prison?' I waited till seven in the morning and then walked the two miles to Shuklaji's residence. His wife was not up yet but the security guard said he had left town on his bimonthly visit to one of our provinces.

'When will he be back?' I asked the man.

'Who knows? Sometimes he returns on the same day he left but always goes to his office first and no one can tell when he'll show up at home. At other times he may stay away for a couple of days. On a few occasions he's even prolonged his visit.' As I turned to leave, he called out, 'What work did you have with my master?'

I was stymied for an answer and said the first thing that came to my mind: 'I'm looking for a bride.'

'You think my boss runs a marriage bureau? Stupid man, he is the Chief of Police. Besides, old man, you really think you're a spring chicken?'

I went home in a foul mood, had a bath and breakfast and for the first time in my life resolved to comb every nook and corner of the capital. I was clueless about why I was setting out but you could say I was following orders.

How many years had I lived in the capital? And yet it turned out that three-quarters of the city was a discovery and an education for me. Panchananda was both city and village, sorry, multiple cities and villages. The ancient lawgiver Manu who had lived centuries or millennia ago and was the father of the caste system was in evidence everywhere. Every super-rich quarter had a tiny hamlet hidden a little distance away from it. After all, while even the shadow of an untouchable was anathema, still whatever came out from the backside of the super-rich as of every caste Hindu had to be cleaned up.

Believe it or not, I was enjoying the tour. I had forgotten that barring the grumpy or laconic types, folks of every variety enjoy talking as much as I do. Class or caste has no role to play here. I met all sorts of people: water carriers, scavengers, traders, tailors, stock market players, moneylenders, jewellers, snooty aristocrats, lawyers, pimps, ladies of the night, washerwomen, priests of every shade and belief. I sat in many a tea-stall, on the steps of temples, on the circular platforms around five- or seven-hundred-year-old banyan trees where the village elders gathered in the evenings to discuss politics or how to deal with miscreants.

It had been a long day. If you want to know what had been my takeaway from the day's confabulations, the answer is zilch. I must have been on automatic, for without knowing what I was up to, I went to the workshop and spent the next two hours weaving on the handloom. It took my mind off how I was going to face HM. Kashmira and I had dinner and by the time I lay down on my bed I was already half asleep.

It was when Kashmira tapped me gently on the shoulder around 7 a.m. and spoke to me that I understood what I had been looking for all of yesterday. She said very softly, 'There's a rumour going around in town that Mubarak Sahab is in prison.'

'Who told you this?'

'The milkman couldn't wait to share the news with me.'

What can I say about Kashmira's incredible intuition and sense of discretion. I have never spoken to her about HM having secretly entrusted me with life-and-death decisions which terrify me, but I can tell you she has known about it for years. She gauges immediately when I am tense and terse and makes sure that no one will disturb me. Don't ask me how she sensed that I had spent the whole day yesterday looking for clues about the Prime Minister's disappearance.

Now that my wife had dropped a bombshell, I knew that I was in serious trouble. How the hell had the news got out? I was certain of one thing. It wasn't Shuklaji. Period. Whatever picayune reservations I may have expressed about him, his loyalty to HM and Panchananda was never in doubt. I finished my bath and breakfast and stepped into the workshop to leave instructions for the day's work.

The supervisor in charge of the colour section, Param, accosted me with a big self-righteous smile. 'I guess you haven't heard that the Prime Minister is in jail for betraying the country's secrets to the authorities in Jehanarabad while we are still negotiating with them?'

Did I hear him right? Is that why Mubarakji was in prison? Had the country gone mad? How the hell did Param come to know about something that I am sure only the Chief of Police and HM knew? Or was Param making up the whole story? On the other hand, I still didn't know why Mubarakji was in prison. Luckily I controlled myself before I snapped at him and chose to laugh his statement off. 'What rot. Who told you this nonsense?'

'I'll take a bet everybody in the country knows it,' Param cackled scornfully. 'The man has been backstabbing the country since the day he was appointed Prime Minister.'

As far as dear Param was concerned, the fact that His Majesty Ramdeoji had chosen Mubarak Sahab to be the second-in-command of Panchananda three decades ago had made no difference. The Prime Minister was a Muslim. Wasn't that reason enough to doubt his integrity? Islam and integrity were mutually incompatible. QED.

'Oh, so the seven peace treaties Panchananda has signed with seven other states under the stewardship of Mubarak Sahab then are as good as invalid.'

'Well, maybe not all. But of course, it's an altogether different matter when Mubarakji is dealing with a Muslim state like Jehanarabad.'

And all of a sudden whatever stereotypes and deep prejudices had lain buried all these years were out in the open. Something else suddenly crossed my mind. Whether I had a Hindu mother or not, I sure had Muslim parents. Where did that leave me? Your guess is as good as mine.

The weavers and apprentices were by now signing the attendance register at the entrance of the workshop and joined the discussion as they sat down at their looms. As expected, they were a divided lot. Most people vote for the faith they belong to and not the evidence or the lack of it. But while many Hindus and even a few Muslims backed Param, it was heartening to see that far more Hindus and Muslims didn't just stand staunchly behind the imprisoned Prime Minister but mentioned why he was unique and invaluable.

The discussion in the workshop was getting overheated and even a little nasty when Kashmira walked in. The acrimonious exchanges were immediately suspended and she took me aside to tell me that a messenger from Shuklaji had come over to the house to say that the Chief of Police was sorry that he was not there when I had dropped in the previous day but he would be happy to see me if I could spare a few minutes. As I was on my way to meet him, I saw posters being put up on every road and corner in huge big red letters saying 'Anyone who spreads rumours about the prime minster will be put in jail for three years of rigorous labour.' Well, in that case they would have to put almost the whole of the population of the capital behind bars.

'I believe you've been scouring the city for clues about how the secret preliminary negotiations for a possible peace treaty with Jehanarabad went off track and resulted in the arrest of Prime Minster Mubarakji. Let me at the outset make it clear that the only reason I will share all the details in this matter with you is that HM has secretly appointed you judicial consultant in the most complex cases.'

'Shuklaji,' I smiled and interrupted him, 'I will refrain

from asking you how you get to know any and every thing that happens in the world even before God does.'

He laughed heartily. 'If I may reply even though you don't want an answer, why would HM appoint a man to my post unless I could peek into if not every citizen's heart, then at least into God's?'

I laughed but he had something more to say. 'Kabirji, let me share a brief memory of the time I accepted the job of Chief of Police. HM made one comment which I have never forgotten. He said, "Shuklaji, get one thing straight, if you are expecting to be loved and honoured for doing a damn good job, I suggest you resign even before you sign on the dotted line at the end of your appointment letter. I'm sure there will be times when even I might end up hating you."

I have to admit this was an insight that had never occurred to me and forced me to look at the Chief of Police in a new light. I am sure that more often than not he was seen as a loathsome villain and not as a hero by the families of petty thieves as well as those of big-time crooks.

No, he did not try to conceal the fact that Mubarakji and he had had the occasional difference of opinion. I must have looked a trifle surprised when he aimed a counter-question at me. 'Are you trying to suggest, Kabirji, that you and HM have seen eye to eye on every single subject?'

What could I say but 'Touche, you've got me there,' nod my head and move on?

'Let me then start at the very beginning, Kabirji. So far the Prime Minister and HM have succeeded in getting seven major countries to sign a peace treaty with us, starting from Samadhanpur. Somehow or other, we had failed to enthuse Jehanarabad for all these years. But the Prime Minister is a close friend of yours and so you must know he does not ever give up on a job once that becomes an item on Panchananda's agenda. After years of pursuing the matter, Mubarakji finally got a tentative yes from the head of Jehanarabad.'

'How did you find out that confidential information was being leaked, Shuklaji?'

'Quite frankly we were unaware of this development despite the fact that there is a 24×7 border post. It was the booking clerk at the Sarnath Inn outside town who noticed that the same Jehanarabad man showed up every couple of weeks or so and reported this to one of the constables on duty in that area. The curious thing is that the constable was reluctant to give credence to the Sarnath Inn clerk and did not report the matter. It was sheer luck that three days later he happened to be going home around midnight after he had signed off in the duty register, when he saw a man with an overnight bag hurriedly harnessing his horse outside the inn. He tried to stop the rider but he galloped off. There was a long chase and it was three o'clock when the assistant commissioner on night duty woke me up at home and showed me the contents of the bag along with the courier's confession.'

'What kind of papers were they?'

'I'm getting to that. As you must know, before the two parties can start negotiating a complex treaty, they have to have several meetings in advance to firm up the agenda to be discussed. I wish every diplomat or student of political science had had the chance to see the clarity and vision with which Mubarakji was preparing the foundations for the talks.'

'I see your point. These were the negotiations which would form the framework for the crucial negotiations to come.'

'Precisely. Don't forget, after a treaty's signed, there's no way you can say, oh, I forgot this. Or we'll need to change this or that clause.

'The next morning I went over to the Prime Minister's office but he was in a meeting. So I left a message with his PA, asking him to let me know when he was free and I would come back as soon as possible. I should have known better. The Prime Minister has never allowed his high office to prevent him from acting as a common citizen. Two hours later he walked over to the police headquarters. I showed him the papers which had been confiscated. Mubarakji's face slowly drained of all blood, his hands shook and he closed his eyes as if in pain. I asked the orderly outside my office door to immediately fetch a glass of water and a strong cup of tea.

'I turned around only to find Mubarakji standing up and holding both his hands in front of himself. I thought he was suddenly feeling shaky and pulled up a chair for him to sit down. "Just hang on for a minute, Prime Minister. The water and tea will be here in a minute and you will feel much better. There's no hurry."

'He smiled wanly and said, "Let the law take its course."

'And I replied, "Yes, sire, the law will take its course. I just wanted to confirm that these were indeed the papers that you had prepared for the next bilateral meeting."

'He now held his hand close to my face as if in supplication and repeated, "Let the law take its course."

'I was utterly confused and asked him, "Forgive me, Mr Prime Minister, for being so opaque, but what exactly do you want me to do?"

'His voice was barely audible. "Let the law take its course."

'I wanted to argue with him or at least tell him that he would have to ask someone else to take him into custody, but he was as much my Prime Minister as the country's and I had no option but to do his bidding.'

I looked the Chief of Police in the eye to share his quandary and for the first time noticed an incipient scar around a wound in his forehead.

'Have you had a bad fall in the last few days, Shuklaji?'

He smiled wryly and shook his head. 'After I followed Mubarakji's instructions, I came back to the office, sat on the floor and beat my head against the wall not knowing how to show my face to HM or my own family. I was bleeding heavily when it struck me that I would have to go over to the Prime Minister's house and share the bizarre news with his wife and son.

'I held my forehead under the flowing tap water to stop the bleeding and then went over to Mubarakji's house. The maid fetched her mistress. As Gunawantiji walked into the drawing room and greeted me, I remembered that Mubarakji always called her Mehbooba, his beloved, and not by her original name. She told the maid to bring me tea and snacks even though I protested and told her a lie that I had just had a hefty lunch. Of course, having known the Prime Minister's household for I don't remember how long, she ignored my pleas and went inside and brought back a first-aid kit with Islamic healing unguents and bandaged my–'

Shuklaji suddenly stopped and said, 'I can't go on. I remember her face crumble as I told her the news about her husband's insistence that I put him in prison. She did not burst out in tears. No, that was against the traditions of the Mubarak family.

'After a while she said, "If that is what he said, then I understand that you had no choice other than to take him into custody. Shukriya, Shuklaji, shukriya from my heart. I can imagine what an untenable position my husband has put you in."

'I told her that I had kept Mubarakji in a state guest house outside the capital and she could visit him any time she wanted. As a matter of fact, I said she was more than welcome to stay with him though in that case she would have to be there till HM returned.

'One detail that I left out was the Prime Minister's anger when he learnt that I had no intention of locking him in the country's central prison or any other one for that matter. He could not understand why he was being treated almost as a state guest when he was nothing less than a traitor to the nation. I told him that since he claimed he was a fifth columnist, as the Prime Minister he would surely know the law: that the current ruler of Panchananda alone, none other than HM Ramdeoj Singhji at the moment, was entitled to take all decisions regarding someone who betrayed the country. Finally I added that for the nonce I would tell the cabinet and the populace that Mubarakji had gone out of the country on an urgent matter.'

When I was at the door of his office, Shuklaji called out my name: 'Kabirji.' I turned around to face him. 'Kabirji, you are older and much wiser than I am. What do you make of what I told you?' This was a different Chief of Police from the one I had known for years. He seemed to be deeply troubled. 'You see I cannot forgive myself for taking the Prime Minister into custody. I doubt I've met a finer human being than him.'

I stood nailed to the ground and then with an effort walked over and put my arm around the Chief of Police.

'Shuklaji, I may be older than you but I am no wiser. Truth to tell I am baffled beyond words by Mubarakji's stand. If I am to come clean, somewhere at the back of my mind I felt that you were responsible for the Prime Minister's arrest. I was hopelessly wrong and I owe you an apology. I am hardly likely to come up with anything new, but if I do, I will get back to you instantly.'

'Where are you headed now, Kabirji?'

'I thought I would pay a visit to the head of the intelligence bureau in case he has some stray information.'

'Don't you know that Kamaljeetji is seriously ill?'

'No, I had no idea. What's wrong with him?'

'He suffered a paralytic attack a few days ago. His deputy Vidyasagar Sumant has taken over temporarily.'

'I'm afraid I don't know him.'

'You don't have to worry on that count. I'll write him a note.'

I had lunch at a roadside eatery and went over to see Vidyasagar Sumant, the temporary head of the intelligence agency. He grasped quickly that this was not a courtesy call and was reluctant to share whatever facts he was privy to till I produced the note from Shuklaji telling him that I was HM's emissary and hence he was to cooperate with me. He was less curt and dismissive now but I could sympathize with his predicament. After all, like it or not, I was a mere weaver and I guess he couldn't fathom why Ramdeo Singhji would entrust me with this delicate task. But truth to tell he really didn't have any new facts or insights to share with me.

I dropped by on a few other ministries on one pretext or another but came back home none the wiser.

The next day was D-day. Ramdeoji had preponed his return and had sent me a missive asking me to see him by nine latest.

I switched off the lights since Kashmira was already fast asleep and was about to hit the bed to spend a night hating myself for having failed both the Prime Minister and HM when there was a knock on the door. My first thought was that only Ramdeo Singhji would presume to drop by at this hour. I opened the door to find Vidyasagar Sumant, the new head of intelligence, standing outside with a shoulder bag.

'Forgive me, Kabirji, for disturbing you so late at night. But I had always taken it for granted that Kamaljeetji would be around for many more years. Then as you know I found myself temporarily heading the intelligence bureau. Now suddenly something has come up and I am unsure about how to proceed, and I felt I should leave it to you to decide whether you wanted to share the information with HM.'

I had no idea what had made Vidyasagarji change his opinion of me but I led him into the drawing room and made him sit down. 'Have you had dinner, Vidyasagarji?'

He looked puzzled by the question and said, 'I haven't

been home yet but I am fine.'

'I'm sure you are.'

'And please call me Vidyasagar.'

'Just give me a minute to get back to you.'

'Kabirji, just one question.' He paused to get my full attention. 'I believe you and the Prime Minister were friends. Do you recall anything, doesn't matter how irrelevant or inconsequential it might be, which Mubarakji may have said to you?'

I tried to concentrate but shook my head after five minutes. 'Sorry. See you in a few minutes.'

I went into the kitchen and walloped three eggs furiously, taking them to be my brains which had gone dead, cut an onion and a chilli into fine pieces and made an omelette and served it with the leftover chapattis from Kashmira's and my dinner.

'Oh really, you shouldn't have,' Vidyasagar said while eyeing the puffed-up slab of omelette.

'I know I shouldn't have but since it's on the plate you might as well eat it.' I went silent for a minute and then blurted out, 'The last time I saw him, he said "Weaver Sahab, you will have to come home and read your poems to me. That cataract in the left eye is giving me a hard time. And anyway I love to hear you recite or sing your poetry."'

Vidyasagar looked dazed and lost. 'What? Who are you talking about?'

'Oh I should have mentioned that I had gone over to his place to give him my new book of poems. Him as in Mubarak Sahab.'

'He had cataract, you said?'

'Yes, that's what he told me.'

When Vidyasagar was done eating, we sat down opposite each other.

'Since Kamaljeetji, the head of the bureau, fell seriously ill so suddenly, I have been trying my best to catch up with the various matters he was dealing with. He was a very methodical man and it has been an education for me to see what brief but precise notes he kept on every subject under scrutiny. About fifty per cent of the stuff is routine and the other half is detailed notes. I'm now at a point that's a week or less before he stopped coming to work and have stumbled upon something that looks like gibberish. I had done a course in encoding and decoding while I was still an apprentice, but even though I spent four hours before landing up at your place trying out various options, I'm still at sea.'

Vidyasagar opened his shoulder bag.

'I suspect,' I told him, 'I am going to be even more at sea than you since intelligence gathering is altogether alien to me.'

I took one look at the text and knew instantly that this was a lost cause. The writing looked as if it was in Hindi but as Vidyasagar, who was fast asleep, had said, it was, no question about it, pure gibberish. I struggled with it for three hours and then gave up. Instead of fretting and fuming for the rest of the night I seemed to have passed out on the floor till I got up with a start at five-thirty in the morning and looked for the pad on which I had tried at least fifty alternative ways, maybe seventy or eighty, to breach the text. It was lying under me.

I picked up my pen and replaced each letter with the

third that followed it. So 'a' was replaced with 'd' and 'd' with 'g' and so on. No luck. I tried three other replacement series. No, I was getting nowhere. One last shot. My attempted final solution was so damned simple, of course it was not going to work. I turned the letters of each word in a reverse order. No, as expected, it was a lost cause. Full stop. I put the pad aside and went to the kitchen to make a cup of tea. A couple of minutes later it occurred to me that I must be brain-damaged, for suddenly it hit me that the writing was in a remote adivasi dialect and as I had conjectured, each word was in an inverse order.

'October 3rd. The Prime Minister paid me a surprise visit. He said he had the feeling that someone was leaking our plans and conditions for the peace treaty with Jehanarabad to the other side. I asked him what had led him to this conjecture. He said it was not a conjecture but a conviction. I once again asked him on what grounds he had come to this conclusion. His answer was unsettling. He said even as we started discussions on every clause of the economic, trade, agricultural and scientific cooperation along with military and maritime exercises, their answers had already been formulated on an intimate knowledge of our plans and proposals. I found this hard to digest but he showed me nine examples from different areas of discussions.

'What do you want me to do, I asked him. He said I have deliberately formulated misleading and obtuse clauses and conditions to test their responses. If they come prepared for that scenario, we will know for sure about the leakage. What I would want from you is to zero in on who's passing the information. Let's not forget we are negotiating with a friendly neighbour just now. But what if it was an enemy with whom we were dealing?

'October 7th. The Prime Minister was back four days later and confirmed that the Jehanarabad team had bought into the deliberately misleading note and were thrown off balance when the points we raised had nothing to do with what they were expecting us to focus on. Quite rightly now he wants to know where the leakages are coming from. I am personally taking charge of this enquiry from tomorrow and we will resolve the matter asap.'

I couldn't believe that we had blundered so unforgivably and put a totally innocent Mubarakji in jail only because the chief of intelligence had suffered from a paralytic attack the very night he made his last notation. I looked at the young Vidyasagar with something like awe, if not reverence. He was breathing softly through his mouth and every now and then snoring. How the hell had he decided to bring this unresolvable conundrum of decoding the work-diaries to the dumbest person in Panchananda? Me? Enough marvelling and roundabout patting of my own back. I woke up Vidyasagar and told him to go home, take a quick shower and wait for me at the Purana Gate behind Alakhnanda Palace since it was hidden behind a five-hundred-year-old banyan tree and used only by tradesmen and suppliers.

Simultaneously I sent a message to Shuklaji telling him there was some crucial new information and asked him to join us at the Purana Gate for a meeting with HM Ramdeo Singhji since it was important to keep the visit as low-key and inconspicuous as possible. The security personnel at Alakhnanda Palace told me that HM had returned at 3.30 a.m. and was already waiting for me.

Ramdeo Singhji was surprised to see me with the Chief of Police and the officiating head of intelligence but refrained from commenting on that since he knew that I would never venture to invite anybody to a private and pivotal meeting unless there was something extremely important.

HM made me go over the series of events twice and then questioned both Shuklaji and Vidyasagar Sumant.

'The best news that we have had in a long, long time is that Mubarakji is blameless. Not just that, it is entirely due to his vigilance that we became aware that someone was briefing the other party about every detail of our strategy.' HM smiled and said we should all drink to that but we would have to postpone it till next evening since 9.30 a.m. was a little early to get smashed.

'The citizens of this country may well ask us why then was Mubarakji taking the blame. Because that's the essence and greatness of the man. He was in charge and so he saw himself as being responsible for the disclosure. Now I leave it to you, Kabirji, and Shuklaji and Sumant to get to the bottom of this leakage of highly confidential information.'

Then he turned to me and said, 'Kabirji, Shuklaji will give you a note for the release of the Prime Minister. After that I will entrust you to bring back Mubarakji from the state guest house and drop him at his home. Can you imagine how relieved Gunawantiji and their son Arman will be? Please tell the Prime Minister that I would be delighted to see him and the three of you tomorrow evening for dinner. We will decide then when and how to honour our esteemed Prime Minister with Panchananda's highest award, the Amarjyoti.'

As I headed for the state guest house I must have stepped into that place called seventh heaven. I couldn't believe that the One-Up-There had been so kind to me that I had entirely by accident decoded those few lines that the head of intelligence Kamaljeetji had recorded in his diary. And that Ramdeo Singhji was now sending me not merely to release my dear friend the Prime Minister from prison, but to declare his innocence to the whole of Panchananda and all our neighbours. As if that was not enough to write a series of joyous dohas, I was going to be the one who was now about to share the news with Mubarakji that HM was going to give him the Amarjyoti or Eternal Flame award. Did I say I was flying? Yes, I was, and yet there was in a dark corner of my mind a strange sense of disquiet or unease that I could not explain.

I was, however, soon at the guest house and face-to-face with Mubarakji. Before I knew what I was doing I gave him a long hug telling him, 'His Majesty has declared that you're free, free, free but I'm not going to let go of you because I don't know what new stunt you will pull on me and take off.'

He laughed and said, 'Well, I'm going to hold you to your word and get Kashmira Mai over to stay with us permanently. You will–'

'One slight change.' I interrupted him. 'One week at your place and another at our home, all three of you.'

I kept holding his hand and we continued our juvenile banter till we reached his place.

'Well, here you are. This is the last time you will have Gunawanti Bhabhi and Arman all to yourself. Make the most of it because from tomorrow the plague and company will move in with you.' I had deliberately left the best news till the last minute. 'Oh, lest I forget, HM's going to honour you with the Amarjyoti award for exceptional service to the nation.'

'I don't deserve it. I really don't.'

'Not to worry. I'll tell HM to give it to me.'

He laughed and said, 'It's yours.'

I looked around for the security guard but he was not at his post.

'Where's your security guy?'

'Oh, he must have gone to relieve himself and will be back in a minute or two. But the key will be on the window sill as always. That way I will be able to surprise Mehbooba.'

I bid him goodbye as he pulled out the key from the sill and opened the door. As he was about to enter the house, I yelled out, 'I will pick you up tomorrow at seven-forty-five for dinner at HM's.'

He stood there thinking for a minute. 'No. Let's go back to our old ways. Come over by five-fifteen in the evening and we'll go for our famous five-mile chakkar. That way I will get to see Kashmira Mai. Later we'll go together to the palace.'

'Deal.'

I had been away from the workshop far too much and now spent time going over with the supervisors on the work done and whether we would be able to keep the deadlines on the jobs due this weekend. Suddenly I was face-to-face with Param, the man in charge of the colour section. Oh, the sheer pleasure of telling him after I had gone over the receipts for the purchases and stocks of colours and he was on his way to his desk, 'Oh, incidentally, I dropped

Mubarakji at his home before coming here.'

He looked at me and said, 'Yeah, sure. A likely tale if ever there was one.'

I had a ten-mile-long grin on my face and asked him to take the day off and check at the Prime Minister's home. That knocked the wind out of him.

'You can't be serious. I confirmed on the grapevine that he was still in prison on my way here.'

'I'm sure your sources are a hundred per cent reliable but what if mine are a hundred and one per cent certain?' I have to admit that I was rapidly slipping into, what do they call it, infantilism? Or is the word dotage? 'So why not take a bet. Two months' salary and a paid holiday for you and your family?' I paused for effect. 'And the same for me and Kashmira Mai on the remote chance that I win.'

Param walked away with an expression of hopeless disgust at my antics. Oh, the pleasure of putting him down. My childish triumph, however, did not last long for it suddenly occurred to me that in the relief and exultation of the Prime Minister's release from prison, all of us had forgotten, at least momentarily, to ask who then had been sharing the secret information with the Jehanarabad diplomatic team.

I got to Mubarakji's place five minutes late and was expecting him to be waiting for me outside near the gate since he was a stickler for time. Nope, he wasn't at the gate. I looked around for the guard on duty but he wasn't there either. Was I to understand that he had again gone to the loo? Was he suffering from incontinence? I walked over to the back of the house where the toilets for the staff were. But there was no one there. I was getting a little uneasy now. Had Mubarakji walked off on his own since I was a bit late? My first impulse was to walk fast and if possible catch up with him. But I thought it made better sense for me to ring the bell on the door. I rang for a while but since there was no response, I went over to the windowsill and got the key and opened the door.

I hollered loudly for Gunawanti Bhabhi and Arman. The place was just too quiet. I was puzzled that the help in the house was not responding. I called out for Mubarakji as I started going through the drawing and dining rooms, the kitchen, the guest bedrooms on the ground floor. I checked the bathrooms and the toilets. Not a soul there, and oddly enough the place looked as if it had neither been swept nor dusted for some time.

I was still yelling as I climbed up to the bedrooms, library and Mubarakji's study on the first floor. Like the staircase walls, the study and the master bedroom were full of bookshelves neatly stacked with hundreds of books arranged subject-wise and alphabetically. The writing table looked as if it had been recently used. It was full of neatly arranged papers, some open books and an envelope with HM's name on it. But there was no one to be seen. It was the same in the four bedrooms, and oddly enough it looked as if the beds had not been slept in.

I was beginning to get the first faint signs of a panic attack as I walked down and rushed through the whole place again. I had passed the pantry twice but this time I noticed a door with a staircase leading to the basement. I kicked it hard out of desperation but it opened without any resistance. The stink was overwhelming as I hurtled down the dark steps. There were two bodies, completely covered with a bed sheet. Several rats ran helter-skelter as I shoved my kerchief against my nose. Mubarakji's body lay with his hands on either side of him on the floor. Next to him were a few hundred, maybe a thousand, tiny torn bits of paper. I pulled back the sheet that covered the two bodies. Now I could see that one was a woman and the other a man. For the moment I took them to be the remains of Gunawantiji and Mubarakji's son Arman though there was no way of telling whether my guess was right or wrong, nor could I tell how long they had lain there. Most of the flesh on Bhabhi's face and an eye had been eaten and so had huge chunks of flesh from the thighs, breasts and the rest of the body. Strangely enough Arman's body hadn't been bitten and eaten so much and yet it was far more depleted and was almost just skin and bones.

I went back to Mubarakji and called out his name in desperation and I felt a faint tremor in his eyes. I put my head near his nose. I thought there was a wisp of air on my cheek. I placed my head lightly on his breast now. I don't know how long I rested it there but then I felt a hand gently lie on my back. 'Khuda hafiz, Kabir miya.' The hand fell to the floor and I knew he was gone. Did I dream that whole sequence up or did it really happen? It's something I will never know.

I wanted to scream till I had woken up Allah, all the gods in the Hindu pantheon, plus Jesus and the God of Creation, wherever they were, but I couldn't take the ghastly rotting smell and the rats scampering over my legs any more. I was about to climb up the stairs when on an impulse I went back to the two bodies and blindly collected three of the hundreds of torn bits on the floor.

I ran out of the house but deliberately slowed down, realizing that the last thing I needed to do was to attract attention. It took me ten minutes to reach Shuklaji's home. He had just got back from work and was a little puzzled to see me.

'Kabirji? I thought we were going meet at the palace at . . .' He must have seen the expression on my face and was immediately alert. He pulled up a chair for me and tried to make me sit down but I just couldn't.

'Please sit down. I'll get some tea for you.'

I shook my head. 'Please come with me.'

'Sure. Do I need to take anything?'

I shook my head again. He whispered something to his wife and was back with me.

He brought his carriage around and helped me climb in and asked me, 'Where to?'

'The Prime Minister's home.'

'Do you want to tell me anything now?'

What could I tell him? I just wouldn't meet his eyes. A few moments later he helped me climb down. I had forgotten to close the door to the house. We entered and I led him straight down into the basement. He took out his kerchief to smother his nose and so did I. He surveyed the place rapidly but with a policeman's eye. He pointed his hand at the Prime Minister's mouth. There was thick froth coming out of it. Shuklaji bent down to smell it. 'He's drunk poison. I suspect his wife and son too have consumed it. One of our first priorities is to locate it. Have you checked out the rest of the house?'

'Yes.'

'Take me with you.'

We did a quick tour but I had the feeling he did not miss even the most insignificant detail. When we reached the study I picked up the envelope with HM Ramdeoji's name on it. Since it was not sealed, it fell on the floor. He picked it up and gave it to me. I read it out aloud.

Dear Majesty Ramdeoji,
Please forgive me for not being able to come for dinner tonight. It's the first time in my life that I am missing an appointment with you. But I am afraid this is also going to be a farewell letter and hence brief. Sire, I am an old man and I can feel the breath and life in me coming to an end.

How can I possibly convey to you my gratitude for taking me under your wing and making me whatever I am today. Everything I may have achieved is because of you and your great vision not only for Panchananda but for all of humankind.

My liege, there's so much more to be done and this is the moment Allah has chosen for me to say goodbye to you and take your leave. Luckily the man you and I chose to be the deputy Prime Minister is one who has not only shown immense commitment to his work and the country but has excellent judgement and a fine work ethic. I do sincerely believe he has great potential and will never fall short of your expectations.

May you live many many more decades, Majesty. While you never ceased to stress that economic prosperity and health care for every denizen of Panchananda were a fundamental priority, you made it absolutely clear that without peace, security and that intangible thing called a thriving culture, our lives would be meaningless.

Khuda hafiz, my liege and friend. I will miss you but will always be with you.

Yours forever,

Mubarak

PS: I am leaving behind rather substantial notes in a confidential file for the remaining agenda regarding our discussions with the diplomatic team of Jehanarabad. Do please take a look at them, Ramdeo Singhji, and jot down your comments, corrections and suggestions and then pass them on to the deputy Prime Minister or rather the next Prime Minister.

PPS: Sire, forgive my handwriting and the number of words I've had to scratch out. As you know the cataracts in my eyes are at an advanced stage. I just hope I will be able to see Allah when and if despite all my flaws and sins he deems me worthy of an audience.

'I know that we're very, very tight for time,' the police chief said when I finished reading Mubarakji's letter, 'but our first priority right now is that we need to take some extremely difficult decisions. Would you agree with that?'

'Yes.'

'Let's deal with one thing at a time. I think one thing is clear: the Prime Minister left the envelope open because he wanted you to read it and perhaps me too, since he would have known that you would ask me to look into the three deaths in the basement. Does that make sense to you?'

'Yes.'

'The letter suggests that he felt his time was up and he was about to die of old age.'

I nodded my head.

'Which means he didn't want HM to know that he had drunk perhaps the same poison that his wife and son had.'

'Oh.' I must have looked a little shocked, for he immediately clarified, 'The foam from his mouth was a clear indication of the intake of ivy poison juice. Let's understand one thing clearly. We will have to choose one of the two propositions I just mentioned: the sordid truth or the Prime Minister's version. But there is a crucial corollary to the one that we decide to go with. All the rest of the follow-up decisions we take will have to be in line with the choice that we opt for. Otherwise it will be instantly obvious that we are being duplicitous.'

'What would you recommend, Shuklaji?'

'I will certainly tell you what my choice is without hesitation. As a matter of fact, I will write it down right now on this chit of paper. But please don't play the "you first" game just now. It will lead us into a blind alley.' He immediately jotted down his preference.

'I will go with the Prime Minister's take on the matter.'

Shuklaji shoved the piece of paper he had written on towards me. It said, 'The Prime Minister's version'.

'Kabirji, we'll have to cover a whole lot of ground in that case in a very limited time. Under no circumstances can we allow anyone to see the Prime Minister's half-eaten wife or son. Thank God it's winter and already dark. And thank God Mubarakji's security guard and servants were not here to witness what happened – they must all have been sent away on leave by Gunawantiji even before Mubarakji was released. I am going out into the tin shed at the back where all the gardening implements must be, to find a shovel and dig a single grave for the two horribly mangled corpses. It will help if you first hunt high and low and locate the bottle of poison and also look for any perfumes that Gunawantiji used.

'Next clean up the basement meticulously and then sprinkle the perfume all over till the smell of the rotting bodies is overwhelmed. Make sure that the windows in the basement are left open so that both the stink and the scent vanish. One last thing. The poison must be poured into the hole in the bathroom with great care so that not a drop is spilt. The reason is simple: any dead mouse or rat will rouse suspicions. As far as possible let's try and avoid that.

'One last thing we need to do. Or rather the first thing. Undress right now and take a bath as soon as our work is done so that we smell neither of perfume nor of sweat.' He looked at the grandfather clock on the wall and said, 'We have exactly one and a quarter hour's time.'

I was sweeping the floor of the basement when I heard Shuklaji calling for me. 'Pick up every single bit of the torn paper on the floor and put it in a bag. Make sure you've got the whole lot.'

I was puzzled, to put it mildly, and would have liked to ask him what on earth he was going to do with that confetti, but he had already disappeared. He was the top sleuth in the country, so I followed orders and added the three fragments that I had collected earlier to the new lot and put them in a large envelope and handed it to him before we left the Prime Minister's home.

We just about made it to Alakhnanda Palace on time. In the mad rush we'd forgotten to take the letter and the file but luckily remembered when we were a furlong away from the Prime Minister's home and went back to pick them up.

'We've got one hell of a hole in our story,' Shuklaji blurted out just as HM Ramdeoji was about to enter the private drawing room where we were waiting for him.

'What is it?' I whispered.

'HM is bound to ask us where Gunawantiji and Arman are.'

Damn, damn, damn. How could we have missed something so crucial, I asked myself in panic, but Ramdeoji was already looking askance at us.

'Where's Prime Minister Mubarakji?'

'Majesty, why don't you sit down first.'

'That I'm about to do, but you haven't answered my question.'

Shuklaji took a deep breath. 'Majesty, I'm afraid I don't have good news.'

'What do you mean you don't have good news. We're here to celebrate the return of Mubarakji.'

'I was supposed to pick him up, Majesty–' I took over from where the police chief had left off – 'and together we were to take a leisurely walk to the palace for dinner. When I got to his home today, there seemed to be nobody around and so I hollered for him. Since there was no response, I climbed up the stairs and to my horror found him lying inert in his bed.'

Ramdeo Singhji looked at me in sheer disbelief. 'How can that be? Both of you told me he was fine yesterday.'

'Yes, Majesty. That's exactly why I ran over to Shuklaji's place to get help so that he could revive him. We got back as fast as we could in his carriage.'

'I attempted very hard to resuscitate Mubarakji,' the police chief spoke up, 'since that's one of the first things they teach at the Police Academy. I tried every trick in the book but he was way past breathing, sire.'

'Where is his family, Gunawantiji and Arman?'

'I learnt that they left the capital when the Prime Minister was imprisoned in the state guest house,' I butted in, 'for fear of the rabble hunting them down as enemies of the State.'

'Do you know where they have gone?' HM asked me.

'No, my liege.' Try as I might I had not been able to come up with an answer earlier. And yet now on the spur of the moment I was making up a story. 'The rumour is that they went to one of our neighbouring states, perhaps to Kamalghad, to escape a possible backlash generated by the bogus rumour that the Prime Minister had been passing state secrets to Jehanarabad. I assure you, Majesty, Shuklaji and I will make enquiries and we'll do our best to find out their location as soon as possible.'

Ramdeo Singhji was lost in his own thoughts for a long time. 'If only I had seen him yesterday when he got out of the state guest house. He was both my left and right hand. What are we going to do without Mubarakji? Do you know how long we've been together? Longer than my marriage to the queen. I doubt if I've taken a single major decision in the last thirty years without consulting him.' He was silent again for a long time. 'Do you know there are some people you can afford to lose only if you have the good sense to die first?' Then he turned to the Chief of Police. 'We can't let the Prime Minister's body rot for days. Please try and find Bhabhiji and Arman as soon as possible. I will make the announcement of his funeral tonight itself. His body will lie in state from tomorrow morning in Alakhnanda Palace and the time of the funeral will be day after tomorrow at 5 p.m. Now let's have dinner and plan the ceremonial last rites and honours. Tomorrow morning I will inform our friendly neighbours of the tragic death of the Prime Minister and invite them to the official funeral.'

A week after Mubarakji's state funeral, Shuklaji dropped in at the workshop for the first time. He was taken aback by the series of handlooms operating there, but even more so by the number of apprentices who were studying to be weavers. It's true that my relationship with him had undergone a sea change, but while I was sure that he was genuinely impressed, I also knew he would not have come over personally unless there was something very important that he wanted to share with me.

'Kabirji,' he said to me as he was leaving, 'why don't you visit me at the headquarters when you have a little time on your hands and we can sit and chat?'

That evening I walked over to the police headquarters after office hours. He was waiting for me. After instructing his secretary that he was not to be disturbed, he showed me into his office.

'Sit.' He got down to business immediately. 'I've something to show you.'

He turned round to face the window and bent down to pull off a white cloth sack and lifted a large transparent glass panel that was about two feet by two feet in size and laid it flat on his work table. In the middle of it was something that looked like a large crossword puzzle that had been completely solved. As I kept staring at it, I could now see that I had got it wrong. The puzzle or whatever it was had been trapped between two glass sheets that were glued together. 'Read,' he told me. 'Take your time.'

It took me a couple of minutes to recognize that it was the torn bits of paper that I had collected from the floor of Mubarakji's basement which had been reconfigured to form a coherent whole. I could only wonder how many days it had taken to put it together till it read in its original form.

My beloved husband and protector (I use the latter word advisedly),

The Chief of Police Shuklaji dropped in this afternoon to give me strange news. He told me that he had asked you over to his office because he had found out that someone had been passing the highly confidential preliminary notes that you had prepared in great detail about the permanent peace negotiations going on currently to the diplomatic team from Jehanarabad. Apparently you took a quick look at the notes and told the police chief that the law must take its course and hence you should be immediately taken into custody.

He was flabbergasted and at a loss to understand what you were talking about. Was he to understand that you were the one who had made the notes and then had passed them on to the Jehanarabad team? That was totally absurd, according to him. You were not merely the second most important person in the country but you were also in charge of the negotiations. But you were adamant and so he was forced to put you in prison. However, despite your vociferous objections, he put you in the state guest house outside town.

He had come over to our place not merely to inform me about your whereabouts but also to tell me that I was at liberty to visit you any time I wanted but on one critical condition: I was not to speak to anyone about your whereabouts.

He said he wanted to ask me if I had any idea what the Prime Minister, who happened to be my husband, was talking about. Of course I realized instantly that you had not only recognized that I was the culprit who had betrayed the country but you were taking the rap for me. After all, I was the one who took dictation from you since the cataracts in your eyes made it difficult for you to write.

I was in a dreadful bind. Ours very likely was perhaps the love story of the century. We set eyes on each other when your cousin Sayyed was to be betrothed to my closest friend, Rehana. I was all of seventeen but it was that terrible cliché, love at first sight, that made me blind to all else. We were not just Hindus but high-class Brahmins. No power on earth could persuade my parents to allow me to marry you. Unfortunately while we may have said hello to each other that day, I doubt if you would have recognized me the next day. And just as importantly, marriage, I am certain, was the last thing on your mind. You were an idealist and your one and only obsession was to get into the civil service and serve the country.

I must confess that I was staggered by my gall and sheer shamelessness. I took it upon myself to serve dinner that night to your cousin's friends and dropped a note in your lap as I was about to serve you biryani.

'You've dropped a note by mistake in my lap,' you told me. 'I am surprised it didn't fall in the lamb curry.'

'No mistake there,' I whispered. 'It was meant to fall in your lap.' I remember you blushing to your gills. Fortunately you pocketed the note instead of trying to read it then and there. When I came back to serve the dessert, you had obviously read the note and said, 'I can't meet you. There's the last bachelor party for Sayyed tonight.'

'I know,' I said, and served you three extra helpings of rasmalai. 'I will come around to your room at 3 a.m.'

'I won't be there.' I could see he was panicking.

'That won't stop me.'

Come three o'clock, the bachelor party was going great guns but I kept my promise and knocked on your door. You opened it instantly and let me in.

'Have you gone mad? I don't know you from Adam.'

'You mean from Eve.'

'Yes, that's what I meant. What do you want from me?'

'Nothing, I just came over to warn you that I intend to marry you.'

'Have you lost your marbles?' You were obviously very nervous about having a young woman in your room while everybody else was at the bachelor party.

'Men have marbles. Women have tits.'

You blushed a perfect purple.

'Relax. You will go back to the party in a minute. I wanted to warn you that I am a Hindu and I have very orthodox parents. I have no idea whether your parents are liberal or even more bigoted than mine. If it's the latter, then you can look forward to hellish times. But I am a tough cookie and I don't give up.'

'You don't know me,' you answered. 'Marriage and everything else is of secondary importance as far as I am concerned. My only priority is joining the civil service.'

'I'm glad to hear that. I'll be following your career. Don't forget I'm in deadly earnest about marriage. Bye.' And I was gone.

Looking back, I realize I had been reading too many women's pulp magazines. But, as you know, I meant what I said and was not fooling around. Every week I dropped by first at the hostel where you stayed while you were training in the topmost administrative service in the country and then later on at the tiny apartment you had got yourself once you started earning. My parents gave me hell since eighteen was already too late in their eyes for me to get married. They showed me to fine, upright would-be grooms and I said no to each one of them. My father beat me black and blue but he was not a patch on my mother who locked me up and starved me for days on end.

I remember waiting behind the door as my mother entered my room the night of my twenty-first birthday when my father had gone out of town for one night. I snatched the key from her hand and locked her in. I took a shower, packed a small suitcase of clothes, had a good meal and got myself a job so I could live on my own.

When I had settled down, I came over to your place.

'Relax,' I told you. 'I know I threatened to marry you when I was seventeen but I am older by four and a half years now and hopefully wiser by four and a half years too. Oddly enough I haven't changed my mind about you. More than your career graph, which is a steep climb, I have been keeping track of you and am happy to see and chat with you when fate or chance brings us together because of our common friends. If I am to be honest, then half the time the get-togethers occur because of my prodding.

'I would like to stress that you don't owe me a thing. You're free to marry anyone you want or stay a bachelor all your life. On the other hand if you feel you would like to spend the rest of your life with me, I am game. I will give you a year to think about it.

If you would care to get to know me better, we can meet as frequently as you want. I've decided to get an advanced degree in education so that I can teach young children since I love to be in their company. Some of my friends are of the opinion that's because I belong to the same age group as them.'

The rest of the story you're familiar with, since a year and a half later we were married. I had three miscarriages but fortunately the fourth time we got lucky when I delivered Arman. I still don't know whether my parents became close to us because of Arman or because you were appointed senior adviser to HM Ramdeo Singhji and three years later were awarded the Prime Minister's post. (Perhaps I am being unfair to them and the grandchild is the sole source of their stereotypical discovery of affection.)

Time has always been a slippery customer and the years advanced unbeknownst to us. Arman took after his father and did brilliantly in school and then shifted to Jehanarabad to do an advanced degree in structural engineering. As expected, he was doing exceptionally well till in his last year he fell in love with an older woman who treated him as a yo-yo. One minute he was right up in the clouds and the next down in the depths of misery. I remember you going to his university hostel and trying to persuade him to come back home.

He was contrite but adamant and promised to stay the course. But he didn't appear for his final exams that year or the next or the one after that. The roller-coaster ride with the lady continued. The port city of Jehanarabad, as you know better than I, is not just the capital of the country but also famed for its gambling casinos. Arman had become a regular there and I need hardly add that he was rapidly sinking into colossal debts. He was perpetually high on opium, liquor and self-pity. There was only one reason he could finance his various spending binges. His father was the Prime Minister of Panchananda.

You will recall that I went across at least six or seven times, hoping to din some sense into him. You accompanied me on one of the trips and told him it was now or never. If he came back with us, we would square up the accounts with the moneylenders and he could start life all over again. He cried his heart out, but you told me that while he may have been earnest at that moment, he was way past redemption.

You contacted Arman's moneylenders, paid up all his debts, and told them that from now on you were disowning your son. They were more than welcome to lend him money so long as they understood that his father or mother was not liable any more to clear Arman's debts. You were true to your word. While you warned me that Arman was far too gone in his addiction, at no point did you try to dissuade me from seeing him.

But how can I deny that our relationship was badly strained at that time? I could argue like a vindictive standard-issue mother that you no longer gave a damn about what happened to your son. Yes, there may be some truth in that but you had spent hours trying to persuade him in the early days that his addictions were depriving him of all the remarkable achievements and joys that life could offer him.

You were convinced that the most dangerous achievement of poverty was that the poor closed all doors and windows to hope and took it for granted that their only option was resignation to their fate. You were very keen that he should revolutionize housing for the poor in Panchananda so that their minds and ways of thinking changed radically. But Arman, I have to admit, was a lost cause by then. I would also have to grant that you worked twelve to sixteen hours every single day, week in and week out, because millions of young people of Panchananda looked as much to you as to His Majesty as father figures who would look after their education, make sure that they got fulfilling jobs and safeguard their future.

A new problem of an altogether different nature cropped up suddenly. The cataract in your left eye needed to be operated upon immediately. However, at that moment it was out of the question since this was the time when you were deep into the initial stages of the negotiations for the peace treaty with Jehanarabad. So every night you dictated to me the notes that would form the basis of Panchananda's stance about the give-and-take that the final peace treaty would have to reflect.

I am sure we were both aware of the contradictions in our relationship. While Arman had come between us, the fact that we sat together and worked together also strengthened the bond between us. I was not merely your amanuensis, I was also the assistant who voiced doubts and questioned and probed some of your assumptions. As always, you were generous enough to thank me when my advice was sound and immediately adopted it.

One day, in the middle of these negotiations, Arman's lady love informed me that Arman had contracted some horrible, incurable venereal disease and I should take him back with me. I had a running battle with myself. I knew how much you loved your son and what it cost you to cut off all ties with him. I also knew it was time I too did so. But despite all his terrible flaws, I loved my son and couldn't disown him.

I packed every single piece of jewellery, solitaires, brooches, bracelets, pendants, tiaras, diamonds, chokers, chains, anklet, nose rings, silver and gold that I had collected over the years, not to mention what my parents had given me after the standard reconciliation between them and me that had followed Arman's birth. I set out for Jehanarabad with just one intention: no matter what the price, I was going to get my Arman back.

I picked him up from above the brothel where he stayed. He was too far gone by this time to protest or refuse to come with me. When word got around that I was with Arman and packing his stuff, half a dozen usurers turned up. I handed over all the goodies that I had brought with me to these six vultures. I waited till they had done their maths on all the items and then said goodbye to them. I couldn't fathom their response. They sniggered and looked at me as if I was either an imbecile or an ace crook.

The youngest of the lot said to me, 'Where do you think you are going, madam?'

'Going back home,' I answered, 'with my son.'

'Really? And who's going to pay back the remainder of the debt?'

'I've paid far more than my son's dues.'

'You've got to be joking. This tiny pile will be less than a quarter of what he owes us.'

'You can't be serious,' I told them.

'Oh but we are,' they piped up together.

Then the eldest of the lot took over. He spoke softly but with a hint of a threat. 'Come over to our shops and we can show you all the receipts signed by none other than your darling son.'

For the first time I realized that they were in deadly earnest. What had Arman gone and done? Surely he couldn't have amassed such a humongous debt? I tried to push them aside and leave but the old man said, 'Don't even think of it, madam. You are not going to leave till you have settled the full amount.'

It was clear by now that both Arman and I were in grievous trouble.

That's when I noticed a man who had been hanging back. He now came over and asked me whether we could talk privately about how to solve the problem. I pointed to the six carrion eaters hungering to pick me apart. He said he would take care of them and took them aside to talk to them. I have no idea what he said to them but all six of them walked away and stood at the other end of the street under the shade of the three-hundred-year-old banyan tree.

'Who are you?' I asked him the question that had been bothering me from the time he had offered to help me.

'Let's just say a friend of your son.'

'What's your name?'

'I am the nameless one. Call me Tom, Dick or Harry. I am hoping that we'll come to know each other better and then everything will not only be clear but the problem of the humongous debt that Arman has accumulated will hopefully be resolved.'

Let me not prolong the suspense but cut straight to the chase. All he wanted from me was a copy of the notes that you dictated to me.

How the hell did he know about our private affairs, I asked myself. And I said to him, 'You can't be serious. They are confidential and meant to be shown first and foremost to His Majesty Ramdeo Singhji, and then discussed with the cabinet. Only then will it be decided what precisely are the points that would be put on the table when our team meets with the Jehanarabad contingent.'

'True, but that's precisely the point. The end result is the same: they are top secret till the Panchananda negotiators talk with us.'

Whoever this man was he was far too smooth a talker for my liking. He could play with words, turn and twist them and bamboozle anybody.

'Thank you for your offer, but no thank you. First of all I am not privy to my husband's notes and secondly even if I was–'

'Oh, but you are.' He was smiling now. 'The handwriting is distinctly yours and not the Prime Minister's. After all, he's suffering from a serious case of cataract. We all know he needs the operation urgently but it has been postponed because of the peace agreement which both our nations are keen to sign.'

'That may be the case but I will not betray my husband and my country.'

'Once again let me state the obvious. There are no secrets and no betrayals here. Panchananda and Jehanarabad are going to be partners in peace.'

'Maybe you are right. But please understand that I am not in a position to be of help to you.'

He looked at me with a glint of pity in his eyes and then told me, 'In that case I'm afraid both you and your son will have to be imprisoned for life for cheating the locals of Jehanarabad of huge sums of money. You will be placed in solitary confinement. As to your son, it's merely a matter of a few weeks before his syphilis takes him away for good. Rest assured you will not be allowed to see him nor will he be given a decent funeral. The vultures will take care of him.'

'You can't be serious.'

'And pray why not? Nothing more serious than money in this mercenary world.' He let that sink in. 'Think about the scandal it will cause in Panchananda if they discovered that the Prime Minister and his son owed four hundred and seventy thousand plus twenty-one per cent interest to moneylenders from Jehanarabad and are unwilling to settle the debt. If that's not bad enough, they will also learn about your son's activities in the gambling dens and the fun and games he indulged in with the ladies of the night.'

I knew I was in a bind but I was silent, trying to figure out if there was some way to outsmart the man.

'I've a suggestion. If you let my son and me go back, I promise that I will pay you a golden package every month.'

'Thank you for the bribe but what about the moneylenders? Who will pay them?'

'Who will pay them if, as you expect, I part with the information you want?'

'Don't worry your head about that, madam. It's a quid pro quo arrangement. So just keep your part of the deal.'

I was about to stall for some more time, hoping that I might get a brainwave, when he shook his head and said, 'Don't try my patience, madam. Say "yes", and I will tell the border guards to let you go. A "no" will of course have unfortunate consequences.'

I copied the notes you dictated to me and supplied them to their courier the first three times, but then my self-loathing got so out of hand, I had a brainwave. I told the security guard to tell the visitor from Jehanarabad that my mother was very seriously ill and I had left town to take care of her. That night I was jubilant. Wasn't I brilliant? I hadn't mentioned the purported name of the city where my sick mother was. Why had I not thought of this earlier? Anyway, what was clear was that I wasn't going to return from my mother's bedside till the main negotiations with Jehanarabad started.

My self-congratulatory euphoria didn't last long. Early next week I had a visitor, the same man who had told me it was a quid pro quo deal. I don't know what he told the security man but he was waiting for me in the visitors' lounge. He did not wish me nor say a word, but handed me the three files I had passed on so far, with a short note on top.

'I'm on my way to His Majesty's Office to inform him that the Prime Minister has been very kind and has been passing all his notes to us in lieu of the money his son owes to the moneylenders in Jehanarabad.'

That I'm afraid was the end of my rebellion.

I have no idea when exactly you discovered that I was leaking secret information. What I know for sure is that thanks to the Chief of Police, I understood that you insisted that you were responsible for sharing the secret papers with the Jehanarabad folks.

Forgive me, my beloved Mubarak, forgive me when even my thirty-three million gods and your

Allah will not countenance my appalling behaviour. You gave me enough love to last me forever and ever and yet I let you down. So I am going to say goodbye now both from Arman and me. I cannot abide myself for having betrayed you. As to Arman, he's just skin and bones and has been unconscious for the last five days and will be breathing his last either today or tomorrow.

Love you for eternity. Think kindly of me, my dear heart.

Your one and only Mehbooba

I had finished reading the letter the third time, but I was so numb in the head that all I could do was keep staring at the glass-encased missive. Gunawantiji, or Mehbooba as Mubarakji called his wife, had broken faith with her husband and that was unforgivable. But I also could not avoid asking myself another question, 'Did she have any choice? After all, she was Arman's mother.' What would I have done in her situation? Imagine being told by the Jehanarabad agent that the only choice she had was to hand a copy of the notes Mubarakji dictated or go to prison with her dying son and ruin her husband's reputation. What was remarkable was that the Prime Minister obviously understood the nature of her terrible dilemma and hence was adamant about being sent to prison. Arman certainly was the guilty party but I think we all know that we can get up to some very, very foolish things in youth, not to mention in our adult years. Those who manage to survive the high jinks of the immature years can then sit on their high horses and judge others.

Shuklaji came over and sat down with me. 'Kabirji, how can I can ever live down the fact that I was the one who imprisoned the Prime Minister? Granted that he wouldn't allow me any other option, but that doesn't absolve me of my guilt.'

'Talk about the Great Betrayal.' I could barely speak but I think he got the drift of what I was saying. 'HM appointed me to sort out terribly complicated cases and get to the bottom of who the real culprit was in diabolically difficult legal proceedings. How can I ever tell him that sometimes it's best to leave the truth alone instead of chasing it? Look deeply into the matter and we'll discover how we are all party to the tragedy that occurred.

'Yes, while Gunawantiji was at fault for not turning her back on her son, why didn't Mubarakji confess that his wife was the guilty party who parted with the secret papers? What is worse is that neither you nor I can confess to HM that we not only betrayed him by telling him lies but even more so by not being able to reveal or explain the tragic choices that the Prime Minister made.'

There you are, Tanmaya, now you know what the Great Betrayal was all about. Now I've a question for all of you but I am not asking for answers. Think about it: how would you have dealt with such a convoluted dilemma?

Chah gayee, chinta mitee,
Manvah beparvah.
Jisko kachhu na chahiye,
Vahi Shahenshah.

Desire disappeared, anxity's gone,
The mind's without anxiety.
The one who wants nothing,
He's the king of kings.

26

'Do you recall Tanmaya asking me to talk about the Great Betrayal?' I asked all the weavers and apprentices as we were about to close shop for the weekend. 'For some reason the subject of betrayal has been on my mind since then and I thought you might be interested in knowing a little more about this inflammatory topic.'

'Do we have a choice?' As usual it was Inayat who was being obstreperous just to get my goat.

I smiled sweetly and said, 'No.' Fortunately that got a laugh from the folks in the workshop and for the moment Inayat piped down.

'The most famous betrayal is of course that of Judas Iscariot who sold the Son of God, Jesus, for thirty pieces of not even gold but silver, and then some sources say he felt so guilty, he hanged himself. Ultimately Judas' betrayal led to the crucifixion of Jesus and that as you know became the origin of the universal symbol of Christianity. It would be interesting to speculate about which emblem Christians would have adopted if Judas had not ratted on Jesus. I will leave that to your imagination.

But betrayal is a far more complex subject than we

give it credit. Perhaps the most revered character in the Mahabharata apart from Shri Krishna is Bhishma who is always accompanied by the suffix 'Pitamaha' which translates roughly into the great father figure. The very name Bhishma evokes not just tremendous respect but symbolizes the very epitome of virtue and sacrifice. Ironically, some of his deeds are not merely questionable but deeply disturbing.

'Take the scene where the elder Pandava prince, Dharmaraj, had lost the kingdom belonging to him and his four brothers in a game of dice with the Kaurava prince, Duryodhan. As if that was not bad enough, the five brothers and their common-law wife, Draupadi, would now have to go into exile for thirteen years. As you all know, the story is that Shakuni Mama had fixed the dice in favour of his sister Gandhari's hundred children.

The dice game was over and the losers were about to depart the royal court of the Kauravas. It was a full house, for along with the hundred princes, all the elders and dignitaries including Bhishma Pitamaha were gathered there.

That was the moment when the Kaurava princes tried to strip Draupadi naked. The five Pandavas watched helplessly since they were now as good as slaves and had no rights. What is incomprehensible is that let alone the other elders, not even Bhishma Pitamaha raised his voice in protest against this vile and shameless behaviour of the hundred Kaurava princes.

But the Pitamaha story does not end there, nor is his honorific title damaged.

The five Pandava princes and Draupadi return after thirteen years in exile. As per the rules fixed after the game of dice, the Kauravas must return their kingdom to the

Pandavas but Duryodhan and his ninety-nine brothers refuse to do so. Once again, all this takes place in the Kaurava durbar and once again the great Bhishma Pitamaha does not utter a word to tick off the Kauravas for going back on their promise. Bhishma as well as the other elders know very well that what will follow is the great war in the fields of Kurukshetra that will kill hundreds of thousands if not millions, but he and the others stand with the Kauravas and once again Bhishma is above criticism.

Over the centuries Bhishma is defended on the grounds that he owed his loyalty to the Kauravas and hence his behaviour was beyond questioning. But this is where the Mahabharata and most folks in the world have failed over the centuries to grasp the fundamentals of ethics; or rather prefer to ignore them. We may talk loftily about ehical values but when it comes to the crunch, almost always our moral compass goes out of the window. Like Bhishma, we Indians owe our loyalty to the family, the house or the party to which we belong, regardless of our indisputable duty to choose right over wrong.

Time and again people refer to me as the Wise One. I've no idea whether to laugh or cry when I hear those two words. But I now have to come out in the open and confess that there is one case which leaves me utterly baffled. I don't know what to make of the Buddha. No, I need to rephrase that. He is the one we call the Enlightened One. God knows . . . sorry, I take that word back. The Buddha, as we all know, totally ignored the subject of God. What he believed in and taught was the path of ahimsa or non-violence and the eightfold path to nirvana or enlightenment.

But here's the conundrum. Within a few centuries after

his death, one branch of Buddhism declared him God. Deification – I guess that is supposed to be the highest honour anyone can bestow upon a human being, but they were in earnest and chose to worship him.

They didn't stop there, they delved into his past and invented the phenomenon of the Bodhisattvas or those souls who made great sacrifices and eschewed nirvana to help mankind understand that the pursuit of enlightenment was the only worthy goal in life. But his worshippers went even further and invented hundreds of secondary deities. Who knows, maybe they felt compelled to compete with Hinduism and invented hundreds, or rather, thousands of gods and goddesses and taras.

The question is, no disrespect meant, but are these later developments a travesty of the Buddha, or rather the greatest betrayal in human history since they deny everything he stood for, or is it the greatest tribute his worshippers can pay him?

You tell me because as I said I am lost.

Ghana guru vishwas bandhavey,
Unki mat sun lena.
Woh thagiyon mein thagiya rehta,
Paar bramh mein rehna.

Many gurus make false promises,
Don't listen to them.
They are nothing less than thugs,
Rise above them and stick with the truth.

27

The Weaver was an old man now. He had announced many a time that he had no intention, none whatsoever, of dying. I plan to carry on, he would say, and get as old and bald and toothless as the Almighty himself.

And yet, in his work nowadays, you could see the threads and colours of old age.

His students and disciples smirked and made faces about the half-deaf, half-blind and half-mad weaver who was their Master. He was only half the man he had been, they said. The trouble was, there was no telling which half you would meet. Sometimes if he happened to hear them, he raged and ranted. 'I am still more of a man,' he would say, 'than all of you young bucks put together. My dong is longer than yours, my hard-ons are harder and they can outlast anybody else's.'

They wouldn't have dared to in the past, but now they laughed openly in his face.

'Hey, cock-of-the-walk,' the troublemaker Inayat said with a sneer, lifting the old man's kurta so that you could see the bulge of his trailing genitals, 'let's go to the brothel and test the matter.'

'You think I'm going to pay for your pleasure?' the Weaver asked, perhaps to put Inayat off.

'No, no. We'll all come along and pay for your pleasure.'

'Well, I'm busy,' he said. 'I get more orders than I can handle. There are so many other weavers but the Nawabs and Rajas insist that I design and weave all their fabrics. Just the other day, the Sultan of Persia sent a messenger saying that I must weave the world's most exquisite and expensive cloth for his son's wedding robe next year. I had to refuse. What could I do? I have only two hands and you people are a dead loss. Can't ever rely on you.'

'Don't give us that cock-and-bull story, old man,' Charatram, usually the quietest of the Weaver's apprentices, said. 'Why can't you admit that you can no longer get it up?

That evening, all seventeen apprentices and the Weaver went to the whores' alley. They took a woman each for themselves and the prettiest, the one they called Sherani because she was a tigress in bed, they kept for the old man. The deal was that at the end of the session, Sherani would give a report to them about the Weaver's sexual prowess.

When they were done, the pupils gathered in the courtyard but there was no sign of the Weaver. Fifteen minutes, half an hour, two hours. They went and listened at the door. The weaver was still at it. Then there was absolute silence. It sounded ominous after all that panting and heaving.

He's obviously overdone it and had a heart attack. Must have burst a blood vessel. We went too far this time, they said, when the door was flung open and Sherani came out swearing at the Weaver in the foulest language imaginable. They had to admit that her vocabulary in such matters was infinitely more colourful than their own limited and repetitive oaths.

'This is not a man,' Sherani screamed. 'He's a tomcat, a billy goat, a sex maniac. He's done it seventeen times and he wants to do it again. The bloody lech says you guys are paying for it, so why shouldn't he get his money's worth? And what about me? I'm as good as dead. He's done it so often, a bullock cart, even the Maharana's chariot, could pass through. Come on, cough up, each one of you. This is no laughing matter. I'm ruined for life.'

That night they had dinner at an open-air roadside cafe: biryani and tangdi kebabs. The Weaver was feeling generous and they ate heartily. He was narrating in great detail his exploits with Sherani when he became short of breath. They made him lie down on a bench. He was pale and a grey shadow was creeping over his face. They wondered if this was the end.

Charatram, the shy one, said, 'Master, you should have some sense at your age. Couldn't you have controlled yourself? Even we can't do it more than twice, and that too after a break.'

The Master could hardly speak but that didn't prevent him from laughing and spluttering. 'I held Sherani's breasts in my hands. They were full and heavy as papayas and I thought God was finally in my palms. I told her if I sleep with you – and I'm not sure I'm up to it today – you'll earn some money but not much. But if, on the other hand, we lie blissfully in each other's arms for a couple of hours and then you scream and shout that I'm a monster and forced sex upon you seventeen times, all my apprentices will pay you seventeen times as much. Sherani is a businesswoman. How could she not go along with my scheme?'

They could have strangled the Master. Instead they laughed, called him a cheat and a liar. Why else would they love him so and follow him everywhere? He was really a child and he never tired of practical jokes.

By now, the Weaver's pulse was unsteady and his breathing was short and staccato. He looked at them, he smiled weakly and he fell silent. A few more breaths and the soul had flown out of him. They touched his feet and asked for his blessings one last time. They sent Charatram to get the wood for his funeral pyre and told him they would meet him at the burning ghats.

But even as Charatram left, Inayat said, 'The Master is a Muslim and he should be buried.' Adil, Rehmat and Suleiman agreed with him. A vehement argument broke out amongst the disciples, but the Muslim pupils were outnumbered by the Hindus and walked away in anger.

Charatram came back with a bullock cart loaded with firewood. The Hindu disciples arranged the pyre and laid the Master gently on it. They performed the last rites, and each one of them lit a torch. They poured the ghee and were about to light the pyre when Inayat, Rehmat and the others returned with a group of Muslim friends. They had knives in their hands. The Hindus and the Muslims were now evenly matched.

'If you know what's good for you,' Inayat said, 'give the Weaver back to us.

'Just you try and take him,' Gunidas retorted.

There was only one way to settle the matter. They fell on

each other. Scalps broken open, blood and guts, both parties were doing pretty well when the Weaver sat up.

'Can't a man even die in peace?' he asked.

The Hindus and the Muslims froze as in a tableau. What was this apparition? They fled in panic.

'Come back, you fools, come back,' the wispy figure called after them.

One by one they returned. Some of them stood at a distance just in case the incubus sprang at them.

'You won't ever change, will you?'

For the first time in his life there was defeat in the Weaver's voice. 'Light me a torch,' he told them. They had to help him down off the pyre. He stood unsteadily and took the torch from Charatram.

'Come,' he said, 'follow me.'

His legs seemed to buckle and he walked drunkenly. He had, after all, just come back from the dead. It was three in the morning when they reached the bazaar. The Weaver stood almost at the centre. He was silent for a minute or longer than that. He was not going to make it, they thought, but his voice rang out.

Kabir stands in the marketplace,
A torch in his hand.
Whosoever will set fire to his house,
Come, join me.

Now, he's really gone off his rocker, his apprentices and disciples said to each other.

'Bring me the town crier's drum,' the Weaver said.

Why not, Inayat thought, this might be fun. He went to the peepul tree where the drum rested when it was not in use.

'Beat it,' the Master said, 'wake up the whole world and the heavens too.'

The townspeople came out of their houses – husbands, wives and children, patriarchs and mothers-in-law, dogs and cats – and soon the whole town was gathered around the Weaver. They looked a little eerie and unreal in the light of the torches.

'I stand in the marketplace,' the Master said again. His voice was steady and it seemed to echo off the walls of the houses.

Kabir stands in the marketplace,
A torch in his hand.
Whosoever will set fire to his house,
Come, join me.

'What the hell is the old man up to?' Ismael asked. 'What's he trying to say?'

'Something symbolic and profound,' Charatram said sardonically. 'Something totally beyond you and me.'

It slowly began to dawn on the townspeople that the Weaver was serious about his invitation. He was always a bit mad but this time he had definitely gone over the edge. They began to close in on him almost imperceptibly, the men followed by the women. There was something sinister about the way they moved, as if the Weaver's madness had touched them too. The pupils and disciples, all but Inayat, slowly shrank away. The villagers bent down and picked up stones, bricks and whatever they could lay their hands on.

Some went back to their homes to get knives, axes, hammers and bamboo poles.

'Inayat,' they said, 'move away, lest you get hurt.' He shook his head but was sensible enough to distance himself from the Master. The Weaver began to run, his right hand up in the air. The flame of the torch sputtered and quivered. The villagers were not about to let the mad old man burn their homes. They began to pelt him. The Master torched his own house. A stone split open his forehead, a bamboo cracked his shin bone. The Weaver did not stop. A boy with a catapult got his left eye. Some of the disciples shouted to the villagers not to hurt the Master but no one paid them any heed.

Gunidas and Rehmat flung their torches up in the air, caught them and set their own houses on fire. The haystacks next to their homes crackled and sputtered and turned into fireworks. Sparks rose in the air like fireflies. Three of the houses were burning steadily now, the conflagration making a racket and rising high into the skies.

There was a battle raging between the Master's pupils and the villagers. The disciples were in a minority and even those who had merely stood aside and watched were attacked; some were badly injured. The villagers had long realized that their houses were safe, but that did not assuage their fury. They continued their rampage.

'Are you happy now?' Inayat asked the Master. 'Why burn our own houses? Makes no sense.'

The wounded Weaver said, 'Fire purifies, my friend. It is our chance to start afresh, to alter the course of our lives. The trouble with men is that the past is always and ever with them, as it was with you, Inayat and Charatram and all your friends at the burning ghats. You were about to kill each other for the sake of a god who you claim is either a Muslim or a Hindu.'

'Is arson, then, the end of all your weaving and questioning, whoring and poetry?' Inayat sneered. 'Or perhaps that is how you conceal your despair.'

'It needn't have been, if even a few of my pupils had changed just a little. We are never fully God's because we are always bound to the world and its ways; to our children, wives, work, pleasures, old habits that don't die; to our pride and sacrifices. Once we are homeless, once we have no past, once there's an end to me, me, me, and there's nothing to hold us back, once we are true orphans, then our only home is God.'

'And is your work done now, old man?'

The Weaver laughed, more like a cackle really. 'Hardly,' he said, 'now we'll burn heaven and hell and smoke and flush out God himself.'

Tan man dhan arpan satguru ney,
Aur guru vachan sun lena.
Aur jo guruji tharo mastak maangey,
To seesh kaat dhar dena.

Offer the body, mind and wealth to the truth,
Listen to the words of the guru.
And if the guru asks for the gift of your ego,
Cut your head and offer it.

28

'We were so much better off with you dead. Your reputation would have remained intact. And we would have grown fonder of you. Nostalgia is not just selective memory, it is the reinvention of the past as it never was. We would have romanticized and idolized you. Your crass attempts at attention seeking and your juvenile desire to shock would have become the stuff of parables and mythology. You were dead. I checked again and again. You had no pulse and you had no breath. Why did you come back?'

The Weaver patted Inayat's back as if to console him. Inayat shook off the Master's friendly overtures.

> It was something of a surprise for me too. I was standing in the queue with thousands of others waiting at the gates for St Peter to check in the Book of Life and tot up and tally my sins and good deeds and decide whether I was to go to heaven or hell. Suddenly, there was a commotion and the doors to God's mansions opened and Michael flew out. It was an amazing sight. The painters and the sculptors have got it wrong. You can't see the angels and yet there's no mistaking them. Their wings are transparent

and insubstantial as air and the beatitude on their faces . . . I can see you getting impatient.

Like everybody else I wondered why he was in such a hurry and why he was carrying a beauteous garland of carnations, or maybe they were roses, the colour of dried blood, when lo and behold, he alighted where I was waiting and put the garland around my neck and lifted me as if I was as light as breath, and took me straight inside.

People were screaming abuses. You would think that they would behave at least after they were dead but I could also understand their anger.

'Welcome Kabir,' I heard a wonderfully mellifluous voice speak to me. God got off his bejewelled gold throne and embraced me. 'We are absolutely delighted to see you here. We must say you kept us waiting so long, we had begun to wonder whether you had given up the idea of dying altogether.' I prostrated myself in front of the glorious presence. I was overawed and speechless. I couldn't believe my eyes. I mean this was the real thing, the ultimate experience.

'Rise, Weaver. No need for you to touch our feet.' He bent down and raised me up. 'I do apologize that you had to stand in the queue with the rest of the crowd,' God said. 'Peter had a bout of shingles and you know what a hypochondriac he is. He still hasn't managed to update the records for the births and deaths and of course while he was recuperating, all was chaos.

'I'm afraid it's no excuse but that was the reason why you were not picked up directly from earth and had to stand in the queue.'

I had the depressing feeling that I was still on earth.

Nothing, it seemed, had changed. If you were in with the bosses you got special treatment.

'Make yourself at home, Weaver. This is, after all, your final resting place, your heavenly abode. Ask for whatever you want, milk and honey; the best fruit in the world; absolutely any kind of cuisine you fancy; wine, women, and song. Anything you need, consider it yours. Any time you feel like company, just call or drop by. It would be a pleasure to spend time with you.'

It was clear that the interview was over but I must have looked puzzled, maybe even a little alarmed, for God asked me, 'Is anything the matter, Kabir? You look pale and not entirely happy.'

'Almighty Father, am I to understand that I have got admittance to heaven?'

'But of course. Was there any doubt about that?'

'I don't mean to sound ungrateful but I thought this place had some standards.'

He looked at me coldly and I could feel the mercury rising. 'You haven't been here over a minute,' he thundered, 'and you already have complaints.'

'You misunderstand me, Lord,' I said hastily. 'I merely wanted to point out that there must be some mistake.'

'What mistake?' His irises had narrowed like a cat's.

'How should I put it? My history of misdemeanours would hardly make me eligible for heaven.'

'Oh,' he said, and his face relaxed and a smile broke out like sunlight from a crack on a grey, oppressive day. 'You mean your whoring and blasphemies, your days as a brigand and a highway robber, your constant lying and your desire to shock and scandalize, anything to be sensational?'

I squirmed at this litany of my misdeeds and didn't dare look up.

'There's more, much more.' He paused. 'Do you want me to go on?'

'No, no. I am well aware that you are omniscient, my Lord.'

'How could we keep you out? You are our annual gesture of forgiveness. Our token sinner and untouchable. We do not subscribe to that dubious doctrine of equal opportunity, but we have to be careful about our reputation. They call you a saint down there. We don't want to disappoint your constituency, do we?'

Then he turned to me and said, 'Besides, don't forget, as our honorific title says, we are all-merciful and compassionate.'

My joy knew no bounds then. This was truly the God of love. I fell on my knees and took his hand in mine and kissed it joyously. 'Thank you, God. You are truly great. Then all those waiting outside, the good and the bad, the sinners and the pious, the whole and the halt, they'll all find a place in heaven, yes?'

He looked at me in consternation. 'You must be joking. What happens to the promise I made to the chosen people? What happens to heaven and hell? What happens to the concept of dharma? If people do not respect the Word and the law, all nature will be out of joint. It will be a free-for-all. The stars and planets will stray from their orbits and crash into each other, spring will follow summer and the sun will freeze us all.' He looked at me indulgently then. 'Enough nonsense, Weaver. We know that old habits die hard and you are merely trying to get a rise out of us.' He clapped his hands and a hundred houris appeared out of the blue of the sky. 'Someone give a glass of ambrosia to the Weaver. Look after him well. He is one of our favourites.'

The cup was at my lips, the elixir of life that would grant me eternal youth and bliss. And a great sadness came upon me.

'Tell me that we are all chosen, Almighty God. Tell me that you'll let all your creatures into the kingdom of heaven, the worms and the weevils, the birds of prey and the sharks in the sea, the lion and the serpent, the vines and creepers, the parasitical plants and the great trees, the cheats and the sanctimonious, all those who walked the straight and narrow and the rest who fell to temptation and ate of the apple. Tell me that no one, but no one, will be left out of paradise.'

I was breathless but continued recklessly. 'Forgive me, Father, but otherwise send me back to where I came from, for I cannot bear the thought of a God who will leave behind a single creature of his.'

'You are an arrogant fool, Weaver. We would urge you to think again. Do not cross swords with the Almighty. We may deal in infinities but our patience is finite.'

He looked long at me as if to give me time and a second chance.

'Let them all in, Lord God,' I said again.

'I see that your mind is made up. So be it, Weaver. You are banished forever to the earth and mankind.'

'Now, Inayat, you know why I came back from the dead.

'There is only one God. And her name is life. She's the only one worthy of worship. All else is irrelevant.'

Afterword

Let me state right at the start that I am neither a Kabir student nor scholar. Yes, we did have Charlotte Vaudeville's book of translations of Kabir's dohas and Bijak at home and I had dipped into them from time to time but I have to confess shamefully that I am not that passionately into poetry. That is odd, to say the least, since the late Arun Kolatkar, one of the finest and most thought-provoking bilingual poets in our country (remember Jejuri?) and I were together at least twelve hours a day. We worked as a creative team in advertising for over twenty-five years, visited bookshops, saw movies, shared silences as well long conversations on every possible subject and then receded into our own worlds. I read his poetry and enjoyed much of it hugely. I even recall pinning some of his hand-written poems on a softboard in my apartment. Every once in a while Arun would recite Kabir's dohas to me. The one that has stayed with me all these years is the one where Kabir asks the mullah why he had to climb the minaret and scream the azan. Did he really think God was deaf?

It must have been towards the end of the last century when I was sitting in my friend Renate's home writing my novel *God's Little Soldier*. My task at that moment was to compose the opening pages of a 'book within a book', by Amanat, one of the two major protagonists. By the time *GLS* was done, it had sixteen pages of excerpts from Amanat's book, *The Arsonist.*

I am not quite sure how Prof Dr Boehm-Tettelbach of Heidelberg University heard of my sixteen-page Kabir and invited me in 1999 for the six hundredth anniversary seminar on Kabir. I recall feeling relieved when I heard that the head of the Kabir Panthis in Delhi had had to cancel his visit for some reason since he wouldn't have cared for my unorthodox depiction of Kabir in *The Arsonist*.

GLS was DOA in India but turned out to be a bestseller in Germany and was much discussed. Around 2010, when I was a Fulbright fellow at Ithaca College, the college decided to produce *The Arsonist* as a stage production in collaboration with Cornell University. Original music and dances were composed and performed while I read out the text.

Every now and then someone who had read *God's Little Soldier* would ask me when I planned to write the full version of *The Arsonist*. My answer was brief and to the point: In my next life.

So what happened? How come sixteen pages became three hundred? Was it loathing and bitterness for the way the world had changed? All of a sudden country after country was returning to fascism. God and religion were both enlisted to kill hundreds and thousands of those who didn't share the chosen faith, whichever one it was in that particular country. Pure hate and hyper-nationalism were fast becoming the common currency across the world, including in my own country.

Is that why I invoked Kabir?

Maybe.

In the last couple of decades, scholars and especially singers, musicians and poets have re-sparked an interest not merely in this most unusual of our Bhakti saints, in metropolises as well as in the most unlikely of backwoods small towns.

But let me ask an embarrassing question: We may sing Kabir but when will we start living Kabir, that is, living by his tenets? When will we raise our voices against the deadly discrimination and hatred for the 'other' that is rampant across the world? In the topsy-turvy universe we live in today, it is the mullahs, the yogis, sadhvis and racists who seem to be hell-bent on lighting the fires of hatred and violence.

For some forty years climate scientists have been warning us about the impending extinction of mankind unless drastic steps are taken to substantially reduce fossil fuel consumption. Finally in 2019, people all over the world heeded the call of sixteen-year-old Greta Thunberg to stand up for our planet, try and force the politicians and their masters, the industrialists who finance them, to allow our children the benefits of a living and not a dead planet. And what did we Indians do? We continued in our comatose state.

Can saints really change human nature? Or are they like God, good for prayers when we are in trouble, or when our consumer-selves are in a demanding mode: I want, I want, I want . . . a Mercedes, a bungalow, a successful business, the right lottery ticket.

Initially I intended to place Kabir in his own period but I kept sliding into different time zones. Jesus crept into the text and so did the enmity between Catholics and Protestants. Let's not forget Kabir himself was half-Hindu and half-Muslim. When I sent an earlier draft of *The Arsonist* to the German couple who have been superb translators of my novels into German, they were puzzled, if not bemused. Why was I bringing Catholics and Protestants, not to mention contemporary events, into the Kabir era? My Kabir though had a very different take on the matter. He asked me – no, he demanded to know – why I was trying to trap him in the past. If I was reimagining him, it was imperative to make him your and my contemporary.

I don't know of any Bhakti poet who has such a robust sense of irony and humour, a deep understanding of the different springs of human motivation and action. Kabir wrote wonderful, surreal verse to deal with the most complex issues of faith and God, and had the gall to question the most precious and revered of our beliefs, received wisdom and our shibboleths. Truly Kabir is unique.

I could see the twinkle in his eyes as he poked a sharp needle into my inflated sense of self-importance, rage and outrage. Wake up and look around, he told me. No malice there but just a plain, down-to-earth reminder that mankind had lost its moral compass. Add to that this earth is the only home man and a million or trillion other species have. We may send airships to land on and explore the moon or Mars but all the while we are making certain that we ourselves will be homeless and extinct.

This was the final call, he said, to choose to fight for humanity and the planet or say goodbye to life.

Did I undertake this book because of these dire conditions? Kabir's watching me, so I have no option but to be honest. The truth is he had got under my skin a long, long time ago.

PS: One of the most curious aspects of the printed versions of Kabir's dohas and other poetry is the depiction of this man of God over the past few decades. Bear in mind that there are no portraits of the man available but he's almost invariably shown as an emaciated and enfeebled, shaky old figure or an elderly sadhu with the mandatory long, white beard. Who knows, he may have lived to an advanced old age, but how can we not grasp that Kabir's mind always remained young, daring and mischievous and kept ticking with the most adventurous, imaginative and powerful poetry?

Acknowledgements

I have always called myself a storyteller and nothing more. Then out of the blue a story happens to you and you are no more. My grateful thanks to those few who have helped to unearth me even as I was being buried alive. A 'thank you' has rarely been so inadequate. My only hope is that my Arsonist will give them an inkling of my gratitude. Thank you Nayantara Sahgal, Suzanne Davies, Radhika Bordia, Naresh Fernandes, Hartosh Bal, Nandini Ramnath, Vasu Jain, Sister Ananda, Vaibhav Purandhare, Amy Fernandes, Anil Dharker, Manjula Padmanabhan, Shilpa, Praful and Suhail Shah, Radha and Daniel Welt, Vinayak Vatsal, Ranjana Ramchandra, Jyotee, Milind, Mala, Jaya, Sneha and Rochelle from my family, Jehangir Sorabjee, Neha Sarna, Alisha Attarwala, Adrian and Hira Steven, Sean Mahoney, Vasundhara Nath and Sidharth Bhatia. A great many other fine souls supported me solidly. Regretfully I am not able to name them since the list would assume epic proportions.

As to the writing of *The Arsonist*, as always my boundless gratitude to Pervin Mahoney for reading and re-reading the text and fine-tuning it. Thank you Chiki Sarkar for reading

The Arsonist within two nights and taking it. Nandini Mehta, Jaishree Ram Mohan and Arushi Singh, thank you for editing the novel, and Shyama Warner for proofreading. And Disha Naik, the publicist, who I hope will sell at least a billion-and-a-half copies.

There is one other person who I frankly don't know how to even begin to thank. I am referring to Tulsi Vatsal. She wouldn't allow me to go into a serious depression and has stood steadfastly by me and *The Arsonist*.

CRAFTED FOR MOBILE READING

Thought you would never read a book on mobile? Let us prove you wrong.

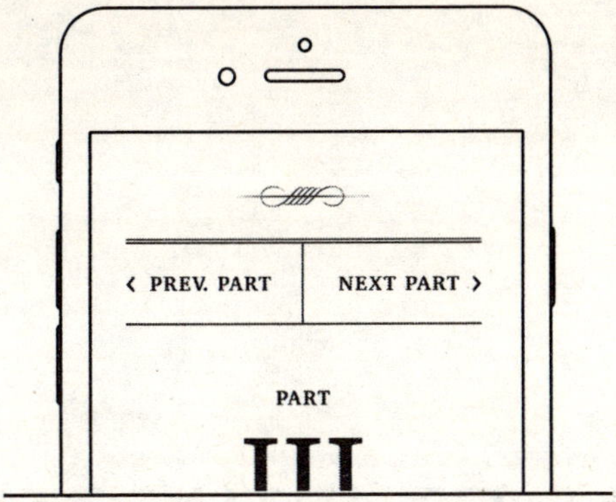

Beautiful Typography

The quality of print transferred to your mobile. Forget ugly PDFs.

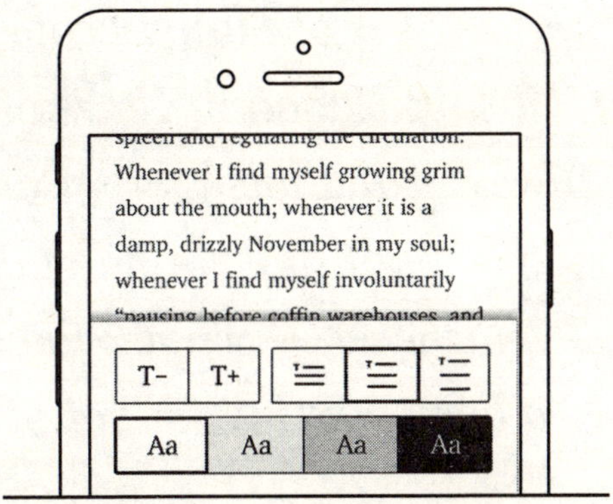

Customizable Reading

Read in the font size, spacing and background of your liking.

AN EXTENSIVE LIBRARY

Including fresh, new, original Juggernaut books from the likes of Sunny Leone, Praveen Swami, Husain Haqqani, Umera Ahmed, Rujuta Diwekar and lots more. Plus, books from partner publishers and loads of free classics. Whichever genre you like, there's a book waiting for you.

juggernaut.in

juggernaut.in

Ask authors questions

Get all your answers from the horse's mouth. Juggernaut authors actually reply to every question they can.

Rate and review

Let everyone know of your favourite reads or critique the finer points of a book – you will be heard in a community of like-minded readers.

Gift books to friends

For a book-lover, there's no nicer gift than a book personally picked. You can even do it anonymously if you like.

Enjoy new book formats

Discover serials released in parts over time, picture books including comics, and story-bundles at discounted rates. And coming soon, audiobooks.

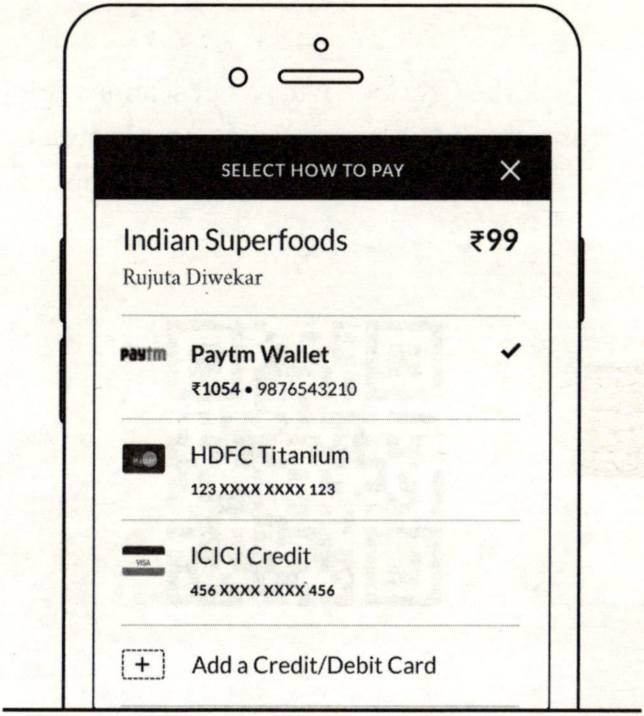

Paytm Wallet, Cards & Apple Payments

On Android, just add a Paytm Wallet once and buy any book with one tap. On iOS, pay with one tap with your iTunes-linked debit/credit card.